JUNTTO

JUNTTO

WAR OF THE DAMNED™ BOOK SEVEN

MICHAEL TODD   MICHAEL ANDERLE
LAURIE STARKEY

DISRUPTIVE IMAGINATION

JUNTTO TEAM

Beta Readers

Dorothy Lloyd
Tom Dickerson
Dorene Johnson
Diane Velasquez
Timothy Cox
Sarah Weir

JIT Readers

Danika Fedeli
James Caplan
Misty Roa
Daniel Weigert
Nicole Emens
Peter Manis
Mary Morris
John Ashmore
Angel LaVey
Larry Omans
Paul Westman
Micky Cocker

If we missed anyone, please let us know!

Weapons Consultant
John Kern
Proprietor
Spurlock's - Henderson NV

Editor
Lynne Stiegler

DEDICATION

To Family, Friends and
Those Who Love
to Read.
May We All Enjoy Grace
to Live the Life We Are
Called.

Geraldine was getting pleasantly drunk in a bar north of 120th Street when the greasy television caught her eye. The news was on, and Geraldine grinned. It was strange how the local news had become her favorite program lately. She was wondering why that had happened when a picture of Katie popped on screen. Yeah. That was probably why.

"In a bloody turn of events yesterday, footage was captured of our very own New York City heroine Katie taking on Juntto, the Leviathan. We learned early yesterday that Juntto had been responsible for not only the senseless and brutal slaying of the two hikers in the Alps but for ravaging the townspeople in a village not far away. Sources say Juntto was on the move and attempting to raise an army for a possible takeover of Switzerland and surrounding areas." The image on screen changed from Katie to one of Juntto holding up a large tree.

"Fuck that dude," someone in the bar yelled.

"Yeah! Kick his ass, Katie," Geraldine slurred, and the regulars gave her a round of applause.

"The video we are about to show may not be suitable for younger audiences," the reporter warned, turning to a video which took over the screen.

There was no audio involved, just pure action. The crowd *oohed*, *ahhed*, and grimaced every time a punch was thrown or a kick was launched. The camera panned the area, showing a small team in the distance, weapons poised, ready to help in any way they could. Katie, who was actually Pandora at the time, was bloodied and battered and barely able to stand. She was caught in what seemed to be a hopeless position as Juntto grabbed a large tree and walked it to her.

Everyone in the bar went silent, and even the music was shut off.

Geraldine stared helplessly as blood ran from Katie's mouth, her body bruised and beaten from the battle. She struggled to hold her head up.

Geraldine tilted her head. "She's calling him in to tell him something."

Another stood up and pointed. "Yeah. Yeah, look at the smirk on her face."

The moment in the fight where Katie rallied had arrived. Although the viewers couldn't see the change, they could all feel the strength roll back through her. When she summoned the angel weapons and armor, the entire bar went quiet. When Katie's eyes flashed blue and she stabbed Juntto through the stomach, the whole bar erupted in cheers. People jumped to their feet and began hugging each other, still watching the fight progress.

Geraldine shook her head. "I wish we could hear what she was saying. I know what *I* would say to that douchebag. He thinks he's so damn tough, but not against our angel."

Katie reared back and kicked Juntto hard in the balls. Everyone groaned and started to slowly clap. The fight continued, with Katie holding her ground. The guns surrounding the Leviathan blasted him as he attempted to grow. Bullets flew from Katie's gun, and his crotch exploded into red mist.

Geraldine covered her mouth and turned her head away, whispering a quick prayer.

A young man next to her grimaced. "Gonna take more than prayers to fix that, lady."

The footage cut out there, and the reporter came back to the screen. "We don't have the rest of the footage, but we are told that Katie is doing fine. As far as Juntto is concerned…let's just say justice was served with the help of angels."

———

Moloch sat in his lair, slumped in one of his large armchairs. He leaned forward, putting his elbows on his giant knees. His beady red eyes stared at the footage playing on his television. Moloch's mouth hung wide open as he watched Pandora and Katie kick the living hell out of Juntto. Moloch hadn't even thought that was possible. The last time the angels had subdued the Leviathan they'd been unable to kill him, and had instead left him buried deep in the ice of the Alps.

Moloch shifted his gaze to Baal, who was sitting next to him in another chair. Baal's mouth was also open, remnants of the small bunnies he had been eating stuck to his lips. He began shaking his head, leaving bits of bunny fluff floating around. He had no words for whatever the hell they were watching.

Moloch shouted and pumped his fist as Juntto slammed Pandora/Katie in the stomach, sending her flying. "My man isn't going down without a fight. At least he is attempting to put those bitches in their place."

Baal swallowed his bunny. "Until she shoots him in the dick."

"What? Have you seen this already?"

Baal nodded. "Yeah. It came out early this morning. I had to look away. My stomach hurt just watching it."

When they got to that part, Moloch scooted to the edge of the chair, watching closely as she pulled the trigger and did just that—shot him square in his man-junk. Moloch jumped back, putting his hands over his mouth. "Holy fucking pickle-thumper, that bitch just shot him in his most valued asset. And that's not even fucking Pandora! That's Katie! It looks like Lilith's bad attitude is wearing right off on her. Shooting someone in the meat stick is Pandora's signature for sure."

"I don't know what he was saying, but I have a good idea he wasn't talking about taking Pandora on a date with flowers and candy. That one might have been provoked."

Moloch shoved his finger in Baal's face. "Nothing short of stabbing someone with the dick-spear would warrant a shot like that. That was literally a low fucking blow."

Moloch clicked off the television and slumped back in

his chair, defeated. He ran his huge claws over his bald head and sighed dramatically. "All I want is to be the king of Earth. To make them bow to me, maybe worship me as their one true dark lord. Is that so much to ask, Baal? Am I reaching too far, here? Do I have delusions of unholy grandeur?"

Baal jumped from his chair and poured a whiskey, handing it to Moloch. "Now, now. You have just hit a tough spot. You are still the most maniacal beast in all of hell, and you deserve ten Earths. Don't start getting depressed now. Buck up." He laid a claw between Moloch's horns and began stroking his head. "Every time you want to quit, think about the 'shot heard round the world, and let that motivate you to kick Lilith right in the damn ovaries."

Moloch patted Baal's hand. "You always remind me how amazing I am and how much I deserve. Thank you, dear friend."

Baal smiled, showing the fur still stuck in his jagged teeth. "Now, come on. Let's figure out where the other Leviathans are. We know Juntto's defeat is bound to piss some of those guys off. We need to get to them before that army of human bastards decides to come for us."

Moloch stood up and walked to a table with a giant map of Earth spread across it. "Do you really think Pandora and the rest of those idiots are dumb enough to attack us here?"

Baal shrugged. "I don't know anymore. It would be smart of us to have the Leviathans on our side, though, in case they do. Juntto was an excellent choice, but he got beat to hell and was shot to shit by her and her brood of super-hero wannabes."

Moloch groaned. "We have endless numbers of troops here, and we know that humans can't come this deep into hell. Other than that, I'm not even sure what strategy we should use to combat those morons. It's not like they will be able to roll tanks and armor in here without us knowing. Those kinds of gates are caught, and caught fast. Still, you may be right—we may need to keep some tactics in reserve just in case."

Baal nodded. "Yes, good thinking. And maybe we should invest in bulletproof cups. You know, just to protect our junk in case of a fight. Take my leg, take my arm, but mess with the lady-killer?" Baal shook his head sadly.

Moloch gaped at Baal. "Really? The lady-killer? What are you, some fifteen-year-old human living in his mom's basement? If you ever say that again, I will rip your arm off and punch your lady-killer with it."

Baal cleared his throat and moved his hand over his junk. "Right, never going to say that again. Got it. But what about..."

Moloch shook his head. "No, don't. Just stop. In fact, that conversational topic is banned for the rest of the week. Put together some of the smarter demons and have them start researching the whereabouts of the other Leviathans. In the meantime, we will focus on our next attacks. We must make them worth our time and energy.

Baal pouted and walked to the table to look at the map. There were Barbie heads with nails through them stuck in all of the locations they had already hit across Europe. Baal flipped one of the doll's hair up to see the surrounding countries. "I would really go for places away from where you've already hit. Shake it up a bit."

Moloch rubbed his claws together. He loved few things more than planning attacks on Earth. "That's what I was thinking. I was considering several places for minor incursions and then one large one on Katie's doorstep. Now, obviously the large one will have to include some of our more nefarious creatures, but we can plan that one last. I want it to be a surprise. While they are looking at the other small incursions, we sneak them into New York."

Baal was excited. "That sounds absolutely evil. I love it. What area of the world are we focusing on first?"

Moloch pointed at Japan. "We will start our world tour here, in Uji, Japan. A little birdie once told me that young Katie was a tea lover. Well, this is one of the tea lovers' most-prized destinations. It's where the first tea seeds were planted. It is also home to a tourist favorite, the Byōdō-in, a beautiful temple the humans can't get enough of. It should be amazingly bloody."

Baal smirked. "Excellent. That meatsack needs a little punch in the throat."

Moloch moved his finger to Muuido Island, South Korea. "This beach town not only brings excessive tourism, but people actually do something called 'camping.' They put up these tiny fabric houses and sleep there on the beach. Strange to me, but they seem to love it. Apparently, humans all over the world do it."

Baal wrinkled his nose. "No shower? No stove? How do they manage? They deserve a stomp in the face from a demon."

Moloch laughed. "And we can use fire too. Fantastic— they will go up in flames in two seconds."

Baal chuckled. "Where after that?"

Moloch slid his finger over. "We will end our Pacific tour in Mullumbimby, Australia, known to the locals as Mullum. It is overrun by those weird hippies with their art galleries and health food shops. The entire place is basically vegan."

"By my hateful balls, vegan? We'll have to nightmare up new punishments for those idiots."

"Down here, veganism is a mortal sin. Up there, it's hip. It's cool. All the kids are doing it."

Baal made a gagging noise. "They are filled with granola and kale. They *must* be terrorized. Scare them right back into their little eco-friendly huts."

"Exactly. We don't need to tell them that peace doesn't win. We just need to show them that blood makes a statement."

Baal pulled out three freshly severed Barbie heads and pinned them to the locations. He picked up another and waved it over New York. "Okay, boss, where is the big one going?"

Moloch knocked the Barbie head from his hand and reached into a drawer of the table. He rummaged around until he found what he was looking for.

Baal grinned evilly when Moloch pulled out a tiny screaming human head and nailed it to the board. The head kept screaming as blood spread out over New York City. "This one is going to be good."

So, can I please start making that sound every time I kick someone? Pandora asked, watching the credits of *Bloodsport*.

Only if I can try that kick where he toe-punches that guy in the eye while he's facing away from him, Katie replied.

I don't know if your body is made for that, honey. Maybe if you'd been getting down with the deed this whole time to work on flexibility, but not now.

Katie's face straightened. *You are damn hopeless with this shit.*

I'm hopeless? You're the one who can't toe-punch.

You know what I mean.

I would say motivating, not hopeless.

Katie looked out the window of the plane and watched the clouds flow beneath them. They were on their way back to New York. She sighed and glanced at Calvin. "You coming back to the condo before heading to San Diego, or are you just leaving from here?"

Calvin stretched his arms over his head. "I'm going to just jet on over there. I want to see my girl and make sure everything is on the up-and-up. She's going into the fall semester soon, like in a week, and I want to spend time with her before she goes."

Katie nodded. "I get it. Tell her we send our love. I can't believe it's almost fall already. Before long I'm gonna witness my first New York winter."

Pandora groaned. *You're going to have to buy an alpaca-lined outfit. I'm not dealing with cold-fucking-snowflakes as we fly around. I'm already gonna have to make sure your wings don't ice up.*

I'm not an expert, but I have a feeling that my wings will be just fine. You need to relax. I am not accustomed to cold, either. Remember, I come from Nevada. We'll figure it out.

Pandora grumped. *You better, or I'm hibernating.*

Calvin chuckled. "Yeah, you can teach Pandora about the white-girl obsession with pumpkin spice."

Katie wrinkled her nose. "Yeah, probably not. Never was a big fan. I'm basic, but not that basic."

Calvin laughed. "Hell, when it comes to pumpkin spice, *I* let the white girl come out. I'm as basic as can be."

Katie laughed along with him, then her eye caught an empty seat. Katie looked at the bathroom door. She wondered what Juntto was doing in there that was taking so long. She was still nervous about having him around. *Are you sure I can trust Juntto like you say I can? I mean, how long could it possibly last?*

Pandora thought about it for a minute. *I would say you've got him under your thumb for at least twenty years. Remember, we think long-term. As far as he is concerned, until he figures out a way to kill you, he has to honor the oath of fealty.*

Katie didn't like that answer. *And if I'm weakened?*

You've got to think of it this way: he isn't a demon, which means he isn't exactly honorable, but he's not a total Lucifer-loving douchebag either. Plus, we will weaken him with Western decadence.

Decadence? Like donuts? That's worked on one woman I know.

Donuts keep me going, bitch. There's nothing weak about me. Besides, Juntto has a lot to learn. He hasn't been here in a long time. Just as I figured he would be, he wasn't too impressed with the people so far. We've just got to focus on the extras.

Katie heard a bump in the bathroom. *And when he gets hooked on decadence, that means he'll stop trying to take over the world?*

Pandora cackled. *Oh, hell no. That man and conquering are like two peas in a pod. That is pretty much the point of his existence.*

Great.

Pandora smirked. *It's not as bad as you think. It'll take a while before he figures out his next plan. Who knows? We might all get killed, and then all bets are off anyway.*

Katie scoffed, rubbing her face. *Great, I kick the bucket, and he's good to go. My parting gift to Earth is a bloodthirsty spear-loving Viking with no conscience.*

Seriously, the real threat are his food intake and his liquor bill. Viking warriors are no joke.

Katie shrugged. *I'm loaded. Like, the money just keeps coming in. It's not like it used to be.*

Pandora wasn't convinced. *You just think you are. That man can eat three times as much as me, and he pays no attention to it. If I were you, I'd...*

The bathroom door flew open, and Juntto came walking out with his shoulders squared and his chin chiseled. He was wearing a pair of white karate pants, no shoes, and a bandana tied around his head. He hadn't been wearing that when he'd gone into the bathroom. Katie tilted her head to the side, realizing he looked like a young Jean-Claude Van Damme.

Juntto turned in a circle and put his hands up with balled-up fists. "What you think? Good, no? Now I can kick demon ass in style. And I can even replicate the noise. Aaaayaaa."

Juntto kicked the headrest of the empty seat, knocking it off. He reached out and caught it, juggling it for a moment and then tossing it back into the seat. He looked at Katie with a guilty grin. "Sorry, I will replace."

Katie rolled her eyes. "As much as I appreciate your love of eighties and nineties cinema, you can't go walking around looking like a famous person. That will draw more attention than anything else."

Juntto wrinkled his forehead. "What you want changed?"

Katie put her hand to her chin and looked him up and down. "I want you to change your eyes to dark brown, your hair to another color entirely, and stand taller. It's more intimidating."

He changed right in front of her, his hair going bright blond, his back straightening, and his eyes darkening. "Better?"

Katie sighed. "Yeah, whatever. You didn't have to lose the pants, though."

"You said you wanted intimidating."

"That's sending the wrong signal."

Juntto clothed himself again and shrugged.

Katie massaged her temples. "I just can't win. I've got a shapeshifting action superhero on my damn team now. What's next? Jackie Chan and Burt Reynolds?"

Juntto laughed, then stopped. "Who are they again?"

"Don't worry about it. At least you're good in a fight."

"And I've got dashing good looks."

Katie just blinked at him. "Oh, and humble."

2

Angie grunted as she set down a large box of food and beer on the counter of one of the condos that Brock's team would be staying in. She looked around the place, making sure that everything was okay. She had been working on it since Katie had left, trying to get everything in place. The guys would hopefully be staying for three days of relaxation before heading back to the base. Because of their hard work, Katie wanted to make sure they were comfortable and felt like they were at home.

Angie started putting away the food for the fourth time. As she situated the beer in the fridge, her phone rang. "Angie's Mortuary. You kill 'em, I deal 'em."

Katie chuckled. "That's gross, Angie. And who are you dealing them to? I need to know this, because they may need an ass kicking or two."

Angie shut the fridge door. "I never reveal my sources. What's up?"

"We're landing, and I just wanted to find out how everything's going."

Angie looked into the empty box. "Well, the rooms here are set up. They have lots of food, beer, cable, and the clothes you said you wanted me to get for everyone. Everything is pressed and put away in the closet."

Katie let out a sigh of relief. "Good. And how about the stuff for the base?"

Angie grabbed her clipboard and flipped through it. "Three new beds, plus enough new linens for everyone in the base, check. Dishes and cookware to feed a multitude of people, check. Delivery of groceries to fill the kitchen, check. Then the little odds and ends I had shipped to them. Everything is accounted for, as far as what you asked me to send. Oh, and I ordered the new SUVs for the team, but they'll take a couple of days. They should be there by the time the guys arrive, though."

"Excellent. You're a gem. I feel like I can trust you with just about anything."

"Why do I feel like you're going to drop something on me here?"

Katie laughed. "Because I am, but I'll talk to you about that when I get there. In the meantime, I need more stuff sent to the base. You got a pen?"

Angie produced a fountain pen, seemingly out of thin air. "Always."

"Okay. I want a barbeque pit, the kind with a smoker attached. We'll need several more fridges and deep freezers so that we can buy food in bulk. I'm thinking we can build another kitchen. We'll need doubles of all appliances. Then get with Korbin and figure out what combat stuff we need to include for the guys. I want the whole shebang."

Angie scribbled it all down. "And *we* are paying for this?"

"Good point. Get with the general on this one. Work out a budget with them, and we will cover the rest. If he has a problem with it, remind him we're housing some of his guys, too. I'm pretty sure he won't." Katie hoped he wouldn't, at least.

Angie saluted the phone. "Ten-four, Captain. Now hurry up and get back here. You guys need some R & R."

Katie watched out the window of the SUV as they passed by the tall buildings of New York City. Pandora was in a good mood. *Ahh, back home. And look, your human counterparts are starting to prepare for the fall season. Little decorations up everywhere. I don't really understand why they don't just leave them up all year round. Pumpkin spice themselves into comas.*

Then it's not as exciting when the season comes. It's only for a short period of time, so that makes it special. As far as pumpkin, I like it in my pie, and that's about it. Katie stared at a Starbucks as they passed. The windows were plastered with pictures of different pumpkin spice products. Drinks, cookies, and more drinks.

They pulled up in front of the condos and began to unload. Katie called to the guys, "Hey, stop in the lobby, okay? I want to just go over a couple of things with you."

Juntto trotted up next to her, and Katie rolled her eyes at his Jean-Claude Van Damme look. "You want to talk to me, too?"

Katie nodded. "Yes, but upstairs. Just stand by the concierge's desk, and I'll be with you in a second."

"Concierge? Who's that? That's the little soldier over there?"

"He's not a soldier. He's like...an assistant."

Juntto's eyes sparkled. "A servant?"

"No! He's just a person you're going to quietly stand next to. And for God's sake, try not to touch anything, okay? As a matter of fact, don't speak, touch, or do anything."

They walked through the doors. Juntto split off from the group and grumbled as he approached the desk. "Treats me like child. Damn angels in disguise."

The concierge beamed at him, "Can I help you?"

"I'm not to speak to you, servant. You do the same. Avert your eyes from my glory." The concierge waited for a moment, then realized the man who looked a little like Jean-Claude Van Damme was serious. He looked away as casually as he could.

Katie heard the exchange, but nobody was bleeding so she thought it had gone well. She did her best to ignore Juntto as she approached the soldiers. Brock gave her a smile she couldn't help but return.

"All right, boys, you have the same rooms as before, and the doorman will leave the keys with you as he takes you up. I just wanted to talk to you about something. I think it's important for you to remember that Juntto was being Juntto."

Turner, Brock's second, grumbled. "He did some terrible things, Katie."

"I'm not saying it's okay, but I need you guys to give

him a clean slate. Judge him by what he does in the present, not his past. Can we do that?"

Brock turned to his men. "That we can. God knows not all of us have good pasts."

Eddie, a short soldier covered in tattoos, piped up, "I got one of those sold-drugs-in-high-school pasts, not murder-tons-of-people pasts." His partner in crime Sean snorted laughter.

"All right." The tone in Brock's voice shut them up. "Nonetheless. We'll give him space to prove himself."

The guys nodded and grumbled agreement. Katie and Brock shared a brief look, then he took his men to the elevator.

Katie let out a deep breath and turned to Juntto, waving her hand at him. He glared at the concierge for a moment, then followed her. The two of them entered the empty elevator and rode up to her floor. Katie watched him out of the corner of her eye. The Leviathan looked wildly at the elevator. "No elevators the last time you came here?"

"Why have you put me in this prison?"

"It's moving. We're going up."

"You have wings. We could fly. I wish to fly." Juntto reached out to touch the glowing buttons, but Katie slapped his hand.

"Just let it go, Juntto. You can't just touch everything you don't understand. You could blow yourself up."

He pulled his hand back quickly as the doors opened and marveled, "The prison was a portal to another world."

"No, idiot. We just went up a few stories."

Angie grinned as she met them in the hall smiling. "Hey, guys!"

Katie hugged Angie briefly. She gestured to Juntto, who was carefully stepping out of the elevator. He suddenly jumped free and whirled on it as it dinged and the doors closed.

"Juntto!" Katie gestured for him to join them. "This is Angie, my right hand. She'll show you to your room."

"She's your servant."

Together, Katie and Angie blurted, "No."

Katie grimaced. "She's my friend. I am going to put my things down. Follow Angie. Respect her, or you'll end up with another bullet in your dick. Get it?"

Juntto shrugged. "Yeah, I got it."

Angie and Juntto watched as Katie disappeared into her apartment. Angie turned and gave Juntto her best smile. He eyed her suspiciously. She kept the smile as she walked him down to the condo across the hall. "This is going to be your place. There used to be someone else living here, but the owner decided to sell. They didn't like the attention Katie was getting, and they were worried."

Juntto looked around the condo. "This is a palace. What could worry one who lived in this place?"

Angie set her clipboard down on the table. "I'm assuming a demon invasion or something. Either way, I bought it at a reduced rate as an investment of sorts. We can use the privacy up here, and the condo will always sell for more than what we purchased it for."

"I see." Juntto obviously did not see.

Angie showed him into the living room, trying her best to treat him with respect and not fear. He turned to her and put his arms out. "I accept this palace. It is very pleasing to me."

Angie smiled and reached into her bag, pulling out a tablet. "Here. This is a computer—a tablet really. You press the little green, red, and yellow ball and then type whatever you're looking for into the search bar. I've pulled up several tabs already. You just select what you want like this, okay? I need you to search for clothes that you like. Just go through the clothes and add them to the basket. I'll take over when you're done and purchase them for you."

Juntto wrinkled his nose. "This technology is strange."

Angie chuckled as she went to the kitchen counter and organized her notes. "It can be. And we will need to take you shopping in public before you leave, too."

Juntto plopped down on the overstuffed couch and grabbed the remote. "Ah! Some of this technology is coming to me." He held it up and clicked on the large flat-screen television. His eyes roamed down to the flowered material under him as he ran his hand across it. "By Crtagul's frozen tits, this furniture! Who in the world picked it out? Was it you?"

Angie smirked. "The people I bought it from sold everything in the place except for their personal items. I left all the furniture and cleaned everything else out."

"I need a man's chair. A throne of iron and wood."

"The couch is fine for now. There are sheets in the cabinet and on the bed, and the towels in the bedroom, and any other linens are all brand-new. There is also food in the fridge and beer and wine on the shelves. I wasn't sure what you liked."

"Tequila."

"I'll look into that. I got you soda and bottled water as well. This is your residence while you are here, and we should be good until you leave. Of course, if you run out of something, just let me know."

"Did you get him soap? The man needs some soap," Katie called as she walked into the apartment. "He smells like a bear dipped in foot fungus."

Juntto leaned down with a furrowed brow and sniffed his armpits. "Hey, it's not so bad."

Angie looked at Katie with a confused look and shook her head, walking out of the room. Katie glanced around the place, making sure everything was as it should be. She plucked the remote from his hand and clicked off the television.

Juntto looked at her standing over him. "Do humans treat all of their prisoners in such a luxurious manner?"

Katie scoffed. "No, you should see the prisons. But that doesn't apply to you."

"True. I am your slave, correct?"

"You are a vassal, not a slave. Pandora told me that I need to consider your type when I am deciding what to do with you. While you are here on Earth, we have Earth customs."

Juntto picked up a frilly pink throw pillow. "I see that."

Katie ignored him. "I'm willing to give you a very restricted second chance and accept your fealty. If you fuck it up, I'll cut your head off, and we'll see if you can grow it back."

Juntto pouted and sat back on the couch. "Such a bloodthirsty angel."

Katie shook her head. "No, just being real with you, Juntto. Regardless of whether I come to terms with what you are, you are exactly what we don't want here: a bloodthirsty Leviathan with no conscience and a willingness to hurt anyone and everything you come across if it suits you. I accept your fealty, but that doesn't mean I won't be prepared for the worst. These people you see around me all the time? They aren't slaves or servants, they are family. I will protect them and the other innocent humans with my life."

Juntto looked at her strangely, as if the idea were foreign to him. "Right. Well, I have clothes to pick out, and I would like to get caught up on my news. See which emperor is reigning supreme these days."

"Good luck with that."

Juntto grumbled and turned the television back on. "Thanks for the stuff."

Katie put her head down to hide the smirk. She walked to the door but stopped in the doorway. "Oh. You need to be ready by eight a.m. tomorrow. If you need help with an alarm, we can do that. Angie will pick you up. Your job is to get what she tells you that you need and make sure she is protected if she can't handle a situation. She is not normally on the fighting side of the team. Most importantly, no killing unless they try to kill either of you. You will be walking through crowded city streets filled with innocent beings. Here in the big cities, if we find ourselves in the middle of an attack, we instantly try to steer it away from the people. You should keep that in mind."

Juntto looked at her, bored. "Right. Do what the Angie lady tells me, don't kill, and protect her. Got it."

"Right. Besides, killing involves paperwork, and I hate paperwork more than I hate most demons. Except for Moloch, of course."

Juntto grunted in agreement. "Yes. Fuck Moloch." He thought for a moment, then studied the remote. He muted the television. "Wait. What is this paperwork?"

Katie tapped her foot for a second and walked over, sitting on the coffee table in front of him. She leaned forward, putting her elbows on her knees as if she were going to tell him something secretive. "On Earth, we try to kill as few as possible, so they set up a system of penance. A punishment, almost. If you kill outside of an assignment, no matter who is in danger, you are sentenced to *the desk.*"

Juntto *oohed.* "That doesn't sound fun."

Katie nodded somberly, trying to keep a serious face. "No, it's not. Suddenly, in front of you, there are hundreds, maybe even thousands, of forms to fill out. You write and rewrite what you saw, over and over again. You can't stop until you are done, but you never really know when you are done. And you only get stale coffee and old donuts the entire time."

"No steak? No tequila?" Juntto's eyes grew wide, and his lip quivered. "What fresh hell is that? It sounds like one of Lucifer's creations."

Pandora was cackling inside Katie. *Oh. Oh my God. This is the best thing ever. Tell him there's a man who comes around and watches over your shoulder.*

Okay.

Tell him the man watches and puts his dong on your shoulder until you're done.

I'm not saying that.

C'mon! He hates being managed.

Katie cleared her throat. "I've heard they got the idea from him. They have a slave driver known simply as 'the

Captain' who comes around and watches over your shoulder. He doesn't say a word, just reads every word you type."

Juntto's eyes grew large. "Oh, fucking *hell*, no. I am Juntto. No one lords it over me like that. I would slash through the paperwork and grow until I filled the space. I would spear the Captain with a leg torn from the vile desk. I might even rescue the others from that damnation!"

Katie patted his leg and stood up. "Just don't do anything to warrant paperwork and you will be fine. Humans have become a bit more ruthless in the days since you were last here."

Juntto shook his head, visibly startled. "I see this. No paperwork. Got it."

Katie turned, trying desperately to hold her laughter back. "Okay, eight in the morning. Don't forget."

She walked out of the room and shut the door behind her, leaning against it. She let out a loud snort and started laughing so hard that tears rolled down her cheeks. *That should do it.*

I love that you fuck with him. Seriously, I have rubbed off on you. Pandora could barely get the words out, she was laughing so hard.

Whatever it takes to prevent him from snapping the hot dog vendor's neck for not having mustard.

Pandora giggled continuously. *They'll appreciate that at the station. Can you imagine them taking a statement from Juntto?*

Katie started chuckling again, deepening her voice. *Uh, yes, Juntto, can you explain what happened? I like mustard, man have no mustard. So, I rip his head off. He will learn to have mustard.*

Pandora bellowed. *Oh, your detectives would be lost. Good preemptive action.*

Gotta make the best of it, right?

The next morning Katie got out of bed relatively easily. She had so much on her mind that she couldn't have stayed asleep any longer if she wanted to. She changed her clothes and headed to the kitchen, where Angie had left two dozen donuts sitting by the drawered toaster.

Pandora let out a sigh of relief. *Thank you for Angie. She seriously saves my stomach from eating itself.*

Katie took out three donuts and put them in the toaster to heat them up. *I would be inclined to agree with you this morning. I was not looking forward to walking all the way to Krispy Kreme. I feel testy, so I might have been the one to rip the wiener man's head off.*

Or something worse, Pandora whispered.

Katie smiled and took the donuts out, grabbed a mug and poured a cup of coffee. *She even put the coffee on a timer for me. That girl needs a raise.*

Agreed.

They sat down at the table by the window and looked out at the bright sunny day. It didn't look at all like it was the start of fall, but that was okay with Katie. She wasn't ready to fight in the cold just yet. She took a bite of her donut and pulled her phone out of her pocket after feeling it buzz. It was a text from Angie.

Eating breakfast. All is good, although he seems to have this strange fear of paperwork?

Katie laughed, typing back, **Good on both accounts. Don't tell him the truth.**

Pandora sniffed. *So far so good?*

Yep. We gotta go to the precinct, though, and update Travers and Schultz on what's going on. Katie grabbed the last donut and stood up, looking around for her keys.

When she arrived at the station, both detectives spotted her and dropped what they were doing.

Katie walked up to them. "You got a minute?"

Detective Schultz ushered them into an office. "For you? We got two. What's up?"

Katie stared at them both for a second and then launched into it. "This has to stay between us, but I thought it was pertinent to tell the two of you. I have Juntto. He is in my custody, and is working for me."

Travers let his mouth hang open, then blurted, "Wait, what? That monster you fought? I thought he was dead. The news said you killed him."

Katie shrugged. "The news didn't wait to get the whole story. The deal is, I need him for this fight. If he goes nuts, which he shouldn't...

He absolutely will.

Don't help, Pandora.

"If anything happens, I will be responsible for putting him down."

Schultz hesitated and traded a wary glance with his partner. "Well, that's a lot to compute. I was pretty happy he was dead."

Katie nodded. "Yeah, well. He is harder to kill than you might imagine."

3

"There were nice drapes in condo. Why you just don't take those down and sew something for me?" The Leviathan sighed, following Angie into the store. It smelled of perfume and was populated by clothed mannequins frozen in impossible positions.

Angie rejected the idea. "You are not going to walk around with drapes on. Besides, I don't sew."

Juntto gasped. "No wonder you are single! What woman doesn't know how to sew?"

Angie grabbed a pack of boxers and slapped it hard against his chest. "Quite a few, actually. Shocking, I know. We don't cater to men's needs anymore. They try to force us to, sure, but we refuse. Most of us, at least. Women have careers, families, and all the things men have."

Juntto looked at her with complete and utter shock. "This is Earth, right? I didn't wake up on another planet, did I? I can deal with women wearing pants, but this sounds terrible. How do men eat or dress?"

Angie stopped and let out a deep breath. "They use their

brains. It's crazy, I know. Absolutely shocking. But you'll get used to it. And you should probably remember that if you talk to any women. They don't like to be talked down to."

Juntto shook his head and followed Angie. "Times have changed."

Angie stopped at a rack of shirts. "Okay, if you are going to live here for a while, you might want to understand clothes. There are basically two levels: Walmart, which is cheap and neither fashionable or durable. Then there are brands like Dolce, Calvin Klein, and many others that cost more, and they tend to be both fashionable and more durable at the same time. Therefore, they will last longer, and you get your money's worth. Then there's fashion, which is going to be a bit trickier. You don't want to walk around with a short-sleeved button-up shirt with a dragon embroidered on the back."

"Even if I killed the dragon myself?"

"It's a cloth dragon."

"I *have* killed a dragon, though."

Angie couldn't tell if he was joking, so she smiled uncertainly. "No dragons, okay?"

"What about this one?" Juntto held up a short-sleeve Hawaiian shirt.

Angie grumped. "This is going to be a long fucking day. Think, here, Juntto: would you kick demon ass in a Hawaiian shirt?"

Juntto shrugged. "I don't know. I kick ass no matter what garment I am wearing. Is there some sort of rule about that?"

Angie put the shirt back. "Let's just say that you want to

back away from most things that have plants printed on them. Trust me. You will look ridiculous."

They made their way to the sock area and stopped in the aisle. Juntto narrowed his eyes and walked forward, staring at the mannequin on the edge of the aisle. It was wearing a tight black shirt, black fatigue-like pants, boots, and had a pair of sunglasses on. "Now, this I like. What are the labels? Is it this Walmart you talk about?"

Angie turned her head and studied the mannequin. "No, actually they don't sell that here. Walmart is its own company. These are Calvin Klein pants, a Calvin Klein t-shirt, and Steve Madden boots. I would have to say that's a good outfit, and it's this season's fashion line."

Juntto began to undress the mannequin, and Angie had to hold him back. "No, we'll get some fresh clothes. From the rack."

"I see. Yes. Fresh." Juntto pulled on his raggedy shirt. "I'll take them in many colors. That way if I happen to conquer any banners, I will have appropriate clothes to match."

"Katie said no conquering."

"Of course. This is just in case. If I happen to conquer any banners in the course of normal events. I want to be respectful of their colors."

"Okay, still—no conquering. And don't skimp on the socks. They should be this Mr. Klein too."

He walked off toward the rack of socks, and Angie chuckled. "Oh, boy, I created a monster here. Juntto the Viking with style. Great."

She ran after him and helped him pick out the right socks for his boots. When he selected ankle socks, she launched into a whole explanation of sports socks versus dress socks.

Turner held up his chicken wing with a proud face. "And then I was like *bam*! Not today, Satan, not today."

The guys laughed, Brock sitting back and watching his friends. They were all finally able to relax after a hellacious trip to the underworld. One of the first things they had done after they woke up was devour some donuts, and then drink beer until lunch. They decided to hit up the Hard Rock Café. Sean had warned them that it was seriously touristy, but the rest of the guys wanted something exciting. Even in the middle of a weekday, the lines had been exceedingly long, but Brock and the boys had come to expect that in New York.

Eddie laughed and took a gulp of his pint. "Right, and then Satan came up and said, actually yes, Turner, today would be the perfect day."

They all laughed, except for Turner, who angrily chomped down on his chicken wing. "Whatever. You're just jealous because your job was to man the damn cart."

Eddie shrugged. "Hey, I got a hot medic out of the deal, and I'm pretty sure you got the white Mr. T."

Turner just narrowed his eyes. "I took one for the team. You guys looked like you needed a bright spot since you struggle to get chicks to touch you on a normal basis."

Sean *ooohed* and covered his mouth. Eddie threw a napkin at him. "I get chicks."

"Like who?" Turner eyed him suspiciously.

Eddie took a moment to think, but couldn't name one. He grinned, and the table burst out laughing.

Brock swallowed the last gulp of his beer and shook his head at the waitress when she asked if he wanted another. The rest of the guys got another round. Turner pointed to Brock's empty beer. "What's wrong with you, dude? It's like two in the afternoon, you don't have work, and the beer is cold and delicious. Why are you being a pussy?"

Brock feinted a punch and Turner ducked. "Don't break my balls. I just want to go back to the room, turn on SportsCenter, and enjoy the quiet and tranquility for a while. I keep hearing bells tolling and demons snarling. I need to recoup."

The table went quiet for a moment. They all thought about their time in hell.

Brock shook his head. "I don't wanna bring the party down." He pulled out his wallet and tossed some money on the table. "I'll catch you guys back at the condos. Don't do anything stupid."

The guys chuckled, and Turner put out his arms. "Hey, it's us here. We would never do anything stupid."

Eddie downed his beer. "Nothing that we could get caught for, anyway."

Brock rolled his eyes as he grabbed his light jacket and headed out of the restaurant. He jumped into a cab and told the driver the address of the condo. As the cab drove through traffic, he almost told the driver to turn around. He could go back and get hammered with his boys. Then he remembered the demonic snarling, and he could almost smell the sulfur. No. He needed to rest.

The doorman held the door and nodded at him kindly

as he walked through and across the large marble entry. He pressed the button on the elevator and stepped inside, hitting the floor his condo was on.

As the elevator moved up, Brock closed his eyes and leaned back against the wall, enjoying the silence. Suddenly the elevator shook and quickly came to a stop, the doors slowly opening to the wrong floor. He glanced at the numbers, realizing he had stopped on Katie's floor.

That couldn't possibly be a coincidence.

He leaned out of the elevator and looked up the hall. Katie was standing there in a tank top and tiny little yoga shorts, propped against the doorframe seductively. He could tell she was definitely getting some of that lustfulness from her demon, but he didn't mind. He stepped out and gave her a questioning look.

She crooked her finger in his direction.

Brock bit his lip and let out a breath. Who was he to say no to an angel? Even when she was acting less than angelic. He walked forward until he stood in front of Katie.

She put her arms around his neck and pressed her body against him. "Did I interrupt your plans?"

Brock wrapped his arms around her waist. "Watch sports? Or play a sweaty, sporty game? I'll take door number two."

Brock leaned in and kissed Katie, and she writhed against him for a moment, then broke off. She giggled and stumbled back into the condo, Brock hot on her heels.

The door slammed shut. The hallway outside Katie's door was silent for a moment, then there was a quick ruffling and a sound like clothing hitting the floor.

A bed frame squealed. Katie giggled.

The sound of the frame slamming against the wall echoed down the hall.

———

Juntto picked up the cloth napkin, looked at it for a second, and stuffed it into his shirt. Angie pulled it down into his lap. "Napkin goes in the lap, big guy."

Juntto looked at the place setting in front of him. "This is different than last time I was on Earth."

Angie was surprised. "You actually ate at a table with place settings and not at an old wooden one where everything was consumed with your hands?"

Juntto glared at her. "Yes. I was a great warrior, but I dabbled in the politics, too. We ate at fancy estates, although they were a bit different than this one. There are no candles or servants here."

The waitress walked up with a smile, dressed in a blue button-up shirt and a knee-length apron. "Good afternoon, and welcome to the Grand. May I offer you one of our bottles of wine?"

Juntto put out his hands. "Ah, here is the servant. Excellent."

Angie looked mortified. "I'm sorry, he's not from this country. We'll take two glasses of water and two glasses of iced tea. Thank you."

Juntto's shoulders slumped as the waitress hurried off, trying not to show her discomfort. "Who eats supper without a bottle of wine?"

Angie put the napkin in her lap. "First of all, no one eats supper anymore. This is lunch. The large meal and wine, if you choose, comes at dinner, which you would have called supper. Secondly, it is frowned upon in this century to call anyone a slave or servant."

Juntto grumbled to himself. "Humans are so picky. You put napkin in serkr, no one happy. You talk to vist, no one happy."

Angie narrowed her eyes. "Serkr? What is a serkr?"

Juntto sighed and pulled on the top of his shirt. "Serkr. This is serkr."

"Oh, okay—your shirt. Got it."

The waitress returned with their drinks. She set them nervously down in front of Juntto and took the rest of their order. When she had left, Juntto looked down at all the silverware on the table. "So many instruments. What happened to one fork and one knife? Why do you need so many?"

Angie pointed her finger at the row of forks. "It's easiest to remember if you start from the outside in. That is your salad fork. It's just manners. We brought it over from the English."

"The English, always so...how do you say it...snob faces."

Angie choked on her water and put it down. "Snobbish? Right. Snob faces, and they weren't that. They were just mannerly and proper. People liked it."

Juntto pushed around the lettuce in the bowl. "You know what I like? Big slabs of beef. You can just tear it apart with your teeth. We should go to one of those restaurants."

Angie grimaced. "Um, I don't think they make those types of restaurants. You want to pull beef apart with your teeth, you might want to learn to cook and eat it at home."

Juntto rolled his eyes. "Men cooking..."

Angie pointed her fork at him. "Don't start with that again."

Juntto took a bite of the salad, slowly chewing it with a pained expression. "You eat like rabbits, too. Oh, and another thing. I was on this internet you showed me last night, and I discovered something."

Angie just looked at him. "You press Enter, and it gives you information?"

Juntto waved his hands. "Yes, that too, but the excitement of that quickly wore off. I discovered these things called me-mes."

Angie just looked at him. She had no clue what he was talking about.

"Oh, this is something the great and powerful Angie does not know! Ha!" Juntto clapped his hands and sat up straight in his chair. "Do not worry. I will enlighten you. Me-mes. they are pictures of something like a cat or a dog making funny face. Then there is something written on it. For example, I found one that depicted a white cat sitting in a table of some sort. This gave one the impression that the table's legs were, in fact, the cat's legs. A cat with wooden legs! Over top of the image it read *Lieutenant Dan, you got new Legs!* I deduce that the cat was once a soldier named Dan. Perhaps some witch or warlock turned him into a cat and took his legs. Modern times are strange. There are many strange and mysterious me-mes."

Angie giggled. "You are talking about *memes*, not me-mes. Ha! Yeah, that's a kind of humor these days."

"Really? I don't like it. The humor is not funny at all. These people have no respect. You make fun of a man with no legs? I had a comrade a century ago missing a leg. He would have pulled your spleen out of your stomach for making small of him." Juntto forced himself to take another bite of lettuce.

Angie pushed the croutons onto a side plate. "I can't argue with you on that. People today are meaner than ever. They feel that sitting behind a computer screen protects them from the outside world. It makes them feel strong and brave, and they say things that normally they wouldn't dare say to someone's face."

Juntto finished his salad and pushed the plate away. "In my opinion that doesn't make them brave; it makes them cowards. Part of being brave is being able to state your opinions and stand behind them. In my world, a man who does that is considered to be of the highest caliber, even if his opinions are strange or foolish. Beings where I come from are not so sensitive. You want someone to tell you the full and utmost truth. Even our women—they want to know what the man is thinking, how he feels. They do not get hurt feelings by it."

Angie snorted. "That sounds like the kind of place the men on this planet would love."

Juntto grimaced. "Men here are too weak for my world."

Angie chuckled. "I got a few you can take back with you, then."

"They would be turned to pets or dinner, whichever was needed."

"What you were talking about? We call them emotions.

They are what makes humans human. We have empathy and sympathy toward other people. That is why you don't see us going around just killing people because they talk too much. We value life."

"And you think my people don't because we don't cry when someone says something mean about us? We reserve true emotions for when they are most useful. Anger, love, revenge, triumph, pride."

Angie thought his people sounded interesting. "Maybe that's why your world does so much more with their time; they aren't worried about what anyone else has to say."

The waitress put their main course down on the table and walked away, seeing them in conversation. Juntto didn't even glance at it. "For example, if I met you today, I would say that you are smart and beautiful. At the same time, I would say that the fit of your dress makes you look slightly like a gifr."

"A what?" Angie asked dryly.

"Uh, uh, the small creatures with long noses and hats that run around in gardens," he tried to explain.

"You are referring to a troll. You just told me I looked like a troll."

Juntto put his hands up. "Yes, but now you are aware that these are my thoughts. So what? Does that make them truth? One makes you feel good, one might not. But they are both true, so far as I think them. However, unless you give me power in your mind, they cannot do any damage to you. So, it is not about what people say, it's about humans' inability to *not* care. Humans give people power they should not.

"Why would you care if someone that you had never

met and would never see again thought you were ugly? Does it change your face? Does it change your life, who you court, who you feud with, what your children think? No, it does not. It changes how you think of yourself. I don't understand why you would allow a stranger to have that kind of control over you."

Angie crossed her arms on her chest. "Right, but why do you feel the need to put those opinions out there? To hear yourself talk? If I shouldn't care what you think, why even say it? You can do so much more with that talk coming out of your mouth. Seriously. There is a place for honesty, but we are taught very young to keep our opinions to ourselves unless we have facts to back them up and they will actually be productive to the conversation. Commenting on someone's looks or someone's personal attributes may reaffirm to you that you like the way you are, but you can do damage to someone else. It is called being a damn bully."

Juntto gave a half-smirk. "Maybe you are right, on this planet. Very fragile and emotional creatures you are. That isn't what we do on my planet. We are much different in that way."

"How many of you are there on your planet?" Angie was ignoring her meal, but she didn't mind.

Juntto thought about it. "Last time I checked there were about...let's see, I have to turn it into your form of numbers. I would say about two million people."

Angie was shocked. "Wow, that's not a lot. We have that many people in just a quarter of New York City. I think the last time I checked there were something like eight billion people on Earth."

Juntto nodded, impressed. He stroked his chin and began looking around the restaurant, sizing up the patrons.

Angie watched him with a straight face. "Stop looking like that."

"I have only this face."

"You know what I mean. You look like you're thinking about conquering. If you want to rule so bad, I will get you an RTS game. Then you can find out how difficult it is to conquer a whole country and how bad it sucks once you actually succeed."

Juntto perked up, intrigued. "What is RTS?"

Angie sighed. "Real-time strategy role-playing. It's... never mind, I'll just show you when we get back. Go ahead and eat your food before it gets cold."

Juntto pulled the plate of steak, potatoes, and vegetables toward him. He looked at Angie and slid his fingers in, scooping up some potatoes. She reached across and slapped his hand. "Fork! Use a fork and a knife. Don't embarrass me."

The Leviathan yanked his hand back. "You dare strike me?"

"What are you gonna do about it?"

They engaged in a brutal staring contest. Finally, Juntto relented and picked up his fork. "Very well, gifr. You win this battle."

4

K atie rolled onto her back and pulled the covers up over her. Brock lay there breathing hard, eyes wide. "Holy shit."

Katie laughed, grabbed the bottle of water off her nightstand, and took a sip, then passed the bottle to him and dropped her head back on the pillow. They lay there in silence for a few minutes. Katie wondered what she would have thought of sleeping with a former rock star if things had been different.

Different how?

You. Us. The whole demon revelation, really.

You probably would have asked for seconds.

Is that a hint?

Oh, no! Not at all. But since you mentioned it...

Katie giggled and rolled back on top of Brock. "Time for round two."

Brock coughed and chuckled. "That's...uh... Well, all right."

Katie went in for a kiss, but their lips had just barely

touched when she heard her phone ring. She groaned, all hot and Brocked, and reached for her cell.

Brock grumbled under her. "Now?"

"Maybe." She looked at the number and put the phone to her ear. "Please tell me this is something important, Angie."

"Are you all right? Did I interrupt a workout?"

"You could say that. Just getting in some stretches and cardio. What's up?"

"We got word that there's an incursion not far from where we are. Apparently, the demons are coming out of the subway," Angie replied.

Katie chuckled. "It always happens that way in my life."

Angie was confused. "Huh?"

Katie shook her head, glancing down at Brock. "Never mind. Call Timothy and get the exact coordinates from him. I am putting this on Juntto. I want to see what kind of power he has and if he is really on our side. You can tell him he has some serious ass-kicking to do. I'll let my guys at the precinct know, so they don't get hurt. Just try to keep the cops out of the way, Juntto gets tunnel vision, and only Travers and Schultz know we have a new teammate."

"Got it," Angie replied.

Katie hung up the phone and fell back onto Brock. She held up her finger. "Just hold tight for a second. Shit is always breaking loose at the most inopportune time."

"Should I call the guys?"

Brock tried to sit up, but Katie shook her head and pushed him back down. "Nah, we're going to let Juntto handle this one. You just lie right there and collect yourself. My energy is already back."

Pandora chuckled. *Damn right, it is. Catch up, rocker boy.*

Oh, he's catching up all right.

You talk to the cops. I'll handle this.

Katie dialed Schultz, who answered on the first ring. "I saw the incursion."

Katie smiled, glad to see their system was still working. "Good, but hold your men back. I'm sending Juntto in, so you want to be on the lookout for him. He tends to go a bit overboard, and I don't want any cops hurt while he's tossing demon heads around."

Schultz cleared his throat nervously. "Okay. How will we know he is there?"

"Oh, you'll know. And besides, Angie is with him. Just find her."

"Got it, boss," Schultz replied, hanging up the phone.

Katie tossed the phone to the floor and placed her hands on Brock's chest. "Now, where were we?"

"Send those to my cell, okay?" Angie asked Timothy.

"You got it, girlie. And take some pictures of Van Damme for me. Mmm, all those muscles," Timothy replied.

Angie tossed cash on the restaurant table and grabbed the fork from Juntto's hand. He looked up at her, shocked. "What are you doing?"

"We have an incursion to handle. Come on, we're only about five blocks away."

Juntto grabbed a roll and shoved it in his mouth, then slid his new sunglasses on. He was ready. They sprinted full speed ahead through the crowds, Juntto impressed by how fast Angie was for a human. He sprinted ahead of her and used his strength to push people aside, creating a path for them. Angie didn't like the way he was tossing civilians, but she knew it was necessary to get to the incursion on time.

When they reached the fifth block, Angie slowed down and looked down at her phone. Juntto slowed next to her. "What's the deal?"

Angie scanned through the information. She pointed to stairs leading to a lower level. "They're coming from an old area of the subway system. Their portal is in an unused section, but we can access it from this entrance. Most likely they've made it to the platforms."

Loud shouting rang out in front of them, and a wave of people suddenly poured up the stairs with terrified looks on their faces. Angie glanced at Juntto. "Looks like they're already here."

They ran to the entrance and started to push through the people. Juntto growled loudly as he maneuvered by, hating how weak the humans were. "Weaklings, move! I am here to help. Move your human asses!"

Angie stopped on the third step and searched through her bag for her flat silver automatic. She cocked the gun and gulped in air. Her heart was pounding, and her hands were shaking. She was terrified, but she had to push through it. She was Katie's personal assistant and right-hand woman, and that meant she had to find her courage.

A woman carrying a baby stopped and stared at Angie. "Are you a cop?"

Angie didn't know what to say, so she just nodded. The woman let out a sigh of relief. "They're everywhere down there—demons just ripping through the people. You need a lot more of you."

Angie nodded and pushed the woman toward the doors. "Just get to safety. We got this."

The crowd had died down. A few stragglers ran past her, then Angie was alone, staring down the staircase. She pulled her gun up and adjusted her grip, trying to remember how to hold the thing—and trying to stop the shaking. She had never been out in the field before. It was the first time she would meet demons face to face.

Juntto looked up from the lower platform of the stairs, squinting at Angie. He could see her hands shaking and her frantic look. It was a look he knew from centuries ago. He liked the woman and even admired her impudence, but she was afraid. If she gave in to the fear, she would be no help to him. There was no time to speak to her. The enemy had arrived.

A horde of teeth-gnashing demons ran across the concrete floor, their talons clicking and clattering on the subway floor. Juntto jumped down the last section of stairs. They were covered in the blood of the innocent and thirsty for more.

Juntto crouched, and for a moment wished he had a spear.

Then he launched himself into the demonic crowd.

His arms grew bigger by the second as he slammed his muscular body through the demons, grabbed one by its scaly throat and pulled up. With a great gout of black blood, he ripped the demon's head off its shoulders. At the same time, he kicked hard behind him, where a smaller demon was trying to sneak up on him, and the demon flew back against the wall.

"Take your train back to hell." Juntto raised the severed demon head high and roared, "Juntto is protecting this subway!"

He pounded the severed head into the charred skull of a charging demon, breaking through it and destroying the twisted brains within. It evaporated into ash in his hand, and he tossed that into the face of another demon that was scrambling toward him. The demon screamed, rubbing its eyes. Juntto's massive forearms bulged as he grabbed the blinded fiend by both wrists and yanked downward hard and fast, disconnecting its arms from its body.

Juntto stood his ground in the subway tunnel. In order for the demons to get to the platform they had to pass Juntto, and he wasn't going to give them the slightest chance. Demons hissed and growled savagely, attacking him right and left.

He was having a blast. He tilted his head back and laughed loudly as he brought his massive fists together to smash a demon's head to ash. He raised his hands and growled at the demons. One fat fiend took a step back, unsure what that meant. Juntto's arms suddenly became skinny. The massive muscles stretched, twisted, and then morphed into long limbs tipped with razor-sharp claws.

He lashed out and sliced the fat demon to ribbons. Howls of rage followed, and the rest of the demons surged against him. The demons traded jabs with Juntto. His skin healed faster than they could cut it, but every swipe of his claws tore a demon in half and brought a shower of dust to the subway tunnel. Juntto ran forward and bounced off one side wall, spreading his deadly arms wide and tackling five demons to the ground. He slashed like a man possessed, slicing and shredding black scales until, one by one, their torn bodies turned to dust.

Juntto stood up and brushed his new pants off. The black blood would stain his new clothes. He cursed and decided to revisit Mr. Klein's store, but he was stopped by snarls. Three hulking figures filled the subway tunnel, twisted and nightmarish creatures still reeking of the pits of hell. Their bodies curled at the spine, their black skin tightly wrinkled like an old leather saddle. Their eyes gleamed brightly, and their pointed teeth dripped saliva.

Juntto took a step forward, his boots crunching through the gravel. "Oh, you came out of your caves just to play with Juntto! So did your friends, but where are they now? Well, come and see."

Juntto pushed his lock of white hair back, waiting. As one, the big creatures charged. He reared back and cold-cocked the first to reach him, knocking the demon's head off its shoulders. Juntto shook his hand, which stung where his knuckles had met the demon's teeth. A small amount of blood ran down his knuckles.

He gritted his teeth and turned to the other fiends. "No one makes Juntto bleed. You came to the wrong town, motherfuckers."

He tackled a demon and dug his claws into the thing's chest. Black, foul blood bubbled from the wound. Juntto grunted with effort and ripped the dark, pumping organ free, screaming, "You ruined my pants!"

Back on the upper level, Angie stood facing the dark staircase. She tightened her grip on her gun. Behind her, armored police officers were assembling, checking their gear and preparing to go in. Angie turned as a cop called, "Ma'am?"

She was met by a middle-aged man with a Kevlar vest over his uniform. He gave her a concerned look. "I'm Chief Poydras. You all right?"

"My, uh, teammate is down there." She was still holding the gun at the ready, and the barrel was still shaking.

The chief pushed down on the top of her gun and looked at her scared face. "Is Katie down there?"

Angie shook her head. "No. She has help now."

Juntto's voice echoed up to them. "Incoming!"

A tall, lanky demon came flying out of the staircase, landing on the stairs just below the chief and Angie.

They looked at the demon for a moment as it stood to its full height, shaking its head to straighten its vision. The chief put his arm across Angie, holding her back, then gave a signal. The department all started to fire at the demon at the same time.

Angie could tell this demon was different. The cops' bullets riddled the beast, knocking him back, but he raised a scaled leg and started climbing the stairs. This demon was a badass. The bullets didn't seem to be doing anything but pissing it off.

The chief yelled, "Reload."

The demon hissed and scrambled upward, claws reaching for the chief.

BOOM. The loud shot rang out in the stairwell.

The chief slowly looked at Angie. Blue-black smoke oozed from the barrel of her gun. She pulled the gun down and slid it into her holster. The demon clapped its claws to the bullet hole in its forehead and screeched loudly before exploding into ash.

Angie swallowed hard and walked up to the chief, who was visibly shaken. "Almost got me," he whispered.

"Nah." Angie shook her head and wiped her sweaty palms on her sides.

The chief opened his mouth to talk, but nothing came out. Angie stepped forward. "You need to keep your men back. It's under control. You're all carrying special bullets, right? If a demon like that comes up again, shoot it in the head, okay? Right between the eyes."

Angie went to turn to walk up the steps, but the chief grabbed her arm. "You're Angie, right? Katie's personal assistant?"

Angie nodded. "I am, but today I'm fighting too. Trust me when I tell you that downstairs is being taken care of, but our team member isn't quite as controlled as Katie. I think it would be best if you stepped back to the top and waited this one out. There is a portal in the tunnel, and our guy is working on taking care of it."

The chief looked at her suspiciously. "And who is your guy?"

Angie thought about it a moment. She couldn't tell them it was Juntto since he had been all over the news. "He goes by Claude, at least for today. If you trust Katie, then trust that she sent in the best team possible to handle this. Now, if you don't mind, there are a ton of civilians up here who need medical attention. The demons attacked before we could get here."

Angie marched up the stairs and onto the street, pride beginning to overtake the fear, then got to work. The street was crowded with wounded, and she bent down in front of the pregnant woman and spoke a few words to her. Grabbing gauze and disinfectant from the case next to the medic now on site, she smiled at the woman and started patching her up.

Below, Juntto went to town.

Katie lay flat on the roof of the building adjacent to the subway, watching everything progress. She didn't want them to know she was there, but she couldn't just leave it to chance. There were too many lives at stake to leave Juntto to his own devices.

Pandora scoffed. *I still don't know why you ding-dong-ditched Brock like that. He was ready for round-freaking-three. I don't think I've ever been in your body and had a round-fuck-ing-three before. This is being handled. You should have handled that back there.*

Katie narrowed her eyes, watching Angie patch people up. She could hear Juntto in the subway below, making karate sounds like he had seen in the movies.

Pandora growled to get Katie's attention. *I am not done discussing this. You should have trusted your minion Angie to handle this. Why even send them out here if you're going to throw away a perfectly good dick just to lie on top of a building and watch from a distance?*

Katie rolled her eyes. *We've had two explosions already. I'm not letting Juntto out without a leash. I trust his fealty, but that doesn't mean I trust him as a person or frost giant or Leviathan or whatever he is.*

Pandora was confused. *Then why not go down there and help him kick demon ass? After walking away mid-sex I have plenty of aggression simmering inside me. I could go down there right now and send some demons spiraling back to the pits of hell.*

I don't want Juntto to know I don't trust him. The more he thinks he is part of the team, and the more he becomes obsessed with our Western culture, the more likely it is that he will not even think about bolting, Katie explained.

Pandora scoffed. *He will* always *think of bolting, but that doesn't mean he will do it.*

And when he proves that to me, I will be more than happy to not sit on a building and watch him from afar. Until then, though, I am going to keep my eye out. Also, think about it this way: he could hurt Angie, and then where would you be with your donut obsession?

Pandora sniffed. *You have reduced me to a food whore. Nonetheless, you are right about Angie. Keep her the hell safe. I am not getting up every morning and walking all the way to Krispy Kreme. And it's not likely we will find another human who is as good at her job as she is. Ugh, you still shouldn't have run out on Brock. He had it ready for you. There wasn't even foreplay needed, which I love. Just straight to business.*

Katie kept her eyes glued to the subway entrance. *Can you take your horniness somewhere else? I'm trying to watch out for our Viking Leviathan, thanks.*

After an hour, everyone was still at the subway entrance. The line of cops stared down at the staircase waiting for this mystery help—or anyone at all—to appear.

Angie stood off to the side and leaned against the railing of the staircase. She heard shuffling, then footsteps, and finally Juntto stepped into the light. He still wore his dark sunglasses, although his shirt and pants were both ripped and stained beyond repair. Angie waved her hand at the cops, and they put down their weapons. Once he was at street level, a team rushed down to make sure no one needed help.

The chief stepped in front of Juntto and put out his hand. "Good job down there. We were told to stand back while you finished up. Please tell Katie we appreciate her sending someone of your caliber."

Juntto looked at Angie, and she nodded at the chief. Juntto stuck out his hand and shook the cop's. "No problem. I like to fight."

The chief looked at him strangely for a moment. "You know, you remind me of someone."

One of the other cops came up shaking his finger. "Yeah, me too. I know, I know! You look like Jean-Claude Van Damme from *Bloodsport*. You have different hair and stuff, but wow, you're almost a spitting image."

Juntto nodded proudly. "Yes, and I can do the kick."

The guys stood back and watched excitedly as Juntto kicked his leg all the way up to his shoulder. If there had been someone behind him, he would have kicked them in the face. The guys all laughed and cheered; Juntto had found his audience. They watching him pull different karate moves, expertly making the exact noises from the film. Angie just rolled her eyes.

When they were done, they all wanted to shake Juntto's hand. He obliged them. As they walked away, Juntto turned to Angie. "I did okay?"

Angie nodded. "You did great. You tore your pants, but great nonetheless."

Juntto's head snapped down, and he ran his hand across the tear. He clenched his fist and kicked the railing, knocking it off the half-wall, then picked up a piece of debris and threw it at the half-wall, crumbling it where it stood.

Angie jumped up and down and waved her hands frantically. "Calm down, Hulk. We can get you another pair. Not to mention, we ordered a pair in every color. The company will be paid for your efforts, so it doesn't come out of your salary. You are reimbursed for anything you may destroy during a battle, at least your personal items."

Juntto followed Angie up the stairs. "You said I would be getting a salary, right? I would like to know what to expect so I can plan my expenses."

Angie furrowed her brow. "What expenses?"

Juntto shrugged. "You know, new clothes when I want them, food, alcohol—the important things."

Angie sighed and kept leading him away from the subway. "Come on, Claude. We can talk about all that with your leader."

5

Angie opened the door to Juntto's condo and stepped to one side, letting him enter first. She went in behind him and shut the door. When she turned around, she ran right into his back. "Damn, why are you just standing there?"

He put his arms out, staring at all the boxes piled around the room. "What is all this? Someone has broken in."

Angie put her bag down on the counter. "Usually when someone breaks in they take stuff, they don't leave things."

Juntto shook his finger. "Makes sense. So, we have a kind thief on our hands. Very interesting."

Angie sighed, walked to the boxes, popped one open, and pulled out a shirt. "These are your clothes, Juntto. The stores have people who deliver them to your house when you purchase either online or you buy enough from their store to warrant it."

Juntto slapped his leg. "That's crafty. I find this type of

slavery is acceptable, don't you think? As long as we don't call it slavery, I mean."

Angie rolled her eyes. "If I didn't already have a bigger dick for an ex-boyfriend, you would rank right up there."

"So, you have already accepted worse than me? I'm an eligible bachelor. I have conquered many lands."

Angie put up her hand; she would not allow him to continue. "No! I've raised my expectations since meeting Katie."

Juntto pouted. "That's sad to hear. It seems that most people who are around Katie and Lilith are proud and strong. Must be something to do with Lilith's wicked powers."

Angie opened another of the boxes and threw Juntto a new pair of pants. "No, we are just secure in the power we hold, whether we are plain old humans or Damned with wings like Katie. On top of that, we call Lilith 'Pandora.' You might want to learn to do the same."

Juntto laid the pants down on the table next to him and dropped his current pair to the floor. Angie covered her eyes and looked away. "Oh, holy hell. I bought you fucking boxers. Let me just make it another rule that you can't go walking around naked in front of anyone."

Avoiding looking at him, she rummaged around in the box until she found a package of boxers and threw them in his general direction. "And you are responsible for washing your own clothes, especially if you're letting the boys dangle in there."

Juntto curled his lip and pulled on the boxers and pants. "There, sensitive human, you don't have to gaze at my magnificent body any longer. Is that better, Your Grace?"

Angie opened one eye just to make sure. "Better. And don't be snide. Human women—well, most human women —are not fond of being bombarded by swinging dick. They usually call that sexual harassment, or even assault."

Juntto tilted his head. "Where do I find the women who don't mind it?"

Angie barked laughter. "Usually between Murray Hill and Midtown, but you have to pay them."

Juntto gasped. "Pay? For sex? Juntto would *never*."

Angie put her hands on her hips. "Stop talking in the third person. It's weird."

Juntto moved some of the boxes around and opened one of the smaller ones. He pulled out a laptop and turned it over and over, looking at it strangely. "What is this metal box?"

Angie walked over excitedly and took it from him. "This is your laptop. It's the new Windows Alienware 17— strongest gaming laptop under five grand on the market. Of course, it will allow you to do other things, but this is exactly why I got it."

She put it on the table and plugged it in, sitting down in front of it. Juntto reached out to touch the screen, but Angie slapped his hand away. She turned it on and leaned back in the chair excitedly. "This has Windows 10 Home on it, overclocked GPU and CPU, NVIDIA GeForce graphics cards, and Intel Core processors. Not only that, but it's also made to be compatible with VR."

Juntto looked around the room. "What is VR?"

Angie looked up at him. "Virtual reality. You can be completely immersed in the game, although we would need other hardware for that. We can talk about that in the future. The keyboard lights up, you can adjust your controls, and it will play almost any game out there. Oh man, this is beautiful."

Juntto ran his hand over his chin. "This makes me think of a me-me I saw. Find someone who looks at you like Angie looks at this Alienware device."

Angie nodded. "Damn right. And it's funny too because it's called 'Alienware,' and well, you are an alien."

Juntto just stared at her as she cracked up laughing. "So now you will teach me these role-playing games?"

Angie logged onto the internet. "I'll teach you enough to get going, but you'll have to figure out the rest just like any other newbie. I want you to learn how to play games where you become the emperor. It turns out emperoring sucks."

Juntto slammed his hand on the table, startling Angie. "I refuse to believe it! That is just some lie to keep me distracted. Emperors are widely respected; they are loved by all. They drink from golden chalices in their high castles and listen to the sweet music played by their servants."

Angie stared at him for a moment before turning back to the computer and laughing loudly. "Try again, Viking. They are inundated by political choices, demonized throughout the modern world, and assassination attempts are an hourly occurrence. You would have to be a really great ruler for the country not to plan some sort of coup. Especially if you strolled in and stole the country from the current ruler."

"But that is where the respect comes from. You conquer, you win, and you rule your people with an iron fist," he argued.

Angie pulled up a game on the screen. "Yeah, you're in for a surprise. Okay, sit down. Let me give you the rundown."

Brock's team piled out of the SUV and started down the street for the next club. Turner, Eddie, and Sean each had girls on their arms. Turner looked at his date with a charming smile. "You know, when we were in hell, all I could think about was getting back so I could find the girl I was supposed to be with, then there you were standing at the bar of that club. It was almost like it was meant to be."

The girl clutched his arm, buying his bullshit as her ankles shook walking in her stilettos and short skirt.

Eddie looked deep into his date's heavily made-up eyes. "Baby, I went through hell to find you."

She snorted. "You were on your way to the bathroom at the last bar."

"Shit. You're right. But I did wait in line to buy you an apple martini."

His date nodded and wrapped herself around his arm. The other guys were walking with their dates up to the door of a new club. The doorman recognized the guys and nodded, opening the VIP ropes. The girls were all impressed, and they led the way, giggling as they ran in front of the guys. Turner and the other two put their arms over each other's shoulders as they stepped into the multi-level club, the music throbbing in their ears.

"This is the life," Sean exclaimed.

Turner scoffed. "I know, right. And to think these mercs get to do this every day."

Eddie mused, "Makes you think twice about reenlistment. I mean, if you can go out in the civilian world and live like kings, why settle for barracks and cold chow?"

Turner shrugged. "Because we have contracts, and we're the only ones in the military capable of what we do. We may not have the money like Katie, but we have the fame and each other. I don't mind serving my country with the military. One day I'll get a pretty decent retirement package."

"If you don't die," Eddie pointed out.

"Don't you let me die, motherfucker."

The guys walked up to the bar and ordered a round of drinks. The girls stood to the side whispering and giggling, enjoying the attention the guys brought them. The team was still just as famous as the first time they had been there. Even with Brock staying behind at the condos, they were able to get into the clubs. It made Turner feel a little better about always getting shown up by him.

Turner raised his glass to the other two. "To slaying demons, taking really hot steps through hell—"

Sean continued, "To spraying bullets, dropping demons where they stand—"

"And to always walking out alive and ready for the next round of action," Eddie finished. "Life is one round on the course, and we make the very best of that shit."

"Hear, hear," the three of them chorused, clinking glasses and taking their shots.

They grabbed their dates, pulling them onto the dance floor. It was the boys' night out, something they had earned through brimstone and fire. They were determined to enjoy every second of it.

The base looked completely different than it had when the team had first moved in. They had upped the perimeter safety precautions, although they were invisible to the naked eye, buried as they were beneath the dirt. The landscape no longer looked like an old military ghost town, but a vibrant and budding military playground.

The main armory building had been redone and fortified so that Joshua could get back to work on ammo and other devices. They had used so many of them between going down to hell and the incursions on land that one huge breakout could leave them almost completely undefended. That was the first and most important project completed.

Earth movers and machines crawled over the grounds, digging and making construction possible all over the place. Teams of military personnel sent over by the general were crowded around several locations. Korbin and his team had given them a detailed plan; every aspect of the compound was to be built to their exact specifications.

Timothy was tasked with making sure the computer system for the new construction was done to his standards. He stood in a hard hat, glowering at a group of workers.

"You have to watch where you dig. Those lines cost hundreds of dollars each," Timothy yelled.

Joshua walked over and put his hand on Tim's shoulder. "Take a deep breath, my man. You're going to have a heart attack out here, and I have no idea what outfit you want to be buried in."

Timothy let out a deep breath and laughed. "I just don't want to have to do this more than once. If these lines and cables aren't done right and they get sealed in, it is going to be one hefty bill to fix the mistake. Ain't nobody wanna call Momma Angel and tell her we got to re-dig an entire building. Nope. Not me."

Joshua laughed. "No, but it's better than you stroking out on the dirt."

Timothy crossed his arms, one hand over his mouth. "Is it? I don't know. Then I would get some rest. The other way around and I would be listening to red devil angel woman lose her shit. Maybe just a mild stroke would get the point across. You know, have everyone worried, and then I make a miraculous comeback and wear fashionable pajamas in the hospital?"

Joshua shook his head. "Nope. Sorry, buddy, not okay. Besides, we need you for security purposes. Not a damn person in this building would be able to figure out the system you have set up. Korbin would just press a bunch of buttons, and Calvin would say fuck it and run out with his guns. Stephanie would do better. She might be able to reconnect our cable."

Timothy sighed. "You're right. I need to do my shit. Okay, putting on a calm face right now. I swear I might just get in there and dig it myself." He snugged his hard hat down and strutted up to the diggers. He waved a hand at the foreman. "Dear, may we have a chat?"

Joshua chuckled and turned back toward the armory. "Glad to see nothing has changed."

The soft sound of piano and strings played in the background as Calvin reached across the table and took his girl's hands in his. He beamed at Sofia, glad to be back in her orbit. It had been a long flight and an even longer explanation as to why he still had burns healing on his forearms. Finally, though, he had calmed her down enough to get her out to dinner.

"It looks like you have a fan club." She laughed, glancing at several tables with people pointing at him.

Calvin smiled abashedly. "People are strange. I'm just a warrior like the rest of them."

Sofia leaned in closer. "You are *not* like the rest of them. You are the bravest man I know. You just walked through hell for God's sake."

Calvin shrugged. "With several other very brave men and women. We will continue to do what we promised to when we decided to join the merc teams."

A twenty-something girl walked up to the table. "I'm sorry to interrupt you. May I possibly have your autograph?"

Calvin let go of Sofia's hands and smiled. "Of course. What's your name?"

"Mia," the girl replied.

Calvin signed the piece of paper she handed over. "Mia, stay safe out there, okay?"

She nodded and ran off to whisper and giggle with her friends.

Sofia shot him a look. "Mia? Does that happen a lot?"

"What?"

"Don't act like you don't love it."

Calvin shook his head and sat back in the chair. "All of this is cool, it really is. Lets me know that people appreciate what we're doing for them. But that's not what this night is about. This night is about you. This night is about being back in each other's arms and being safe, even if it's just for a little while."

The waitress walked up and refilled their glasses before setting their salads down in front of them. Calvin put his napkin in his lap and took a sip of his wine. "How is school going?"

"Better. I'm glad I didn't transfer this semester. Just want to get enough of it done that I can, you know?"

Calvin nodded. "I'm glad you didn't too. There is a lot of danger everywhere, but the new base isn't even finished yet. I would have been worried about you the entire time."

She smiled her perfect smile. "You're always worried about me. I could be in a metal box with fortified demon-killing metal, and you would be worried about me. I need you to focus on *you* while you're out there. I don't want to be a distracting thought. That's what can get you killed."

Calvin smirked. "But you are so hard not to think about with that low-cut sparkly gown and that ruby-red lipstick. I don't even want my salad anymore. Let's just get it to go."

She giggled and swiped her hand at him. "You are crazy."

"That's what my team counts on."

Near Las Vegas, down an old dirt road, were the remnants of Katie's Killers' old base. The traps in the field were sprung and open, the guard shack empty. The armory door swung back and forth in the breeze, squeaking and banging against the brick walls. Dust blew across the empty ground with no lights shining overhead. It was abandoned. Every last bit of the merc team was gone.

Lightning shot across the desert sky and a rumble of thunder sounded overhead. There was often lightning and thunder from the heat, but there would be no rain. Between the strikes of lightning, it was dark, just a light breeze blowing sand across the abandoned lot. In the distance, beady red eyes began to glow. At first, there were two pairs, then four, and then they began to multiply as small animals of all types gathered in the shadows.

Beneath the trembling thunderous sky, the orbs grew closer and closer until a horde of small furry animals ran sniffing across the ground. Demons had infected the wildlife and were now looking for any sign of Katie and her team. They had taken over foxes, birds, bunnies, and rodents and now ignored their usual predator/prey relationship, snuffling the ground for a hopeful lead.

They moved in and out of the ammunition building, their small claws scratching on the cement floor. Others searched the guard shack and the landing pad, but the team had been very careful not to leave even a shred of paper on the sands. One coyote scurried to the emergency hatch and began scraping around it faster and faster until his paws began to bleed.

He leaned his head back and howled loudly to catch the others' attention. Suddenly, his body began to shake and twist, and his skin became tighter and tighter until the demon inside him ripped through his thin, furry flesh. Two sharp claws protruded from its front paws. The coyote howled, then snarled, then screamed as the demonic head burst through the coyote's jaws. Its crooked back legs broke through the coyote's bones until all that was left of the animal was a shred of bloody pelt hanging from the demon's body.

He reached down and grabbed the hatch, opening the thing wide, then beckoned to the rest of the creatures, who ran, hopped, and flew to him. He pointed them down the shaft into the empty halls below. The demon slowly climbed in and hung on to the ladder, pushing the hatch door all the way open. He looked at the large moon emerging from behind the clouds and growled, his eyes flashing bright red as he descended.

The demons were going to find Katie and the team for Moloch. It was their quest.

Korbin sat back in the new base and wiped his face. The kitchen was still being renovated, so they had ordered pizza again. Nobody really minded. Stephanie and Joshua were across the table from Korbin, tired from the day's work. Timothy had already gone back to his room, exhausted from having spent the day pushing diggers around the base and supervising the cable-laying.

"You know, things are a lot different now than they used to be back in the day," Korbin mused.

Stephanie picked a piece of pepperoni off her pizza and ate it. "Oh, yeah? How so?"

Korbin sat forward and grabbed another piece of pizza. "For starters, we have to go *to* the incursions to wage war. Back in the day, your job was to defend. Your castle was built, every place had an army, and you were equipped to defend your city to the death."

Stephanie grinned. "Castles? So you're talking *way* back in the day."

"Yeah. Way back in the day. You didn't want them to get anywhere close to the top of your wall, so you built great big things. Now, we put up defenses where we are, and we have police, but demons can walk right into any city they want."

Joshua nodded. "That's true. If you were attacking someone else, it wasn't to save the people inside the walls of that kingdom, it was to take over. Otherwise, the enemy came to you, and you had to defend the rights of your people and your city or kingdom. There isn't any of that anymore. We live in a world where we hope that demons don't come to our town, and then we chase the enemy, trying to hunt them down."

Korbin took a sip of his soda. "Yep, it's not the same."

Stephanie winked at Korbin. "We can build you a moat if that will make you feel better."

He looked up thoughtfully. "I've wondered if we could turn the tides, you know? If we could use our place to both defend and attack. They come to us, but we are ready for them. Then we turn it on them and attack them all until they are dead."

Joshua thought about it. "That would mean us never

leaving our castle. We would have to let them pretty much burn down the rest of the world and wait until they came to our doorstep. It would really only work if we somehow convinced every other country in the world to take it back to the Middle Ages."

Korbin looked disappointed. "They did have some badass defenses back then. The big giant gates, the moats, the fire cannons."

Joshua laughed. "My favorite is the hot oil. They had buckets at the ready all across the walls. In this day and age, we could come up with some hot-tar sprinkler system. It would just douse everyone. We could put them on the grass and the bridge too. Then, *poof*, light them up."

Korbin giggled like an excited schoolboy. "And then load the cannons and just blow them up. *Boom!*"

"It would be interesting to watch Joshua constructing cannonballs out of the special metal," Stephanie replied.

Joshua's eyes went wide. "We would need several facilities for that."

Korbin pointed at Joshua. "I feel like you already need more facilities. Have we gotten anywhere with the thought of expanding our manufacturing to more locations? Now that we're connected to the military, I would think it would be easier to figure it out."

Joshua shrugged. "To be honest, I kind of gave up on the thought. Besides General Brushwood, I haven't met any leaders who are trustworthy. It's been kind of a crapshoot. The general can't always be there, and there are a lot of corrupt people in the government these days."

Korbin thought about it for a second. "What if we didn't do it on military installations? What if we did it through us and just placed them in different locations we felt comfortable with all over the country? We would run, manage, and secure them, and then we could exponentially up our production."

Joshua leaned forward and wiped his hands. "Right, but think about it this way: if we hadn't been the ones defending the last attack on our base, what was the likelihood we would have been able to save the armory? I think that the more locations there are, the better the chances of the process and weapons dropping into the wrong hands."

Korbin pursed his lips. "I agree. We could never take that chance, and given the way they've been targeting multiple locations at once... Well, they could hit us in every location. We couldn't possibly successfully defend multiple locations at once. We just aren't big enough for that."

Stephanie cleared her throat. "If you think about it, in the past we didn't even have enough security on our *own* base. We didn't always have the military support we have now. If you could imagine us fighting off all those demons on our own...that would be a shitshow for sure."

"Not only that." Joshua rubbed his hands over his face. "But can you imagine if the demons started using our weapons? Or if they got the ability to manufacture the bullets and use them against our side?"

All of them shook their heads, and Korbin tossed his crust in the box. "It would be the end of the war, in my opinion. We have Katie, yes, but other than her, we rely on having more advanced weapons than the demons. I can't even imagine what the fight would be like with special bullets turned against us."

Stephanie shivered. "I don't want to think about it. We would be exterminated in three seconds by the hellbeasts. They would have no reason to even send as many as they do. They would just line up, fire, and be done."

Korbin reached across the table and took Stephanie's hand. "Let's hope we never have to face that."

6

The news had really started to sink in with people around the world as more and more attacks happened in random places. The general populace had started to reach a breaking point. They were beginning to realize that the war had grown so large and so unpredictable that they could no longer sit out the action and think the mercenaries would save them. They had to take action and prepare their people for attacks.

If an incursion happened where they lived, they wanted to have a fighting chance.

All across the world, groups set up town meetings, all centered around the idea of bringing defense to the demons' offense. The meetings were planned in the early morning since most incursions seemed to happen in the evening. Droves of men, women, and children came to learn more and give their opinions on how to fight back against the demons.

Videos of the war had been broadcast to all corners of the Earth ever since Incursion Day. The attacks had started in the US, but over time the rest of the world had seen more and more attacks. Demons waded onto the shores of every continent.

In a small town on the outskirts of London, they held the meeting at the high school gym. It was the only place large enough to hold the number of people who wanted to come.

The speaker took to the podium, cleared his throat, and read from a piece of paper. "Dear citizens, I am so glad you have chosen to come out and participate in this meeting. Every day we see a new place destroyed and ripped apart by the war—towns not much different than our own. We feel secluded from these terrors because we are so small, but that is no longer the case. In fact, we seem to be the ones that are under the most threat."

Several of the people in the audience shouted, agreeing with the speaker. He put his hands up to quiet the crowd. "I will not lie: for the first few months, I did not allow my children to watch the news. The hit-and-run tactics of the demons were gruesome and unforgiving. However, as small villages all over the globe fell victim to these attacks, I found that the only way for me to truly drive home their serious nature was to allow the kids to view these terrible events. The world we live in is no longer peaceful or serene. We are under attack by creatures that do not belong here. I will not allow my family to perish during one of these attacks without at least equipping them and everyone else with the means to fight back. We will not die in vain."

Everyone clapped.

The speaker gestured to a woman standing behind him.

"To explore this more, I would like to turn the floor over to demonologist Eliza Dewberry."

The woman was nervous, constantly fidgeting with her long mouse-brown hair and touching her glasses. She put a stack of notes on the podium and cleared her throat. "Hel... Hello, everyone. My name is Dr. Eliza Dewberry, and for ten years now I have been studying demonology. Obviously, a lot of new information has come out since Incursion Day, and my team and I have been sifting through it as quickly as possible."

"How do we fight back?" someone yelled from the crowd.

Dr. Dewberry put her finger up. "This is an excellent question. After studying their moves, their strength, and the randomness of their actions, we have come up with a couple of options. Now, just so you understand, this is not simply my opinion. I sit on a panel of experts from all over the country. I know many of you want to fight, but as we've seen from the videos, it's a futile gesture, followed by a brutally quick and painful death. So, to negate that, we are suggesting a system of shelters. These shelters will be prepared, readied, and manned twenty-four hours a day. There will also be Demon Sirens to warn you."

"Like the old air-raid sirens?" someone yelled.

The doctor nodded. "Yes, precisely. When those sirens go off, you make your way to the shelters as quickly as possible."

A woman in the middle of the crowd stood up. "But won't that just put us all out in the open?"

Eliza pointed her finger. "Excellent question. We believe not. We were able to partner with local and international government, and they have a system created by Katie's Killers that detects openings between worlds, often five minutes or so before the demons arrive. This will allow us to sound the alarms and, as long as you are prepared, enable you to make your way to the closest shelter. Obviously, this is quite risky, but we won't survive in our homes, and we are not strong enough to fight back, so we have to look for better ways."

A man in the front raised his hand, and Eliza pointed to him. "Yes?"

"And then what? We wait?" he asked.

She took a deep breath. "Yes. We wait. We wait for assistance, or we wait for the demons to go back through their portal."

He nodded approvingly. "So, these buggers would be like post-apocalyptic demon shelters."

"Absolutely. They would be fortified and stocked, and we would issue weapons to those responsible for protecting the shelters. This is a foreign enemy: creatures from a completely different world. We cannot stand in the streets with guns and expect to survive. We will create enough shelters from existing structures to hold the entirety of the town. Once inside, we will have a check-in system to help... Well, help us figure out who didn't make it." Her voice managed to grow even smaller somehow. "The carnage these creatures has produced is not easily forgotten. Oftentimes, identifying bodies has been difficult."

The whole room nodded, talking back and forth. They loved the idea.

Time was the only thing against them. The shelters had

to be completed and stocked before the next demon attack. And who knew when that would be?

The alarm went off bright and early, even before the sun had risen. Katie yawned and stretched her arms overhead, then smacked the button on the top of the radio. She had almost forgotten what it was like to wake up to an alarm rather than Pandora's constant nagging. Incessant beeping or incessant bitching? Katie wasn't sure which one was worse.

Pandora yawned, just waking up herself. *I'm not usually one to complain about this, but remind me again why we are up before the sun?*

Katie sat up in bed, breathing in the smell of coffee from the kitchen. *We're heading to the base today, remember? We have to get the boys up and going so we can catch the jet.*

And Juntto?

Katie walked across the room to pull on her clothes for the day. She had already packed the rest of her things. *As far as I know, Angie helped him pack last night. He will probably need a wake-up call.*

Just then the sound of Juntto's deep laugh echoed through the house. Katie wrinkled her nose and stuck her head out of the door. From her room, she could see into the kitchen. Sure enough, there was Juntto munching bacon and drinking coffee as Angie prepared the rest of breakfast. Katie ducked back into her room. *I feel like Angie is taming the dragon.*

Pandora scoffed. *Impossible, unless she castrated him or something.*

Katie started dressing. *Maybe it was mental castration. All I know is, the more laughter, the better off we are.*

I guess.

He's not murdering anyone.

He can laugh and murder at the same time. I've seen it.

Katie finished getting ready, pulling her hair back into a ponytail and putting her two smaller pistols in their holsters. She had packed Tom and Harry, figuring they wouldn't be necessary on the plane ride. She collected her things and took her bags to the door, where the concierge would pick them up.

As she set the bags down, there was a knock on the door. She opened it up to find a smiling Brock .

Why, hello. Morning wood, anyone?

Katie gestured for him to enter, and Brock winked at her. He was followed by the rest of his team, half-awake and half-hungover.

Oh, and the boys too? Don't mind if I do.

Katie laughed internally and ushered them into the kitchen, where Angie was dividing the last pieces of stuffed French toast between a heap of plates.

"Good morning," Angie chirped. She waited for a moment and then gave Juntto a side glance.

Juntto sighed. "Good morning, humans."

Angie smiled proudly, like a kindergarten teacher who has just heard her students recite the ABCs.

The soldiers halted in the middle of sitting down at the table. Angie giggled and put the carafe of OJ on the table.

"Juntto is working on manners. He figured it would cut down on paperwork."

Brock gave her a questioning look. "Paperwork?"

"Paperwork." Katie nudged him in the side meaningfully. "You know. It's a terrible thing."

Brock caught on. "Oh. Right. Absolutely." He looked at the other guys, who immediately started to mumble about the trials of paperwork.

"Shit, yeah."

"Hate the stuff."

"The last dude who gave me paperwork? I punched him right in the dick."

Katie glared at Eddie, who fumbled for words. "I mean, I did that, and I just got more damn paperwork. It's, like, never-ending. Terrible. Yeah."

Juntto nodded in grave agreement. They all sat down together, human, Damned, and frost giant, and ate breakfast.

The concierge had the SUVs packed and waiting by the time they got down to the first floor. Katie looked in the direction of the condo and sighed. "Hopefully it'll be okay until we get back."

Angie heard a mournful note in Katie's voice; her tone was different than it normally was. She gave Katie a big hug before she left, but somehow, she wasn't reassured.

"...it doesn't feel pity or remorse."

Katie leaned her head back and looked at Juntto. He

was sitting in the seat across the aisle from her on the plane. "They're talking about you."

Juntto narrowed his eyes and cleared his throat, the words of the Terminator coming from him. "You are terminated."

Everyone chuckled except Turner, who hushed them, having never seen the first *Terminator*. The ride to the base was pretty long, so they drew a movie name out of a hat and put it on to pass the time. Pandora was completely bored by it. *I don't know why we couldn't have watched* Batman.

Katie rolled her eyes. *Because you've watched all of them a thousand times.*

And I've learned so much from them, yet you still won't let me be who I am meant to be. I am...Slut Girl!

Katie shook her head. *Still no. Nice try.*

You know you want to be my sidekick. I've seen your moves.

I'm nobody's sidekick.

What about Brock over there? Eh?

Hmm.

See? You've got a little Slut Girl in you, too.

They sat laughing at the terrible special effects. Juntto was completely enthralled by the unstoppable bad guy, of course. When the movie was over, they were close to the base. Juntto stood up and stretched. "I am done with Van Damme. I think it is time to go Terminator."

Angie stood up and got in Juntto's face, crossing her arms over her chest. "Oh, hell no."

Brock leaned toward Katie. "She's about to go angry shopper on his ass."

Angie put up her finger. "You better change into a shape

that fits those clothes, or I'm taking you to Walmart to get your replacements. You'll be fighting in sweatpants and Dickie overalls."

Juntto wrinkled his nose. "That would be terrible."

Angie nodded, but Juntto started to smile. She stepped back as Juntto changed anyway, making himself into an Arnold Schwarzenegger look-alike. However, instead of ripping his clothes to shreds in the process, he used magic to make them fit the new frame.

Angie tilted her head to the side, wheels turning. "So, wait, can you do that for other people?"

Juntto chuckled and stood tall, almost hitting his head on the ceiling. "I can use my magic for anything, really. I could do that for anyone. It's kind of my specialty. I once created a full wardrobe for a giant. Not me, a different giant. And I changed a dress for a fairy so that she could walk tall around the others. It was pretty sweet."

Angie had a mischievous smirk on her face, so Juntto quickly shut up. He realized that Angie just might have cornered him, now he'd admitted he could do that. The last thing he wanted was to become a clothing designer for women.

7

A s the plane taxied onto the base hidden in the hills of Colorado, everyone got up and started collecting their things. Juntto and Katie were the last ones off the plane. Katie stopped at the door and turned to Juntto. "Whatever happens on this mission, if I suspect you of having one thought outside of being helpful to our side, I will personally take your dick and throw it in a lava pit."

Juntto gave a gap-toothed smile. "I'll be back...on your side."

Katie sneered and exited the plane. Pandora was cracking up at Juntto, but Katie found it less than comical. *I am surrounded by fools all the time.*

Oh, lighten up. A laugh is good for you sometimes.

They dragged their gear toward the building and piled it up in one of the hangar bays. The captain running the operation came up and shook Katie's hand. "Good to see you doing well. The doctor and his assistant are waiting for you in the gate building to go over the plan. Is your team ready to get going immediately?"

Katie looked at the others and back at the captain. "Locked and loaded."

He nodded. "Good. When you are done with the debriefing, we'll get everyone suited up."

They followed him back to the room from which they had, just weeks before, entered hell. The doctor and his assistant stood up and shook everyone's hands. Dr. Thorough nervously sat back down. "This mission should be much simpler than the last, and Alice and I will not be accompanying you. I think we will just get in the way if we do."

Katie liked that idea but wasn't going to say it out loud. Pandora just laughed. *Thank you, Lucifer. Babysitting is hard work. Unless it's this baby, sitting on Brock's face.*

Going to hell soon. Focus.

Okay. I'm focused, Mom.

Katie ignored her as Thorough pulled out one of his drones. "This is a drone we specially designed. It's meant not only to withstand the climate of hell but also to be as inconspicuous as possible while sending data back through the portal. They are easy to set up. You place them on the ground, click the white button until it begins to blink, and hit the green button. All in all, the whole thing should take fifteen seconds per drone. After that, you want to make sure they are communicating. That is the trickiest part. As soon as I get the signal, I will turn them on. When you see the blades spin, you know it's communicating."

Katie looked at the drone. "And if it doesn't spin?"

The doctor looked at Alice, who cleared her throat and flipped the drone over. "You flip it upside down and press the only button on the bottom. It will reset the circuitry.

Then press the white button and then the green like you did the first time. If, after about fifteen seconds, there's still nothing, just pick it up and bring it back."

"But please try. We need these images," Dr. Thorough added.

"And how many at each of the three locations?" Brock asked.

Thorough nodded. "You will be dropping twenty-four at each location, so six each. You can do them as fast as possible. I have a whole system in place. I'll be able to respond as soon as I get the signal. I designed it not only for ease of use but for swiftness, especially since I know you guys will be inside. The entire operation should take, hopefully, no more than ten minutes tops. We tried to pick locations away from any activity. After you're out, the drones can fly deeper in for observation."

Katie clapped her hands. "Good. Is there anything else we should know?"

Thorough shook his head. "Nope. There are six sacks laid out, one for each of you. Grab your sack and..."

Pandora chuckled. *Grabbin' sacks and taking names. It's our new motto.*

Katie kept the smirk off her lips. Thorough continued. "...get in and out as fast as possible. We will be standing by and will be ready if you run into any kind of problem. We thank you for this."

The team nodded and got up from the table, going to where the suits were. They quickly changed and tested their gear, then threw their satchels over their shoulders.

Sean grumbled, "Heavy gear, bro."

"Heavy mission, bro," Eddie responded. He looked at

Juntto, still in Arnold form. "Don't you need a suit or something?"

Juntto shrugged. He wasn't wearing any protective gear, just a headset so he could communicate with them. "I'm not a weak human. I am a frost giant. A Leviathan. A conqueror of stupid, squishy beings such as yourself."

"Oh. Right." Eddie and Sean exchanged a glance, and Sean rolled his eyes.

The team stood in a line facing the area where the first portal would be made. They looked down the line, giving each other the thumbs-up until it reached Katie.

Katie squared her shoulders. *Okay, Pandora, do your work.*

My pleasure. Abracadabra, reach out and grab ya'.

Pandora reached out through Katie, and the air in front of the team shuddered and shimmered and tore open. Heat and the smell of sulfur billowed from the new portal. Katie waved them forward, and everyone ran into hell as fast as they could. They fought through the blast of heat and knelt on the edge of a cliff overlooking several wide lava rivers. Jagged mountains stretched up to a sky glowing with an eerie light that seemed to have no source. Without talking, they went straight to work. Each took out drones, turned them on, and waited for the signal.

All along the cliff, drones began spinning their blades. In a moment the hellish sky was filled with small drones. They had no problems with any of them. Katie talked into her microphone inside her helmet. "All right, team, round up and get out of here."

The portal had been left open, so one by one they jumped back through. The whole team took a knee to relax, their armor steaming from the unbearable heat of hell. As soon as Katie and Juntto were in the hangar bay, the portal snapped shut behind them. Several military members ran over, placing new satchels in front of each of them.

Doctor Thorough was on the headset frequency as well. "Excellent job. You ready for placement number two?"

Katie gave a thumbs-up. Pandora opened a second portal, this one in a flatland area covered in hardened lava. They jumped through and went straight to work, doing the same thing all over again. It went easy-peasy, with no fuck-ups, and within fifteen minutes they were back on Earth.

The military members again gave them new sets of drones and Katie looked at her team. "You boys ready?"

Juntto beat a fist against his chest. "I am a frost giant. I was born to war, not to free little metal bugs."

Sean turned to Eddie. "Dude is super weird."

Eddie shrugged. "Badass, though."

Sean nodded reluctantly. "True."

Katie called, "Let's get to it. Two down, one to go."

The dust billowed out in dense clouds as a UPS truck charged down the gravel road. The driver took a big hit off his vape and added his own smoke to the dust cloud. He tapped on his steering wheel to the beat of the radio, keeping one eye on his GPS. He frowned, trying to find the location of his next delivery. The device kept glitching, so he reached up to tap the screen. "Come on now, good buddy, don't die on me out in the middle of nowhere. I'll end up being someone's supper." He drove on at a snail's pace.

Just as he rounded a hill, he slammed on his brakes. The truck was right in front of a guard shack. Where had that come from? A long metal fence stretched from either side of the shack. As a bulky guard with a scar on his cheek came over, the driver did his best to hide his vaporizer.

The guard put his hand out. "How can we help you?"

The driver made a show of looking through his notes. "I've got some shipments here for Timothy...the IT Gal? Huh. That's what it says, though. Hey, I didn't actually think that I would find you guys. The GPS went all haywire. I didn't even know there was a military installation out here."

The scarred guard just stared at him. "We are everywhere, sir."

The driver blinked. "Yeah, well, where would you like me to leave the boxes? With you, I mean? Or can I go on base?"

The squeal of tires brought their attention to the road behind the guard shack. The jeep stopped at the fence and a man in tight pants, a lime green shirt, and a tan sports coat hopped out of the car. He walked through a gate in the perimeter fence, holding a handkerchief to his mouth and nose, and looked at the guard. "Because of all of the dust."

"Oh."

He stopped next to the guard and stared at the driver. "Well, it's about damn time. And what is he doing just standing here? I need my packages."

The guard looked a bit thrown off. "We were told no unauthorized personnel beyond this point."

Timothy waved the idea away with one hand, the other firmly placed on his lower back. "Can't you see that this is an emergency? I cannot possibly operate without new clothes. Since we decided to be out here in the middle of fucking nowhere with dust and bugs and grass and shit, I took matters into my own hands. You either bring me to the stores or the stores to me, and I'm a busy bee. I've got things to do, and I'm not doing them in off-brand crap. Jesus, Mary, and Joseph, I would hyperventilate looking down at knockoff Marc Jacobs. I can't *even*."

The guard shrugged, and the driver hopped out of his seat and pulled down four boxes. He helped Timothy load them into his jeep.

The driver was getting ready to leave when Timothy put his finger up and hurried back to the jeep, where he grabbed his wallet. He smiled as he sashayed back to the driver and stuffed a fifty into his pocket. "For all your trouble. Having to make this hellish drive."

The driver smiled widely. "Thank you. I'll keep an eye out for other boxes."

Timothy winked. "Excellent. Drive safe back out of here, honey. It's a doozy."

Timothy ran back to the jeep and hauled ass back toward the base. The driver turned and hauled ass away from the base.

The scarred guard stood there for a moment. He was joined by a young guard. "No trouble?"

"No, but it was strange."

The young guard ventured, "Should we call it in?"

The other guard nodded. "That would be the safest thing since I have no fucking clue what just happened here." The scarred man walked over and picked up the phone. In a moment the general's gruff voice came on the line.

"What do you want?"

"General, it's Lieutenant Briggs at the front gate. Just wanted to let you know the UPS guy came to drop off Timothy's clothes. We didn't let him in, as per your orders, but we let in several boxes. They *could* be clothes, but I was thinking they could be something else."

"Something else, Lieutenant Briggs?"

"Like contraband."

"Contraband?" The general groaned. "For fuck's sake. Deal with these issues on your own. And for the love of all that is holy, don't piss off that IT guy."

———

Pandora opened the third and final gate, and the team stepped through into hell. This location felt a hell of a lot hotter than the other two, and Katie exchanged a look with Brock. He waved his team on to check their surroundings.

Katie had a bad feeling in her gut, but she figured it was just the heat. *This one is scalding.*

Pandora sniffed. *Yeah, because you are much closer to the rings of hell. Keep an eye out, and just get this shit done.*

Katie nodded and looked at the others. "All right, team, let's get these down and get the fuck out of here. I've had enough hot, molten days in my life."

Brock pointed across the ledge they were on, and he and his three teammates went to work. Juntto lumbered up next to Katie and began setting up drones with his fat fingers. "This was a really stupid place to land. Who picked this, the human in the lab coat?"

Katie looked up. The gate they'd walked in through had already shut behind them. Pandora couldn't hold it open forever. "I don't know, Juntto, but if we concentrate we can get out of here in one piece."

Suddenly Katie gasped and grabbed her chest. She could feel the surge of an incoming portal opening. She stood up and turned quickly as a gate began to open in the distance.

For a moment the portal stood there like a shimmering wound, then the demons came pouring out.

Katie groaned. "Fuck, fuck. Everyone, where are we with these?"

Brock looked at the other guys. "We are struggling with the connection over here. We need more time."

Katie glanced at Juntto. "All right, big guy—you said you wanted a war."

Juntto pounded his mighty fist into his other palm. "I'll give them more time. Those fuckers are going to get their heads slammed together."

Katie took a deep breath and walked to the guys. "We will buy you as much time as possible, but get those drones in the air. Our future on Earth is at stake. Work quickly."

Brock caught her eye and nodded gravely, then sent his team back to work on the drones.

Katie turned toward the droves of demons coming toward them and cracked her neck. She pulled out her two pistols.

Juntto flexed his muscles. "Let's do this, angel bitch."

8

Juntto leaped forward, ready to run headfirst into the swarm of damned fiends. Katie grabbed his arm and found herself pulled along with him.

"Shit!"

Juntto stopped and lowered her back down. She straightened herself with a perturbed look. Juntto put his hands out. "So, what are we doing here? You want to have tea or something?"

Katie groaned. "No, I want to know what your strategy is going to be. You're unarmed, and you have this huge, slow-moving body."

Juntto looked down at himself. "Not slow. Muscular and powerful. What are you going to do in that frail human body?"

"Point taken," Katie replied.

Juntto put both fists in front of him and flexed his muscles, green moving up his arms. "I can do that Hulk character. Hulk *smash*!"

Katie put her hand on his arm. "No! Just stick with

what you have. Green monster is too much, dude. Too much."

The green faded as he relaxed his muscles. He shrugged. "I'm gonna head right into that large group and rip some heads off. I will also watch your back in case you find yourself slashed and crashed."

Katie sighed. "Where are you learning all these sayings?"

"The internet...mostly me-mes."

Pandora sniffed. *Dude, just let the big bro loose on their asses. You will see what his plan is. We can do our own thing. Trust me.*

Katie wasn't sure about it, but she was going to trust Pandora. "All right, Terminator, go...terminate."

He nodded and stepped forward, but turned back to Katie. "I'll be back."

"Go!" she shouted, pushing him.

She watched as he started to run, picking up speed. His momentum carried him forward like some huge, insane cannonball. He jumped over large rocks and landed on others, crushing them to small bits. He leaped straight at the first group of demons and slammed his fist into the ground, creating a crater. Demons flew in all directions. Juntto snarled and lashed out with his large hands. He grabbed demons and pulled them apart, their limbs flying off and their heads rolling until they turned to ash.

Katie found herself just watching the carnage. *Damn, that dude is rollin' out there.*

Pandora laughed. *See? I told you, now get your shit straight. You have some demons to kick. Don't let that fool outdo you. You are Katie, the demon angel, the sex goddess. You are* Slut Girl.

Katie shook her head and took off at a run toward the oncoming surge. *I'm not sure if that was meant to be a motivational speech, but it sucked. And I'm not Slut Girl or a sex goddess, although I can live with that one.*

Pandora thought about it for a minute. *I'm now picturing us more like Wonder Woman, only without that stupid lasso.*

Who needs a lasso when you have a demon? Katie leaped into the air and pulled out her guns.

Juntto let out a loud roar and beat his hands against his chest. His eyes shimmered brightly, but not the searing red like the demons. They flashed through all the colors, looking almost like cat eyes for a moment before turning a bright ocean blue. He slashed his fists back and forth, knocking out demons. Given his sheer alien strength, everything he touched pretty much turned to ash. Those who didn't writhed on the ground with giant holes in their bodies in the shape of fists.

"Arnold hates demons," he screamed and grabbed two demons by the throat.

He threw one on the ground and kept his boot on its throat until ash billowed up. He lifted the other demon high in the air and reared his fist back, letting loose with all his might. Black blood splashed his shirt as the demon's head exploded, and he gritted his teeth and threw the dead demon to the ground. Claws reached for him, and Juntto started throwing powerful punches as fast as he could.

Right, left, right, left. Heads flew off scaly black bodies and went rolling across the ground. Black goo splattered all over the place, but it didn't faze the frost giant in the least.

The demons started trying to run from him instead of

attack him, so he chased them down. His hands were like stone vices, and once he gripped a shrieking demon, he would not let go until the thing was ash. He grabbed one from behind and popped its head off like it was a plastic doll. He threw the body at a trio of fleeing demons, spraying the demons with blood, and then dust. A small band of braver fiends began to gather to his right, and Juntto turned to meet them.

He grabbed a large demon by the horns and shoved his knee into the thing's chest. Bones broke and the demon howled in pain, encouraging his comrades to retreat. Juntto snarled at the group and slammed his knee into the demon one more time. His leg went through the demon's body and stayed there. Juntto growled, pulling and pushing the body to free his knee. He finally twisted out of the thing as it exploded.

He spat on the pile of ash before giving it the middle finger. He turned to the group of demons, growing bolder with numbers. Juntto waved at them. "Watch Arnold."

He put up both his hands and turned them back and forth. The demons peered at them as his fists grew larger. When he finally stopped, he looked more like Wreck-It Ralph than Arnold. He laughed as he sprinted toward them, raising his huge arms over his head, then jumped into the air and landed right in front of them. The demons roared at him. Juntto roared right back and brought his hammer hands down on their heads.

His hands battered through their tough, unholy bodies forcefully, ripping several of the demons in half. He tilted his head back and laughed loudly, filling the ears of everyone in range with his mirth. Over and over, he chased the demons and used his fists like he was playing Whack-a-Mole. He slammed his fists into their heads and split them completely in half. The piles of ash were growing larger by the second, and by now most of the larger demons were keeping their distance from him. One ugly brute hissed in the demonic tongue, "He's not human."

His horned companion shook his great head. "No. Moloch will want to know what he is, though."

"You go ask someone."

"Fuck yourself, angel-bait."

Their heads exploded as special bullets tore through them, and then the demons were ash.

Katie landed with one knee on the ground and quickly stood up, pulling the trigger over and over. Six demons teetered in front of her, and she leaned forward and blew lightly on them. That was all it took to send them tumbling like dominos before turning to dust. She smiled, extending her other arm without looking and blasting an approaching demon in the forehead.

Pandora was actively watching Juntto, not to make sure he was doing the right thing, but to gawk at his sick-ass moves. *Duuude, he just grew giant arms and is splitting demons like they're fucking logs. That is a sick-fucking-move. I forgot how awesome he can be.*

Did you happen to forget that he talked about violating you and then killing us both?

Pandora scoffed. *Meh, just Viking talk. We survived without his grubby hands touching us, right?*

I suppose.

Katie ran forward, firing her gun into the crowd of demons. They went down all over the place, but finally, her guns clicked, no bullets left. She hadn't even put an extra clip on her belt. She had been told the mission would be quick.

Pandora tsked. *Coming unprepared. Guess you will just have to go full Juntto on them.*

Katie smirked and put her guns back in the holsters, then pulled two short swords from the sheaths on her back. Like her other weapons, they gleamed with special metal. She slapped them against each other, sending sparks flying everywhere. She reared back and sliced through the air, spinning in a circle and coming to a stop back where she'd started. She looked around at the demons still standing, albeit with no heads, and grinned darkly.

They turned to dust, and she raced through the floating debris. She flipped over a large boulder and landed on the shoulders of a medium-sized demon.

Katie spun her swords and shoved them into the thing's spine. He roared and slashed at her, but she dodged his claws, pushing her blades deeper. She rode him to the ground, and when his knees touched the stone, she pushed off him. She turned to the crowd of demons without looking back. She knew he wasn't getting back up. The crowd of demons kept flowing toward them.

Katie fought, but they weren't trying to kill every demon in hell. They were just trying to buy enough time for the drones to get into the air.

Katie sliced her swords, stabbing whatever got into her way. A larger demon at the back bellowed toward her, and she stood her ground until he was close enough. As he raised his leg, she slid on her knees and brought her swords out to both sides. The metal cut through the demon's thick black scales like butter, and he toppled face-first to the ground. She quickly ran up his back, pushing one of her swords through the base of his skull. He growled loudly, and she dove off as he exploded into ash.

Unfortunately, her movement was anything but graceful, and she flew headfirst into a snarling horde of demons. Juntto saw the whole thing and bounded forward, catching her in mid-air.

They landed on the hard ground, and there was a moment of calm in the storm. She looked him in the eyes. "Thanks."

He shrugged nonchalantly. "No problem."

Then he jutted his arm out, his eyes never leaving her face. His fist slammed into the two demons charging her from behind and turned them to dust. She laughed and shook her head, giving him a high five. Katie looked at the top of the hill as several of the drones began to shimmy upward.

Brock gave her a thumbs-up.

Katie turned to Juntto. "We are almost there, but we have to push these bastards back, or we aren't going to be able to get out."

Pandora cleared her throat. *I think I can handle that. Let me out, and I'll push them back with my magic as we get everyone out of here.*

Katie looked at Juntto, but he sensed that something was wrong. He pointed a massive finger at her face. "She's coming out, isn't she?"

Katie nodded and closed her eyes to concentrate. She reached inside her chest, into the core of her being, and pulled Pandora out. Pandora, Queen of hell, burst into being with a loud growl.

Juntto put his arm out and stabilized Katie so she could catch her breath.

Pandora stepped in front of the sea of approaching demons, and the fiends slowed when they saw her. She was known.

She extended her arms out wide and began chanting in demon, "*Ozz ya zokiy aem ya gont* realm *yaeza qae za ir yiz knaoq saeun. Xnirdh ya daelabbi aem lith oth* thunder *qae zes palms. Dul't xoyt ya* hordes charging *yiz juaar aem sazz oth* thrust *yaz xoytlong iaiae ya knaoq* abyss."

The wind blew wildly around them as sparks shot from Pandora's palms. She turned her head toward Juntto and Katie. "Go! I'm right behind you."

Juntto grabbed Katie and sprinted toward the others as the last of the drones took off into the sky. Pandora slammed her palms together, sending a shock wave rolling toward the demons. The ground cracked and burst apart as lava spewed up from new fissures. The demons squealed, terrified, but they could not avoid the molten rock. Some landed in the streams of lava, screeching and sizzling. Others slammed into the cliffs and slid down to the ground half-conscious.

Pandora turned and ran toward the team. They had set up a perimeter and were fighting off the demons that had broken past Juntto and Katie. She knew the spell wouldn't hold the demons long, but she only had one burst of energy left, and she needed that to get back into Katie's body.

The team was battling viciously in front of her. More

demons had appeared, their claws bright as they slashed and snarled at the team. Eddie and Sean had pinned a small group of larger beasts down, but Turner was being backed against a ledge. One gnarled and twisted demon appeared over him and leaped onto his back, slashing wildly.

Turner managed to get his gun around and he pulled the trigger, blasting the demon between the eyes. With its dying strength, the demon raised a wicked claw and jammed it into the base of Turner's neck.

Turner screamed. The demon burst into ash, but Turner dropped to his knees, blood pouring from the back of his neck.

Pandora knew it was bad when human blood began to spill, but just how bad had it gotten? She wasn't sure. She just knew they had to get out of there.

9

Pandora ripped open a portal to Earth and leaped back into Katie's body. She leaned against Juntto and let him help her along. Pandora was weak and Katie wasn't much better, but Pandora held the portal open for the rest of the team.

Sean came through first, holding Turner's legs. Eddie had his upper body, clutching the wounded man under his arms. Eddie's gear was splashed with blood, and not the black ooze the demons leaked. Brock was the last through, watching their back and firing shots into the depths of hell as he left.

"We need help," Brock yelled.

Katie mustered her strength and hurried over as Brock and the other two laid Turner on the floor. She kneeled on one side of the kid and Brock dropped down on the other, holding onto his hand. Blood gushed from the wound at the base of his neck and shoulder, and a trickle came from the corner of his lips.

Katie didn't know what to do. *Pandora, can you talk to his demon?*

Pandora coughed. *I can try. I am very weak.*

Pandora mustered as much of her strength as she could, pulling from Katie's reserves as well. Katie gasped and fell. She tried to prop herself up, but her strength was gone. Pandora reached out, calling out to Turner's demon. *Help him. Help him now.*

The demon was indignant. *Why should I?*

Do you know who I am? I will not only send you to hell if he dies, but I'll call in the last few favors I have and make sure that you suffer greatly for this. You won't see the light of Earth's sun for centuries.

The demon quivered, stuttering, *Yes, Queen. I didn't realize... Yes. I'll do what I can.*

Pandora curled up inside of Katie, exhausted. *That should help.*

The stream of blood from Turner's neck began to slow. Katie backed up as the medics rushed out and wrapped his neck and shoulders with bandages. They put him in a neck brace and loaded him onto a plastic board. Brock stood by helplessly; he could only watch. Katie walked around and grasped his arm. When the medics carried Turner out of sight, Brock pulled away angrily.

Katie could feel the anguish vibrating from him. "Pandora talked to his demon. It's going to help heal him. He may have been close to death, but now I think he'll pull through."

Brock threw his hands out. "This is bullshit. This should never have happened." Everyone stood still, letting him erupt. "We need better suits for fighting and weapons that handle the heat better. My gun stopped working after six shots because of the heat. Turner was throwing fists because his knives were too hot to hold. Sean couldn't even kick out or use his hand-to-hand combat skills because the suits are too restrictive. Eddie was throwing *rocks*, for fuck's sake. Rocks! At demons! We are going to die down there one day, and it can be avoided!"

Katie staggered up to him and put her hand on his arm, trying to calm him. "I'm sorry about Turner. I don't want to see that happen to anyone else. We're doing our best."

Brock shook his head, deflated, and began tearing his protective gear off. "I gotta go make sure." He walked off in the direction the medics had gone, Eddie and Sean following him.

Juntto ran his hand across his chin and looked at the men standing on the sidelines. He walked up to a soldier, who was staring at him with his mouth open. "Do we have any weapons like the ones I saw on the RTS game I've been playing?"

The soldier looked around. "I don't know what that is."

He looked at Katie, who just shrugged. "I don't know. I don't play those kinds of games."

"I do," a voice called from the back of the room.

They looked over as one of the soldiers jogged forward, two more in tow. "We all do. What game are you playing?"

Juntto thought about it for a second. "I lead soldiers into battle. Does that help?"

Angie's voice rang out from the back. "He's playing *StarCraft II: Wings of Liberty*."

Juntto nodded. "Yes, that one."

All three of the guys nodded in recognition. A kid with glasses gave him a thumbs-up. "That's a good one, man. Lots of action and way better graphics. StarCraft has always been a go-to for these games."

Juntto stared at them. "There are a ton of badass weapons in that game. Where are these weapons?"

The guy in glasses thought for a moment. "Actually, you know the P500 pistol? So, in the game, the thing is strong enough to blow a head off above the jawline. Originally, they were only given to the military, but Special Forces Major Esmerelda Ndoci got one before it was even cleared for military use. The thing looks like a handgun on steroids. It's fucking fat and heavy as shit, but packs a fucking punch. And they are engineered for heat. All our stuff is."

Juntto pursed his lips. "Yes. This will do. Do we have something similar to that?"

The guy nodded. "Yeah. They call it 'the King Slayer.' There are like five or six floating around the military demon hunters."

Juntto glanced at Katie, who sighed. "I'll ask the general about them."

Another guy pointed at the back case. "We have something else similar to one of the weapons, too. You know the AGG-12 grenade launcher?"

The other guy snapped his fingers. "*That's* what I was thinking of. The one passed down from Rhett Shearon to his daughter Ritt, who used the last grenade to kill the zerg spire at Anvil Rock."

Katie was clueless, but Juntto and Angie were nodding.

Juntto cleared his throat. "And we have something like that?"

The first guy chuckled. "Even better. The one we have launches grenades encased in special metal. They not only throw out shrapnel of the demon metal, but they release a toxic gas that has the metal in it. You don't really want to use it around infected mercs, but if we're redoing the suits, we could talk to the techs. Make the suits double-lined so nothing gets through, and they can fight straight through it."

Juntto slapped two of the guys on the backs, causing them to tumble forward. "I like you guys. You know your game, too. I'm just a newb."

Katie groaned. "Good Lord, start the nerd convention somewhere else."

"Hey, this shit could help us. Simmer down, angel." Juntto walked to the weapons area and looked over what they had lying there. "Do you have anything like the Hellfire shotgun?"

The young soldier in glasses nodded enthusiastically. "That gun works through mini explosions, giving the shot an incredible arc. That would be amazing, but I have to say we do not have anything like it. I mean, we have launchers for nonlethal ammo, but nothing like that."

One of the guys pulled a large handgun out of the cabinet with a barrel that looked more like a flare gun. "This one, though, is like the—"

Reaching for it, Juntto interrupted, "Slugthrower."

Moloch kicked the broken lava hard, punting a piece of rock into the back of one of the demon's heads. The demon yelped and ran off to join the others, unsure what was going on. Baal picked up a slab of ash and let it sift through his claws.

They stood at the scene of the latest fight. The humans had ventured deeper into the bowels of hell than they had the time before. The heat radiating from the space had to be at least twice as hot as the outlying areas. Still, Moloch couldn't put his finger on why they had been there.

He looked at six small burn marks on the ground and rubbed his chin. "I don't get it. That demon scum and her meatsack friends come to hell, they fight my demons, and then leave in the blink of an eye. I know that they left something here; I can sense it. But what?"

Baal looked around the area. "Cameras, maybe? They want to watch us?"

Moloch shook his head. "What would they see? Black stone and rivers of fire? Besides, there isn't a tool out there I can think of that would burrow that fast into this stone. And we would see them."

Baal shook his head, rubbing his chin. "Yes, you may be right. What about a weapon of sorts? Mines, maybe. I've seen those humans use mines against each other. One idiot steps on one, and *boom*! Blows the person to bits."

Moloch stopped in his tracks and looked around at the ground. "Again, you idiot, where would they bury these mines? In the lava pits? No, there is something much more nefarious going on here. They snuck into our home again and did something to better their chances. They didn't come to attack; there were too few of them. But what the fuck did they do?"

One of the smaller demons ran up, stopping and sliding across the rock. Moloch put his hand out to grab him and flung him to his side. The little creature looked like he wanted to say something, but Moloch didn't have the patience for his tribe of idiots that day. Instead, he stomped to the edge of the ravine and looked over the edge. His eyes were growing redder by the second, and he ground his teeth.

Baal walked up next to him. "Maybe it was another excursion to check out the land? Maybe that was all it was. We scared them off."

Moloch slammed his fist into his palm. "They brought an extra human with them, a brute of a man. He crushed our demons with one swing of his arms. They didn't come for a scouting expedition. Fuck Lilith. Fuck her human/angel meatsack! I am tired of sitting back and letting them walk all over us. They came to our lands and attacked our demons, and I won't let another moment pass without retribution."

Baal slowly lifted his head and looked at Moloch, who had eyes only for revenge. "What is our next move?"

Moloch turned to Baal. "We attack. We hit them in the gut in their most beloved towns. We shred their humans worse than this mystery human shredded our demons. We bring anguish to their homes, and we make the world see that their human heroes are just bringing pain down upon them with their senseless war."

Moloch stomped to a group of beat-up demons. Most

were battered and limbless, but those who could stand still jumped to their feet. "Tell me about this man—this person Lilith had with her."

The demons looked nervously at each other, and one stood up. "Uh...yes, sir. He...he was very big for a human. He had a square jaw, and his eyes flashed different colors."

Moloch's eyes shifted back and forth. "He had a demon?"

The demon nodded in fear. "He had to. He wasn't wearing a suit, his strength was out of this world, and he knew exactly how to kill us. He got slashed and bashed, but his skin just regrew, and he laughed the entire time he was fighting. He talked to Katie and Lilith like he had known them for a long time, but we have never seen him before."

Moloch growled. "Put together a sketch of this man. I want everyone on Earth working to find him. Whoever has infected him is using his body like Lilith uses Katie's. We aren't missing any of our higher demons, at least not that I know of. If we can figure out who this is and who his demon is, we can kill him on Earth and bring him back here."

The demons nodded their heads, swaying nervously. "Yes, sir."

Moloch looked at them for a second and then stomped his foot. "Well? Get going, fools!"

All the demons yipped in terror and went running off toward the inner ring. Moloch sighed and walked to Baal. "When I find this bastard, his demon is going to spend an eternity strapped to the torture wall in my personal dungeon. Go against me in my own home? Please. I'm going to discover new worlds of pain with this idiot."

Baal nodded, dusting the ash off his hands. "And in the meantime?"

Moloch's eyes flashed vibrantly. "In the meantime, we strike with force and show Lilith just what she gets for crossing me."

10

D octor Thorough sat in a room packed with his gear. Screens flickered and flashed with images of hell, from the obsidian plains to the cavernous reaches of the realm. The drones flew high and quiet in order to not give themselves away. They crept through the fogs of acidic air, flying right over the heads of demons without any of them realizing they were being watched.

Thorough kept busy. His fingers were a blur of movement on the keyboard, recording every bit of information that came through. Next to him on a separate set of machines, his assistant Alice did the same. She scoured each new area thoroughly, pausing occasionally and taking notes on new anomalies.

Alice paused one of the videos and tapped Thorough on the shoulder. "Do you see this area here? I think this would be a really good area for defense purposes. It backs up to a large mountain cliff and overlooks the entire valley here. You could have a barrage of snipers perched on this ledge blasting demons with missiles and gunfire."

The doctor rolled his chair over and leaned forward, narrowing his eyes. "Do you still have a drone in that area?"

Alice clicked some keys and grabbed the joystick, showing one of the drones' footage as it circled back around and hovered over the ledge. It gave a 360-degree view of the area. Thorough pursed his lips as he made some notes, copying down the exact coordinates. "Yes, very good, Alice. That is exactly where it should be. If we can find fifteen places like that, all moving like steps down into the lower levels of hell, we could have an excellent line of defense. Here, look at the few I've found."

Alice moved to the monitors to join Dr. Thorough. He began pulling images up, asking her what her thoughts were. Alice pointed to one of the images. "This one seems good from the outside, but look here. You can tell there is a gap in the rock in the ridge. It leads to flat land. A team stationed there could easily be taken from behind. We want to make sure that they have cover on all sides. Really, we want to box them in. Normally that would be a terrible tactic, but we want to give them cover. Entry to escape won't be a problem, because we have Pandora to open portals directly into these areas."

Surprised, Thorough leaned back in his chair. "You sure know a lot about the tactical side of things."

Alice chuckled. "Well, you didn't pick the dumbest intern out there. Besides, my father was a Navy Commander and used to play all kinds of strategy games with me when I was a kid. He made me think of every opportunity the enemy would have to attack me before I made a move. Luckily for us, the demons have strength but not smarts. They aren't going to be rappelling in from above. They also aren't very stealthy. Everything I've seen shows them just running straight in."

The doctor deleted that image. "Let's get some of the military specialists' thoughts on these. I think with our time limitations, we need to start cataloging these spots."

Alice nodded. "I agree."

A few moments later, two tactical specialists came into Dr. Thorough's lair. The doctor barely looked at them. "Good. You're here. We found something." The specialists looked at one another, confused.

"Don't mind him. He's not used to real people." Alice took over. "Gentlemen, we are developing a few locations that we believe will be of interest. We would like to get your thoughts on them. With any luck, we will be able to present Katie and the team with a line of defensive positions throughout the hellscape."

Alice pulled up the first image. "This image is the same depth as the last entrance into hell, but a location much farther in. It's a peak on a mountaintop, so our troops would be fairly isolated. When you are looking out from this ledge, you can see where hell begins to deepen. It's an excellent vantage point."

One of the soldiers had her turn the image so he could see the surrounding area. "This looks great. My only concern is married to the site's strength. It's an isolated area, but what if the demons somehow reach our troops? We don't know what kind of creatures live in the inner ring of hell. Where do our soldiers go if they are overrun? They are too high to jump, and we couldn't fit enough men up there to ward off a major attack."

Alice bit the inside of her cheek. "Hmm. Maybe you're right. Maybe this would be good as an entrance point for Katie since she can fly and all."

"Yes, those fucking wings. Angel shit."

The doctors and the soldiers all turned to see Juntto, in Arnold mode, standing in the doorway and frowning at the screens and monitors. "Hell. I was just there. I won a great victory."

"Right. We know." One soldier gestured to a lava pit on one monitor. "Hey, you know hell better than most of us. Can you take a look at the locations they've developed and tell us which of them would work for an attack?"

"An attack? Into hell."

"Yeah. We're going to leap-frog in, moving from one highly defensible spot to another. If we can find enough of them."

Juntto looked at all the technology, unsure of himself. He hadn't meant to join them. He had taken a wrong turn looking for the galley. He grunted and crossed his arms, puffing up his chest. "Sure. What do we have?"

Alice marveled at the sheer size of the man. And he really did look like Arnold. "Are you actually..."

Juntto glared down at her. "Actually what?"

"No. Never mind." Alice turned and pulled up another location on the monitors. "I've learned it's better to not ask questions. Here is another vantage point deeper down below the acidic clouds. You can see how it's not far from the ground level, but at the same time, the ridge provides protection from the back."

Juntto stared at the screen. "Yes, that would be perfect. It is especially appealing if we have to fuck with the medium-sized demons. Those fat bastards could climb that ridge, but it is too tall for them to jump. They would be stuck climbing up here. Easy targets for your modern weapons. They would be stuck between your guns and running back into the rivers of lava over here." Juntto rubbed his chin thoughtfully. "It's a good spot, but very deep into hell. The only potential problem that I see is Lucifer."

They all stared at Juntto. Alice ventured, "As in, the devil? Himself?"

"Yes. We would be in his territory. There is always a chance he could decide to battle us himself." Juntto stared off into space wistfully. "It would be a great battle and a fine death."

One of the soldiers scoffed. "Yeah, that's like their nuclear option. Right?"

Juntto shrugged and walked off to find the galley.

The soldier called after him. "Right? We're not going to fight Lucifer. Right? Hey! Come back!"

Moloch grabbed a human by the throat and ripped her in half, throwing the mutilated corpse to either side of the highway. He turned his head and snarled at the large welcome sign for Lake Tahoe. "See how much they like their vacation spot now."

He threw up his arms and beckoned the demons from the gate behind him. They swarmed like hellish ants, spreading out over the town. Baal stepped over half of the woman's corpse and walked up next to him. He ate from a bag of candied camel toes. "This looks like a healthy way to express your anger. Are we doing multiple shots, or are we focusing on just this place?"

"I'm focusing on this right now. Do one thing at a time, and do it right, Baal."

"Got it." Baal popped a camel toe into his terrible jaws. "These camel toes are very chewy. I'll have to talk with the demon that makes them."

"Are they made from real camels, or are they the other kind?"

Baal peeked into the bag of candy. "If you bake them right, you can't tell."

Moloch reached down and grabbed the arm from the woman he'd ripped in half. He bit a chunk off her upper arm and started to chew. "I crave meat when I'm worried. Stress-eating is a bad habit."

Baal nodded in agreement. "I just eat all the time. Cuts the stress right down."

Moloch curled his lip and spit the meat out, throwing the arm down. "She must have been one of those hippy chicks. Tastes like kale and curry. Yuck."

Moloch glowered as Tahoe began to smoke. Even the screams and shrieks of the people below didn't make him feel any better. He was livid. Lilith and Katie had undermined him at every single turn. Sure, he'd gotten in a few good hits, thrown a few good punches, but when he looked at his plan as a whole, it was a disaster. They had stopped the major incursions, exorcised important entities placed amongst the humans, and killed their Leviathans. Now they had another human running around smashing his dumb fists through hell's army.

Moloch turned and punched the welcome sign, sending it toppling over. He whistled for the troops, calling them back to the gate. They stepped through and directly into another small town in western Alabama. It was a cozy little village tucked into a pine forest. Quaint.

The demons shrieked and hollered as they ran onto the town's main street as if they were children running into an ice cream shop. Moloch stood there, his face set as he watched his minions tear humans limb from limb.

"You're brooding again." Baal sighed, munching his candies. "I really think that you need healthier ways to express your anger." He pointed to a demon slowly tearing the flesh off of a corpse. "See that guy? He's taking action. He's found an outlet for his emotions."

"We need to figure out what the hell these assholes are up to."

"I was sure that when you destroyed that town with the tea, Katie would be pissed. They didn't even give you a head nod or curse your name."

Moloch scoffed. "Sure, they did. They came rolling into hell with their new friend and did something fucking sneaky. For all I know, they placed little tiny trackers on everything. Hell, maybe they are here. Maybe they are disguised walking among us." He glowered at Baal. "Maybe you are Katie."

Baal shook his bag of candies. "Would Katie eat camel toes?"

"She's tricky. Maybe they're still in hell, down there setting a sneaky human trap for us."

Baal shook his head. "Nah, they are too human for that shit. They wouldn't be able to stand the heat down there for this long. Not unless they left Lilith, and you know that bitch doesn't have the patience to just sit around and wait for a plan to unfold. She would have made herself known by now."

Moloch dropped his arms by his side in defeat. "I just don't know what to do anymore, Baal. This bitch is spoiling everything."

Baal patted Moloch on the shoulder. "I know. I know. Just remember, her human won't live forever. Eventually, she will have to die, and then that threat will be gone. Until then, we need to keep a close eye on everything down below. Sure, these incursions are fun, but we've got responsibilities."

Moloch whistled again, calling the demons back to the gate. "My only responsibility at this point is taking over Earth. I have promised myself that."

Baal walked behind Moloch as they lumbered through the gate. He stepped out onto a long beach studded with long rows of houses on stilts. "The coast of North Carolina. These people love their Outer Banks. This will definitely ruffle a few feathers. And look—seagulls."

Baal grabbed one midflight and tossed it into his big jaws. He stepped aside as a snarling band of demons rushed by him to attack the sunbathers on the beach.

Moloch snarled as sand covered his gnarly black claws. "I hate sand and sun."

"Do you really think the humans are in hell?"

"You're the one that said they wouldn't survive."

"But you're right, the humans are tricky." Baal swallowed and pointed his claw at Moloch. "You know, Lucifer isn't going to be happy if the humans do any damage down there."

"Damage?" Moloch snapped his head toward Baal. "To what? The rocks? Are they going to dam some of the rivers of lava? It's not like I give a shit about the damned place. Lucifer will just put things back the way they were. He'll create some more volcanoes, and go on decorating the only space he is allowed to have. It's not fair to him or to us, really. Taking Earth would give us all a new playground. The old man has been underground for far too long."

The snarling demons were working on the beach houses now. With a great crash, several support beams snapped at once. One of the houses went tumbling down into the waves. "If I take Earth, I would be doing him a favor. I would be opening up a whole new world for him. I'm sure if God can't send his angels down here, then we can bring Lucifer to the surface." As he talked, screams echoed around them, but they didn't faze him in the least. "It's not right that we have been shoved off this planet, that this one place is set aside for God's little playthings. What the fuck about us? We have to stare at the same old scenery day in and day out without a break? Why? Because we questioned God? Curiosity is a natural thing! He's a damn terrible parent if he thinks this is punishment. The humans would call it abuse."

Just then a small child ran across the sand in front of Moloch. He reached down and picked the boy up. The kid was too terrified to scream.

He gently held the child in his palm and ran his claw over the boy's bright blond hair. "They were given every-thing, and we were left to pick up the crumbs. I'm not concerned with the damage they can do to hell. They have done far more damage than they could possibly know."

Moloch closed his fist with a wet crunch. He tossed the child into the water, skipping him like a rock on a pond.

Baal clapped appreciatively. "Just a warning. Everything is fun and games until Lucifer shoves your own dick up your ass and uses it as an enema."

Moloch turned slowly and looked at Baal. "I don't think you know what that means."

Baal crossed his arms. "It's short for unmitigated pain."

Moloch nodded as he opened another gate. "Oh, new definition. That will work."

The demons all stepped through and out another portal into a small country town in France. The silence was broken by the blare of sirens blasting all around them. Moloch walked into the town. Barely anyone was on the streets. There was only a small group of humans behind a makeshift barricade, and the humans were armed to the teeth. They were shooting at the demons as the fiends tried to take the town.

"Well, look at that. They are fighting back." Baal chuckled.

Moloch was shocked. "Huh. Precious. And it looks as if they have found a way to put their people into hiding. This is just adorable."

Baal thought about that for a moment. "You know, it wasn't that long ago that we would attack a place and be met by little more than screaming and running."

Moloch waved his hands. "I wouldn't read into it too much. Probably just a bad choice on my part. We probably stumbled into a town willing to fight, but they are few and far between."

He opened another portal and stepped through, letting the demons follow along behind, ignoring the sound of gunfire.

He paused for a moment in hell and tapped his finger against his lip. Moloch waved his hand and opened a portal to the other side of Australia, not too far from where they'd attacked just a few days before. There too were sirens blasting and armed militants in the street.

Moloch looked at the demons huddled behind him. They were hesitating. "Well, what are you waiting for? Go on get out there and get it done. I don't have time for your fear."

Baal watched as the first few demons rushed out, screaming. They were met with sharp blasts from a shot-gun, and the first wave was blown to bits. Baal gaped. "Oh, man, that was Larry! He was one of my servants."

Moloch patted him on the back. "It's okay, buddy. We will have plenty to choose from when we get back. What did he do for you?"

Baal pouted. "My chef. He was my chef."

"That's rough."

Moloch walked along the streets of the town and came to a stop at one of the restaurants. He lifted the roof off the building and looked down into the kitchen, where several men in white jackets stood. "Which of you is the chef?"

Most of the others shied away, but one short, round man lifted his shaking arm. Moloch nodded and reached down, lifting the man out by his shirt collar. He handed the fat cook to Baal. "There, now you have a new chef."

Baal grinned widely, a horrific look for him. He walked back toward the gate cradling the chef like a newborn. "I'm going to go see what he can do with puppies."

The chef screamed as he disappeared with Baal into hell.

General Brushwood sat at his desk replying to an epic list of emails he had been putting off for weeks. Things had just been too hectic in his life to focus on them. There were incursions to deal with, and then the trips to hell. Emails just didn't rate when stacked against those priorities. He knew, though, that his political connections were as important to the cause as anything else. He did his best to keep the idiots in suits from doing anything that would get them all killed.

"General, you have a call on line one," his secretary informed him over the intercom.

The general sighed. "All right. I'll take it."

He finished up an email before picking up the receiver. "This is Brushwood, how can I help you?"

"General, this is Lieutenant Rafter from Second Command. We are watching the screens and monitoring any possible incursions."

The general straightened in his chair. "Yes, and?"

The man's voice was shaking. "There have been several short hit-and-run attacks. One in Australia, one in the Outer Banks of North Carolina, and one in Alabama. That seems to be what we have so far. However, they aren't really killing as many as normal. Several places have implemented new measures to protect the towns. It seems to be working. To be honest, the demons seem to be just destroying stuff and running away."

The general groaned, rubbing his face. "It's vandalism now?"

"Well, there was one instance of kidnapping."

The general was starting to wish he had stuck with email. "Okay. Well, that's new."

"Two very large demons stomped through the town in Australia, pulled the roof off of a restaurant, and took the chef back to hell. They didn't kill him or anything."

The general had stopped trying to figure out the ridiculous antics of the beasts. They did what they wanted to do with little rhyme or reason. "I want you to watch this. If there is another incursion of any kind, we'll send a team. Also, I want you to figure out who the two large demons are. They don't usually make an appearance at these kinds of events. It's usually hit-and-run with small demons."

"Yes, sir. I'll call you back with updates."

The general hung up the phone and began pacing the floor. It was never a good thing when the demons went wild, attacking towns and cities, especially in the United States. The shock value, on the other hand, was starting to get old. They were no longer surprised when demons attacked. The public was no longer shocked and distraught by the deaths. Instead of shock, there was a still anger, one that the general was getting used to. They couldn't win every battle, and the demons had come up with a way to cause damage without leaving enough time for the mercs to get there.

He knew that the demons were attacking them this way

because they couldn't beat Katie and her team. *They* knew that if they faced her they would lose, even on the plains of hell. This was a good thing, but it didn't stop hundreds from dying during incursions. Something was eventually going to have to be done, but when?

11

The man on the television screen was shuddering. His clothes were torn, and his eyes were bloodshot and puffy as if he had been crying. "I was standing at the bottom here, and this giant demon came walking through this portal thing. You could feel the heat just wash over the whole town. He grabbed a woman, ripped her in half, and then picked up her arm and started eating it. It was absolutely horrible." The man broke down into sobs. The reporter interviewing him held the microphone right under his nose to capture every sniffle.

When the man was done bawling, the reporter patted his arm sympathetically. "This has been Randy Waid in the devastated town of Lake Tahoe." He smiled at the camera. "Back to Greg with sports."

Moloch and Baal were silent for a moment. Suddenly, they both burst out laughing. Baal folded over and bellowed. They were sitting in their large armchairs in Moloch's lair with glasses of blood wine and plates of puppy-head cheese.

Moloch slapped the handle of the chair. "That guy...oh, that guy...he saw me eat the hippy. Oh, Lucifer, that's hilarious."

Baal cupped a hand over his mouth and tried not to spit out the big gulp of wine he had just taken. He finally swallowed and leaned his head back. "Oh man, Moloch. You really got a home run on that one. That's fantastic."

Moloch wiped tears from his cheeks. "A home run?"

Baal nodded. "Yeah, you know. Like that human sport, baseball. The one where they use their bats and hit balls and then run around bases."

Moloch rolled his eyes. "Leave it to the humans to come up with something so stupid. Now, if they hit heads from the shoulders of the damned and had to jump lava runs, that would be hilarious."

Baal shrugged. "I kind of like it. And they have this catchy tune too. Take me out to the ball game, take me out with the crowd. Buy me some peanuts and Cracker Jacks, I don't care if they never..."

A knock on the door drew their attention. A small demon stuck his head in.

Moloch sighed. "Yes? What is it?"

The demon came just inside the room and looked down. "Your evilness, I think we might have figured out who the new human is."

Moloch's face darkened. "You might have? Or are you sure?"

"Pretty sure, oh terrible one."

Moloch nodded. "Well?"

The demon edged farther in. "He's a famous actor and politician. His name is Arnold Schwarzenegger."

Baal waved his hand at the television, and the news program blinked off. The screen filled with a young Arnold Schwarzenegger walking through a packed nightclub with sunglasses on. He began shooting the dancing fools with a shotgun. Moloch watched curiously as Arnold chased people through the streets.

"Does seem like a bad sort," Moloch admitted.

Baal pointed at the television and the screen flipped again. Now Arnold was standing next to a short, round man wearing a Hawaiian shirt. Arnold was grinning, the short man didn't seem to be happy at all.

"He's a friend to trolls, too?" Moloch asked.

"And a politician," the small demon reminded him.

Moloch growled at the screen. "And a politician too? What party?"

The demon rubbed his claws together nervously. "Republican, sir."

Moloch slammed his fist down. "I hate those guys. They are always preaching, reminding the humans what God wants. The liberals are so much easier to bring to our side. They're all about sinning. They even have rallies for it. Now Katie has recruited some human superstar to her team. What for? Vanity? No, I think they are mocking me. They are showing me that even some action hero from the television can come to my land and destroy my demons. I won't allow it!"

Moloch stood up and stomped his foot, knocking Baal's glass over. Baal looked at the spilled wine. "Aw."

Moloch turned. "Baal!"

Baal jumped up. "Yes?"

Moloch rubbed his chin. "I want you to go after this

Arnold character. You find him, slap the glasses off of his stupid face, and I want you to fucking kill him. Bring the body back here. Try not to mangle him too much. I want to have a good look at this son of a bitch. Understood?"

Baal saluted him. "Yep. I'll take some of the small demons with me if that's all right?"

"You, mighty Baal, can't handle this actor on your own?"

"I could," Baal admitted, "but I'd like to bring along a few demons to go shopping. My new chef has been asking for specialty ingredients."

"Fuck me. Chefs."

Baal shrugged, helpless. "He's an artist, Moloch. He's a tyrant."

Katie paced back and forth outside of Dr. Thorough's office, waiting for the doctor to tell her anything useful. Turner was still in sickbay, and the research team was still looking over their data. Katie had nothing to do. So she paced, and it was driving Thorough and Alice absolutely nuts. Finally, Alice let out a deep breath and swiveled around in her chair, staring at Katie.

Katie stopped in the doorway. "What? Did you find something?"

Alice put on a fake smile. "It's going to take us a really long time to get all of this together. You might want to consider going back home, and then we can call you whenever we are done."

Katie's eyes shifted to Thorough, but he was too

entranced by the data. She looked back at Alice and shrugged. "All right, sounds good. Don't mean to be in your crosshairs. I just get itchy when there is something going on and I can't jump right into it. You know? I'll collect the team."

Katie hurried off down the hall. She would actually be glad to get out of there and head back to New York. She burst into the common room to find the team talking trash with Turner. The young man was still heavily bandaged, and he looked pale, but he was alive.

Katie took in the sight and smiled. "Pack up. We're heading back to New York."

Brock started barking orders to his men, and they hurried off. Juntto walked up to Katie. "Do we get to watch a movie on the flight?"

Katie shrugged. "Sure? Did you have something in mind?"

Juntto shook his head. "No. Just ready to get out of this Arnold character. He's a bit bulky."

The team gathered in the hangar, loaded down with their gear. The plane was already prepared. They said goodbye to Alice and the doctor but got the feeling that the two were ready to be left alone for a bit. Everyone took their seats on the plane and relaxed, letting the staff take care of them. As the plane took off from the runway, the lights dimmed, and the screen in the front lowered.

Juntto clapped his hands. "Yes!"

Pandora snickered. *If he's going to pick his characters from the movies, I'm going to start requesting Disney Princess films. He can walk around looking like Abu.*

Katie giggled. *Or the white rabbit.*

The music on the screen blared, and Katie was confused for a moment. She slapped her forehead when she realized they were about to watch *The Matrix*. This would not be good. She turned to Angie. "Well? Which character do you think Juntto is going to be?"

"Agent Smith has a certain Juntto-esque quality about him."

"I'm putting my money on Neo. Juntto likes to be the star of the show."

"Neo's skinny."

"He likes the attention and praise from it all. I don't think it really matters what size the character is. Juntto is strong regardless of what he looks like."

Everyone joked around and talked during the movie, except Juntto, who moved up a few aisles. He was totally focused on the film. He glanced back at the others whenever the volume of their voices went up. By the time the movie was done, Juntto was clapping and asking for the next one. "This can't be the only *Matrix*. There are too many unanswered questions."

Brock chuckled. "It's not, but we didn't bring the other ones with us."

Juntto slapped his hand against his leg. "Next time, then. We will continue this epic saga. I'm going to use the bathroom."

Katie and the others watched Juntto lumber to the back.

Turner shifted in his seat, trying to get comfortable. "Seriously, this guy would have movie marathons that lasted years if he could. I love *The Matrix*, but I'm not really ready to binge the movies. My head would hurt by the end of it."

Brock grinned. "Your head hurts at the end of *Sesame Street*."

Turner pointed at him. "Hey, no jokes against the injured guy. I'm off-limits here, dude."

Brock scoffed. "Please, you aren't dying. And even if you were, you know I'd rag on you on your death bed."

Turner smiled. "I know. That's why I love you, man."

Eddie turned to Sean. "They're so sweet."

"Near-death experiences bring that shit out in you," Sean explained.

"I'm getting emotional over here." Eddie grabbed Sean with both tattooed arms, pulling him into a bear hug. "So emotional." The hug turned into a head-lock, and soon Sean and Eddie were wrestling in the aisle. Sean struggled against him, but Eddie cackled and held him in the head-lock. "I love you man. Why won't you accept my love?" Sean burst into laughter and tapped out.

The door to the back opened and Juntto came walking up to the front, then sat down in the chair. Everyone turned and looked at him. They were no longer staring at Arnold. Sitting there was Morpheus, straight out of the movie. He had the boots, the long trench, the whole nine yards. "I like this character. He's a badass." Even his voice sounded like Morpheus. "Neo?" Juntto shrugged. "He is kind of a wimp all the way up until the last scene. Juntto is never a wimp and never has been. Oh, and look at this."

Juntto jumped up and whipped around, opening up his jacket. There strapped to his hips, were the same samurai blades Morpheus used. Juntto smiled and winked, very proud of himself.

All Katie could do was shake her head. She had to admit, the guy had some serious talent when it came to shapeshifting.

Brock stood up and walked around Juntto. "That's a pretty good likeness. Though I have to say if anyone sees you, they are going to be a bit confused. Probably ask you for your autograph and such."

Juntto shrugged. "I can give autographs. How do you spell Morpheus?"

"Laurence Fishburne," Eddie guessed.

Juntto just looked at him with confusion. "What?"

"The actor that plays Morpheus is Laurence Fishburne. You can't sign something Morpheus," Turner replied.

Katie put up her hands. "How about I make a rule: no autographs. This is already a tricky enough situation. If you go signing autographs, then people are going to catch on. No pictures, either. In fact, if you're going out, I would appreciate it if you looked like someone else. Someone not famous."

Juntto placed his arms behind his back and considered this seriously. Or at least, he appeared to consider it. "No."

Katie closed her eyes and counted to ten. "At least ditch the outfit and wear something else. We have enough attention as it is."

Brock went back to his seat. "I like the fact that we're fighting with Morpheus. Makes us seem a lot more badass than before."

"He's Morpheus," Eddie mused. "Maybe I'm Neo."

"Maybe you're Trinity." Sean giggled.

"Shit." Eddie shrugged. "Still a badass."

Katie sighed and looked out the window. "It's like working with a bunch of children."

Pandora laughed. *Hey, you're the one recruiting all the dudes. You have to expect there will be some level of nerdy action in this group. I'm surprised they haven't pulled you into a rousing game of D&D.*

No way. I would refuse. Next thing I know I'm on the front page of the newspaper with my wings out, beating some nerd senseless because he beat out my level whatever mage with his stupid goblin.

Sheesh. You're a sore loser.

I have a competitive streak. Nope. I'm going to stick to movies at the most.

Pandora sighed. *Fine. But I want to watch something with Catwoman in it. Something besides the newest* Batman.

Katie groaned. *But Catwoman has been seriously underrepresented in cinema. Every Catwoman I've ever seen has been absolutely terrible. She's not a good guy. She basically does good things to get her way. I don't like her.*

What about the blonde one?

Michelle Pfeiffer? She wasn't a hero. She was a goth BDSM kinkster with a thing for cats.

She sounds right up my alley.

Juntto stood up and cleared his throat. "I would like you all to know that Morpheus and I will be coming to the next battle. We are both great leaders. In this form we will subjugate the people, and I will fight for control of the world."

Katie stared at him with wide eyes. "First of all, you have Morpheus all wrong. He fights *for* the people, not to subjugate them. Secondly, you will never control more than your Xbox while I am around. Take a seat, big guy."

Juntto pouted. "Fine, but one day..."

Katie just shook her head.

Arnold Schwarzenegger sat happily at LA Prime, one of the finest restaurants in Los Angeles. The off-white linens matched the floors, and ultra-modern techno-jazz pumped through the sound system. His agent Bryan sat across the table, carefully cutting a piece of his filet, eating it, and sipping his red wine. "Perfect medium rare."

"You see the fat? This will kill you one day." Arnold swallowed his bite of fish and shook his head. "You were saying they want me to continue doing these spin-offs of *The Terminator*."

"They think this one is going to be huge. So, yes, they're already working on the next one."

"Do they have a script?"

"No." Bryan swirled his wine. "They'll shoot the action scenes and write the script later. You know how it goes."

"You would think that with how old I have gotten, they would back away. But no, here I am, getting ready for shooting in three days. It's fantastic."

His agent gave him a grin. "Well, CGI is an amazing thing. Besides, Arnold never gets old to the people. They elected you governor, for God's sake. Governor of a Democratic state, and you are a Republican. It just goes to show that clout counts for something."

Arnold ate a piece of fish and sighed. "True. Though I

am not sure how many more times I can say, 'I'll be back,' without feeling like an idiot."

Bryan put his fork down and pointed at him. "Hey. Hey. What kinda talk is that? You'll say it a million more times if it gets you these acting gigs. Seriously, what else are you going to do with your time? Golf?"

Arnold shrugged. "I've been getting pretty good at my game. But no, I like being in the studio. I would like something more. A serious role in a serious film. Shakespeare, maybe?"

"Something like, I don't know, *Commando and Juliet?*"

"No, no Commando. Maybe King Lear?"

The waitress came to the table and dropped the check. Arnold stared at the bill, but Bryan grabbed it and handed her his black card. "Arnie, people love the action stuff."

Arnold thanked him. "Look, Bryan. I am in my seventies. I want to work, not only my body but also my mind and my abilities. I know that you want me to make more movies, but this one is good for now. We can talk about things later. Don't be so glum. You still get paid."

Bryan chuckled. "That I do. You ready to get out of here? Your assistant told me not to let you stay out all day."

The two of them pushed out of the restaurant doors and into a huge crowd. Flashbulbs popped and sizzled. Arnold smiled, waving at everyone. A TMZ reporter leaped in front of him. "Can I have a couple of minutes?"

Arnold shrugged. "Sure. I'll catch you later, Bryan."

"Arnold, what do you have to say to the people who are claiming you are too old to act in the next *Terminator* movie?" the reporter asked.

Arnold looked directly into the TMZ camera. "I'd say

they should stop worrying about me and my age and worry about what they can do to save the planet. If the directors want me, of course, I will be in the movie. *The Terminator* is historic. In my opinion, they have all been successful. I can't imagine anyone else continuing to act in their seventies while also being a leading figure in the political arena."

"Does this mean you have further aspirations in regards to your political career?"

Arnold laughed and patted the reporter on the shoulder. "It means nothing like that. It means I have a lot of different directions I am currently exploring. Now, if you'll excuse me, I have a meeting to get to. Thanks, guys."

Arnold pushed through the crowd and waved as he stepped into the back passenger door of a blacked-out SUV parked on the curb. His chauffeur closed the door, and they sped off. Arnold relaxed in his seat.

He watched out the window as they drove through the hills back to his mansion. They pulled through the giant privacy gates and parked. The driver opened Arnold's door, and Arnold slid out.

Arnold shook the driver's hand. "Thanks, Mike. That will be all for today."

An unearthly howl cut through the air. Arnold and the driver both turned to see the very air in front of them tear open. The tear expanded into a huge portal, and Arnold shielded his eyes against a rush of hot air.

Baal, huge and scaled and charred from head to foot, stepped through the portal. A band of smaller snarling demons rushed through, hovering around his ankles.

Arnold put his hands on his hips. "This is private property." The demons didn't care. They scrambled across his driveway. Arnold pushed his driver to the side as one of the demons leaped forward. The driver fell to the ground, and Arnold grabbed the demon by the throat. He swung the demon, whipping the thing back and forth like a rag doll. Arnold slammed the beast into the side of his SUV over and over, until the demon burst into ash.

Arnold frowned at the dust covering his sport coat, then took it off and laid it carefully over the hood of the SUV. He spun around to face the giant demon. "How dare you come to my home? Who the hell are you?"

Baal tilted his head back and laughed loudly. "Kill him."

The rest of the demons ran for Arnold, who grimaced and started throwing punches, knocking the smaller demons around. One slashed his shirt to ribbons. Arnold gritted his teeth and pulled the beast's head off.

While Arnold was occupied, Baal grabbed the driver. He casually ripped the man apart and ate him like a handful of pretzels.

One demon ran up the side of the SUV and dropped onto Arnold's shoulder, slicing him across the cheek with his claw. Baal winced. "Careful, Moloch wants him back with as little outward damage as possible."

The demon was so busy listening to Baal that he didn't see Arnold pull a knife from his boot. The actor reached back and grabbed the demon's head, then pulled him forward and stabbed him repeatedly in the neck. The demon teetered and then fell, turning to ash before he hit the ground. Baal was impressed that this human could do such damage, but as he looked closer, he realized the actor had no red in his eyes. In fact, Baal couldn't sense a demon inside the man.

"Take him!" Baal shouted.

One of the demons flipped through the air, knocking the knife from Arnold's hand. Another kicked him in the backs of the legs, dropping him to his knees. A medium-sized demon sauntered up and grunted at the others. They grabbed his head and pulled it back, exposing his large throat.

Arnold thrashed, but it was too late. The demons had him, and as strong as he was, he was no match for them. "You will regret ever doing this, demon scum. I am guilty of no crimes. I promise, you may get my body, but never my soul."

Baal swished his arm, tired of hearing his Austrian accent, and the medium-sized demon drew his claws across the actor's neck. He watched dark blood spill out and soak the front of Arnold's blue shirt. The demons let the big man go and he grabbed his throat, gurgling and spitting. He fell to his side, coughed, and rolled over on his back. He looked up at the cloudless blue sky overhead and whispered, *"Ich komme wieder."*

After a moment, his eyes shut. All life had left his body.

Baal walked over and stared down at him. "Good. Now bring him back to hell. Moloch wants to see the body."

Baal opened up a gate and walked inside. The rest of the demons gathered around Arnold's body and picked him up. They carried him over puddles of blood and into the portal.

It snapped shut, and the day was quiet. On Arnold's house, the green lights of his security cameras blinked.

12

Moloch was in his study, staring down at Arnold's corpse. Baal stood next to him. Both of them had their heads tilted to one side, their hands on their chins. The blood had coagulated on the actor's neck, and his body was starting to turn blue.

"He *is* pretty big for a human, I guess."

"Absolutely."

Moloch raised a finger inquisitively. "But you say he was killed and didn't turn to ash. No demon came out?"

Baal shook his head. "No, but he did kill two of ours bare-handed. It was pretty badass. For a human."

"He looks pretty lame to me. Maybe it's the death part."

Moloch stepped back and flicked his fingers. The corpse rose on its own, dangling there like a wooden marionette. Arnold's head lolled back dangerously, threatening to fall right off. Moloch flicked his fingers again. Arnold's head straightened out. "He just looks so much smaller than the Terminator."

Baal wrinkled his nose. "And old."

Moloch put down his glass of whiskey and rubbed his hands together. "Okay, okay. Maybe if I just give it a little something, here."

The corpse twitched, as if on strings. It quickly moved into a bodybuilder's pose. His arms were curled on either side of his head, biceps flexed rigidly.

Baal squinted. "I guess I can see it. Maybe in the movies, they put a bunch of makeup on him or something."

Moloch was determined to see the guy as he was spotted. "All right, step back. Let's see him in action."

Moloch moved the body to the center of the floor. Arnold's head continuously flopped. Moloch snapped the body to attention. Suddenly Arnold was dancing across the floor, kicking and punching as Moloch controlled him. "It was like this, and that, and then he punched like this." When he was done, Arnold's body hung in empty space like a puppet.

Baal started to chuckle. "You should make him dance."

"This is serious stuff, Baal."

Moloch looked at Baal and then back at the corpse. A smile crossed his lips. "What shall we have? The waltz?"

He flicked his wrist, and the body whirled over the ground. His wobbling head was the only thing that gave away his body's state of being very dead. Moloch laughed and stopped the body.

Baal clapped his hands excitedly. "Oh, oh. Do the YMCA song."

Moloch flipped his hand. In one motion he created a disco soundtrack and a mirror ball spinning overhead. Arnold danced across the floor to the beat. Moloch moved his fingers like a puppet master, his tongue hanging out of the side of his mouth as he concentrated. Arnold's arms moved to the sound, making each letter. Baal towered over the corpse, making the same movements.

Moloch stopped him again, laughter bringing tears to his eyes. He sat down in the chair and flipped his wrist. "Let's see some street dancing, yes? How about a head spin?"

Baal's face fell. "I wouldn't do that."

Moloch had Arnold upside down already, both hands supporting him. He dropped the corpse to do a head spin. As soon as his arms retracted, a loud pop echoed through the room as Arnold's neck broke, oozing old blood onto the floor. His body fell in a heap.

Moloch grimaced. Baal gasped and covered his mouth with one hand.

Moloch reached over and rang his bell. After a moment, several demons hurried in. "Take away the body."

The demons looked at it strangely for a moment. It took three of the fiends to carry the collapsed actor away. Baal and Moloch both turned to the fire of souls and stared into it, thinking about what they had just witnessed. Moloch took a sip of his scotch. "I think that we can agree, that was not the right person."

Baal nodded. "I believe that is the consensus. He did die a glorious death, though. He fought until the end, and he did a damn good job of it, too. I thought that with the flash of bravery in his eyes he might have fought off the larger demon, but he was dead before that could happen."

"A brave death! Good for him." Moloch began to laugh. "We aren't the bad guys here. We offer the humans the opportunity to live a life that is special, based on how well they accept their death."

Baal lifted his glass. "Very true. We should be lauded for our efforts to help humans ascend to the next level…"

Moloch smirked. "Of hell."

Baal cleared his throat. "Well, most of them. I have to point out here that when Arnold died, he went to heaven. I could feel it. What they did with him after that is anyone's guess. I definitely felt the burning in my veins from the white light."

Moloch sighed. "We can't win them all, that's for sure. He was a Republican, helped the mentally disabled, and fought to save the Earth. It was like a slam dunk for him. There wasn't much we could have done."

"Wasn't there some business with a maid?"

"Don't ask me how the heavenly calculations work."

Baal shook his head from side to side. "Too bad he didn't have a demon in him. He would have been unstoppable. We could have used him."

Moloch walked to the window overlooking hell. "Yes, well, we have plenty more down here to choose from, and fresh ones coming down every day. Since the forties, they rain down here like no one's business. I knew the creation of pop culture up there would brighten our days."

Baal nodded. "Oh yes, that was your greatest achievement. Next, you have to take Earth. Then there is no tricking them, it just is what it is."

"Perhaps, although I think once we take it, it will be centuries before they decide to worship us. There will still be those God sneaks through when they die. Nothing like now, though. We will be in control of Earth. Besides, he has a ton of other pet projects. He should just let the humans go."

Baal shook his head. "He is stubborn. This was his creation, and he doesn't want to see our grubby hands on it."

Moloch turned quickly. "Right. But this time, the big guy might not have any choice in the matter. He won't come down himself, and angels aren't quite what they used to be."

Baal considered the pool of human blood on the floor. "One thing does bother me."

"What's that?"

"If this Arnold didn't come to hell and beat our demons to shit, who did?"

"Right, go right, you fucking idiot," Juntto screamed into the computer microphone.

"Looks like you're going down again, asshole," a kid's voice echoed from the speaker.

Juntto was astounded by the vocabulary the prepubescent teen on the other end of the computer had. He had learned how to play online against other people, and found his rivals to be from all over the world, but mostly children. At first, he had been a bit shocked at the language the kids used, but he admired it. Juntto wondered if he would have the same smart-ass mouth in person.

"Why do you sound like the guy from *The Matrix*? Are you one of those goth freaks who sits at home and faps it to pictures of Matrix code?" The kid laughed loudly.

Juntto was confused. "What the fuck is 'fap?' Wait... fuck, no, pick up the sword, you fucking asswipe."

The kid sighed. "You really need to control your anger. You sound like my dickhead stepfather—and you're yelling at your own character, who is controlled by you."

Juntto slapped his hands on the keys, moving his head right and left with his character. "Maybe your stepfather should teach you some manners, kid."

The kid chuckled. "Or maybe I should just put your character out of its misery. Seriously, dude, you look like a Viking with Downs syndrome. Who picked that skin for him?"

"Shut up and play the game," Juntto growled.

The kid laughed even harder, demolishing the troops Juntto had lined up to protect his castle. He had switched games and was finding that he didn't much like being the emperor of his own lands. Maybe he liked the title, but the actual duty was bullshit. He bit his lips and made a couple of shifts in his players, trying to get them to do what he wanted them to. Unfortunately, he wasn't as good as the kid on the other end.

"Dude, you put your main defense right in the path of my cannon." The kid chuckled again as the cannon fired.

Juntto slammed his hand on the desk. "Fuck. I still have a shot. I'm not going to give up yet."

The kid made another move. "Unless this is one of those war movies where you're going to pull some sort of crazy shit and bring in hidden troops, you are going down. Your shit is mine, bro. Just give in."

Juntto gritted his teeth. "Even if I go down, I'm taking some of your men with me."

The kid sighed. "Fine, embarrass yourself."

They both made move after move. The play was like an elaborate game of chess set in a medieval time period. Juntto made the last move he could, a Hail Mary, and held his breath. The kid moved into position. His cannon blasted through the frost giant's troops and the wall surrounding his castle, and the enemy troops poured in.

Juntto's head hung low. "By my frozen balls!"

The kid cheered. "That's what I'm talking about. What you got in here? Better be some good shit."

Juntto pulled off his earbuds and threw them down. He had spent days searching for the goods he had hoarded, days building his castles and villages, and all for some pimple-faced kid to steal it right out from under him. He thought about tossing the damn computer right out the window.

Then he thought about fashioning a spear and hunting the child like a wild boar.

He sighed and wiped his face. "They would kill me if I did that. Paperwork."

Instead, he sat there tapping his fingers on the tabletop. He eyed the stats screen and watched his name drop.

He closed his eyes and started replaying the game in his mind. He wanted to know exactly where he went wrong. Juntto knew this human kid wasn't smarter than he was. His people were leaps and bounds above the human race, intellectually. He just had to calm himself down enough to see what he did wrong.

He reached across the desk for a pen and piece of paper, his eyes still closed. He began scribbling notes on the paper. His mind replayed the game, and he commented on his own play. Everyone on Earth called his abilities "magic," but the truth was, he was just a more advanced being. He had three times more brainpower than the average humans. Because of that, he could totally control his body, both physically and mentally. He could force memories to surface and study those memories from afar.

The strength he had was fairly normal for his people. The rest of his talents were just the way they were. He couldn't really explain it. After ten minutes of constant writing, he opened his eyes and glanced over the sheet. He smiled and nodded his head, knowing exactly what he was going to need to do.

Juntto began typing swiftly on his computer. He opened a control screen and set up several additional hotkeys. "I have to get to these actions far quicker. If I had them as an option before, then I could have beaten the child no matter how much stronger that fool was."

He hit the last key and saved the changes. Juntto sat up in his chair and cracked his fingers, moving the mouse to start a new game. He smiled as he picked his characters, weapons, and armor. This time he was determined not to be undermined by a twelve-year-old kid with lots of time on his hands.

Juntto picked up the pen and scribbled the kid's screen name down for later. He was definitely going to give the kid a rematch, and he wasn't going to make the same mistakes again. "I will get my loot back, you shit goblin, and much more."

"The attacks left only devastation in several locations, but fortunately due to demon shelters that had just been put into place, the death toll was not nearly as high as in former incursions." The newscaster was sitting at a desk, photos from the incursions playing on the screen beside her.

The general stared at the carnage and destruction, shaking his head. He still couldn't believe that the US had fallen victim to the same kind of hit-and-run tactics Moloch had used on other places. Not just that, but the reports made it sound like Moloch himself had made an appearance. The general couldn't figure out what in the world would have prompted him or angered him to the point where he would have done something that drastic. Then again, Brushwood knew there was no real rhyme or reason to the demon's path.

"In other news, former governor and movie star Arnold Schwarzenegger was found in the driveway of his home, along with an overturned vehicle."

The general shook his head. "That's a damn shame. Liked that man."

He turned the volume down and picked up the phone, dialing Katie. "Katie, it's the general. You have a minute?"

"For you, General, I have more than that. What's up? Did you see that Arnold died? I wonder if—"

The general cut her off. "It's a shame, it really is, but that's not why I'm calling. Three different locations were hit. More hit-and-run tactics like before, only this time I'm pretty sure Moloch made an appearance."

"Really? That son of a bitch is taunting me," Katie fumed.

The general nodded. "Possibly, or he is getting too brazen for his own damn good. I'm assuming this had something to do with the battle in hell. He really had no strategy for any of this, and the hits seemed random. Either that or he has figured out our tracking system."

Pandora's voice came through the phone. "Not likely. Fucker is a complete moron. It sounds like a hissy fit on his part."

Katie cleared her throat, taking back over. "Yeah, he doesn't seem to be too interested in our technology. He is focused on the weapons and the takeover. But as far as the timing, I would say he was probably throwing a hissy fit. He has no idea why we were there, and until they start snatching drones, I'm going to assume that they are still oblivious as to our purpose there."

The general stroked his chin. "I agree. The only problem is, we cannot just sit here and let him attack our lands and our people without some sort of retaliation measures. We have to show him and the people of this country that we are doing something to combat this. We have stood up during every other war, and I don't want us to look weak to the demons or to the rest of the world."

Katie understood. "I agree with you. We can't let the country or the world feel that we are weak. It would help if they understood just how hard it was to fight these battles. I want to show them we are watching without killing too many of our own. That's difficult walking into these situations because the demons are strong, even more so on their territory."

The general tapped his pen against the desk. "Right, but we know that now. What we need to do is regroup. We need to look through our ammo, our weapons, and use the best strategists that we have to come up with a plan. We can't leave this one to chance, and we can't just send you and big boy in there and hope for the best. I want these fuckwads to know that we are all on the same side over here, and that side wants to kick their fucking asses."

Katie chuckled. "I don't think I've heard you this upset before, General. You okay?"

The general snorted. "I am sick and tired of this shit. I'm tired of losing good innocent American souls to these cowardly attacks. Collateral damage is one thing, and it always has been a tough one to swallow. But this isn't that. This is just cold-blooded murder, with this Moloch fellow going after anything weaker than him or his demons. He wastes human life to laugh in our faces."

Pandora coughed her way to the surface again. "Remember one thing, General. No life means anything to Moloch, except his own. Power and winning are the only things that mean a damn to him. He may get angry when demons die, but he doesn't really give a fuck. He cares when he is deemed the loser. Katie and I make him a loser, but we can't just stop trying to fuck their world up because they might attack. We have to stay the course."

The general knew that was true. "I understand. We will see many more casualties before this war is over. Let's just attempt to minimize them as much as we can. Focus on what we can control."

Katie came back to the phone. "True, and I have some ideas. What if we set a trap for Moloch and we get the whole thing on video?"

The general shifted uncomfortably. "I don't know. That could go very badly very quickly."

Katie smirked. "Or very, very right. Look, let me talk to some people, get a plan together, and then I'll put it up for your approval. Just keep your mind open on this one and keep the troops and the cops steady. We are going to get this guy. We're going to end this whole damn war, but we have to be patient with each other."

The general nodded. "I trust you, Katie. Get back with me when you have the details."

The general hung up the phone and leaned back in his chair. Things never seemed to end, but he knew one of these days, one side would fight their last battle. He just hoped that it ended well for the humans, and not for the demons.

K atie stretched out on her bed and closed her eyes
briefly.

*I don't understand why Brock and the boys couldn't stay
with us.*

*They're adults, and they're military. They have to be
debriefed.*

But I want to debrief Brock.

If you're not going to let me rest, then I have shit to do.

She groaned and grabbed her phone. No matter how
tired she was, if she didn't make the call now, she never
would. After a few rings, he answered. "How is my favorite
mercenary doing on the other side of the country?" Katie
asked.

Korbin chuckled. "We are holding tight and putting in
work. How's New York?"

Katie sighed, leaning against her headboard. "Oh, you
know, complicated as always. Trying to take care of fifteen
different things at once. You know how that is, though."

Korbin snorted. "No, I can't even imagine. I remember

being the leader of this territory, sometimes venturing off to other parts to help when needed. I was never leading a task force of four or five, covering places all over the globe. You're handling things on Earth and in other realms, from what we are hearing."

Katie winced. "Yeah, sorry for not keeping you up to date. Things happened at the last second. One minute I'm on my way home, the next we're rerouting to hell. It's definitely been challenging for us."

"I can imagine," he replied.

"How is Joshua doing? Is the armory up and running?"

"It is. We just got the last of the machinery hooked up, and from what I've been told, they are blowing full steam ahead. Of course, they pretty much had to start over, but they knew what they were doing this time, so things are a tad easier. We have orders backed up. They're coming from all over the world. We are filling the government orders first and then moving to civilian. From what it looks like, people are starting to take matters of protection into their own hands."

Katie smiled. "Normally, in historical reference, that would be a bad thing. When it comes to demons, though, I think it's good. We can use all the help we can get, and if it means the citizens are arming themselves, that might mean one less casualty."

Korbin wasn't sure. "Yeah, but that could also mean more brave people standing in the streets instead of finding shelter. We don't necessarily want militias. That has never turned out well. The last thing you want is people gunning each other down in the street because they thought they saw red eyes."

Katie grimaced. "Yeah, I suppose not, but at this point, we don't have the people to police that sort of thing. It was bound to happen. Humans' number one instinct is survival, and that is how it has always been. Either it will hurt us or help us; only time will tell. What about Timothy? Is he keeping his shit together over there?"

Korbin laughed. "As much as he can. I've been keeping him busy with extra things to accomplish. Stephanie is thinking about grabbing him for a movie night soon. She thinks he might pop a blood vessel if she doesn't."

"We wouldn't want that. It would be a lot of glitter and rainbows to clean up," Katie pointed out, laughing.

Korbin choked, then burst out in laughter. "Wow, it's been a while since I've laughed like that."

Katie was glad to hear it. "It's been a while since I've heard you laugh like that. We all need to remember that even with distance, we are still family."

"Very true. So, what can I do for you?"

Katie wished she was just calling to shoot the shit, but that never seemed to be the case. "I need to talk with you about things, but not over the phone. I'll need to come out there. You have time for that?"

Korbin glanced around at the base. It looked like an actual military installation, and they were getting close to being done. "Sure, anything for you. Come on out. You can see what we've done with the place. That extra push from the general lit a fire under these boys' asses, and they are getting shit done."

Katie grinned. "Good. I was hoping it would happen that way. Okay, I'll be down there later today. I'll be flying into the airport on the jet and then over on my wings, I suppose."

"We'll keep an eye out. Be careful."

"Always."

Katie hung up the phone and walked to the dresser, grabbing her guns and putting them in her holsters. She looked at her tired face in the mirror and sighed. Pandora could feel her pain. *Girl, I promise when all of this is said and done, we're going to have a KatieDora demon spa day. A little demon nip and tuck here, some demon botox there. By the time I'm done with you, you are going to be rolling around like a twenty-year-old porn star.*

Katie laughed as she pulled her hair back. *How about just a woman who doesn't feel like she got hit by a truck? I'll take that. Though, I would say, I like this body. If you ever leave me, you better put your voodoo on my metabolism so I stay like this.*

Oh, hell yeah. And to think you fought me on it from the beginning. I'm telling you, Slut Girl is not a bad name for you.

Katie wrinkled her nose. *Or you could call me "Hot Girl" and leave it at that.*

Pandora grimaced. *That's terrible. I fucking hope your major in college wasn't marketing.*

Katie shook her head and headed through the apartment and out the front door. As she shut it behind her, she jumped slightly when she heard Juntto yelling from across the hall. She slowly walked toward the door, one hand on her gun.

She could hear Juntto pound on the table. "Fucking little weasel. You stole the Jewel of Amaranth right out from under me. I'll fucking *find* you, punk."

Pandora scoffed. *You turned the world's most dangerous merc into a game junkie.*

Katie reached up and knocked hard on the door, but there was no answer; Juntto just went on screaming at his computer. She brought her fist up to knock harder when the elevator dinged and Angie came walking out carrying two bags of groceries. She didn't say a word, just walked past Katie, hipping her to the side, and used a key to get into the room.

She just booty-shoved you.

She did.

We're not going to take that, are we?

Katie decided she was *not* going to take that. She followed Angie into the condo.

Angie put both bags of food in the fridge without unpacking them. "I got you food."

"Thank you," Juntto replied without looking up from his game. Then he let loose a string of curses directed at his computer.

Angie sighed. "Stop threatening the challengers. It's just showing how bad you suck."

Katie was perplexed. *I'm not sure whether to be amused or do something about this.*

Pandora was just as confused. *Uh, I mean, we wanted him to love the Western world, but I'm not sure if this is harmful or helpful. Are those cheese poofs around his chair?*

Angie walked over to the frost giant. "You want to fade right, build a small army really fast—ones that take two minutes—and then strike. They will all die, but it'll lessen his hit status. He will be weaker, and then you can strike with your strong weapons."

Katie tilted her head to the side. *He looks badass as Morpheus, though. I can't deny that.*

I know. I just wish I could come to terms with that, Pandora replied with a shiver.

"Yes! I beat that little bastard," Juntto bragged, throwing his arms in the air.

Angie narrowed her eyes. "You won the battle, but the match is still going on. You need to teleport to the other section of the map and help your teammates."

Juntto nodded and went back to typing feverishly. Over the speakers came the sound of several kids cussing at their screens. "Where the fuck are you? We are getting murdered."

Juntto sighed. "I'm hurrying, I'm hurrying. Don't get your training pants in a wad."

Pandora chuckled. *That's an interesting thing to say. He is quite the conversationalist.*

Yeah, except all his conversations are with elementary school kids, Katie replied.

"Right there, right there. Put your cannon there," Angie urged, pointing at the screen.

Juntto typed faster. "I'm trying. It's not up to level yet, damn it. No, no, noooooo!"

The computer made a strange beeping sound followed by a trumpeting tune that made Katie guess he had lost. Juntto pushed back from the computer and shook his head. "Lost again."

Angie patted him on the shoulder. "You got major points for winning your battle. Good job."

Katie cleared her throat. "Guys?"

They both turned. Angie crossed her arms over her chest. "What's up?"

Katie lifted an eyebrow. "Pandora and I have some instructions. I have to jet to the base for a bit to talk to Korbin about the next attack. You guys are going to stay here. I need you guys to be the main protectors of the city while I am gone. Angie has constant contact with Timothy, and I'll put her in touch with Schultz and Travers too."

Pandora butted in. "And look, Juntto the magnificent. You better fucking keep your shit together, or I'll come back here and wrap your entrails around the whole city."

Juntto waved his hands at her. "I am assuming that was Pandora."

"It was, but I'll help her," Katie replied.

Angie pulled out her phone. "Okay, we got this. We have the special equipment stored up here, and we will keep our ears open to everything. If we need help, we'll call you, but there shouldn't be anything too dire. How long will you be gone?"

Katie shrugged. "Hopefully not too long."

Juntto grumped. "I don't like this. No offense to Angie, but she isn't a fighter, so basically you leave the heavy work to me."

Angie nodded. "No offense taken. Though I can hold my own when needed."

Katie smiled at Angie but turned on Juntto. "I know you're doing the hard work, but that's part of why you joined this team. Or, rather, were forced to join this team. You are a heavy—you can take demons out almost better than me."

Pandora chimed in. "Almost—she said almost, Juntto.

Deflate your head, it makes your dick look small. Oh wait, it *is* small."

Juntto faked a laugh. "Funny coming from the Grand Canyon of vag—"

Katie put her hands up. "Enough, you two. Think of it this way, Juntto. The more demons you slay, the bigger your bank account grows. We agreed on a salary plus part of every kill, and I will keep my word on that."

Juntto nodded. "I plan to hire Angie part-time if it doesn't affect her work with you. She will help me, and I will teach her a few things. I will turn her into a warrior."

Angie gave him a look. "We'll see about that."

Katie laughed. "Sure, why not?" Katie nodded her head at the door, signaling Angie to follow her.

Angie did, then stopped at the door and turned back to Juntto. "You should buy an Xbox, and we can get down with some Halo."

Katie went back to her room and finished gearing up as Angie stood in the doorway watching. Katie clipped some extra magazines to her belt and glanced at the woman. "Are you cool with this arrangement? I didn't mean to make you a full-time babysitter, but I gotta handle some shit, and I trust you to keep an eye on him."

Angie smirked. "He's a moron, but I think I can handle him. You scared the shit out of him with paperwork; I think I can come up with a few of my own. By the time you come back, he'll be scared of the laundry monster, the dish brigade, and the killer mop-man. It'll be shiny as hell in there."

Katie laughed and put her bag across her chest. She gave Angie a hug. "You are the best. You need anything or anything goes down, call me immediately. If you can't get through on my cell, call Timothy. He'll be able to get me."

Angie smiled. "Yep, I got it. Be safe, and try to relax on your flight. You are so high-strung, you gotta take every second of peace you can get."

From across the hall, they heard Juntto curse loudly. Katie shook her head. "Good luck."

Katie walked to the balcony and opened the doors, taking in the cool almost-fall air. She decided since the plane would need a second to get fully ready, she would take a flight around the city and clear her mind. She stepped outside and onto the railing, spreading her wings wide.

Pandora giggled. *Look at your fan club down there. I think they scared off the haters.*

Katie gave them a wave and leaped off the balcony, flapping her wings as she soared between the buildings. She took a loop around the city, flying over the river, across Central Park, and over to the 9/11 Memorial. She looked down at all the people visiting, putting their hands on the memorial wall, paying tribute.

She felt a slight ache in her heart. *Ten years from now, you will see those memorials all over the world. People will be paying tribute to all the brave souls who fought hard against the demons.*

Yeah, and sitting at the feet of a mighty statue of you and me —with wings, of course.

Katie smirked. *I hope they don't do it to actual proportions —the damn thing will tumble over, tits first.*

Pandora laughed. *Hell of a way to die. Crushed to death by Katie the angel/demon's stone-hard tits. It'll be a beautiful thing.*

Katie laughed. They flew higher into the sky, waving at a few people who noticed her from the ground. The leaves of the trees scattered throughout the city were starting to change colors just slightly. Katie couldn't wait to see the oranges, yellows, and reds of fall. It was her favorite season.

She banked right and did a quick loop around the Empire State Building. People working in the building pressed against the windows to get a better look and she waved at them all. Normally she felt ridiculous doing things like that, but it had been a while since the public had seen her outside of paparazzi videos. Just like the general had said, the world needed to know they weren't backing down from anything. Katie also needed that moment to see all the innocent faces of the city and remember why she was fighting so hard against Moloch. She needed to make sure she wasn't doing this out of revenge, but instead, from a need to protect the innocent.

It was times like that she wished she had Damian there to give her one of his insightful pep talks, but she knew he was playing an important role in London with the church. She turned and headed for the airport, waving at the tower guards as she flew past them. She lowered herself down to the ground, flapping her wings backward to slow down. She closed her wings and let them disappear, then jogged down the path to the hangar where her plane was waiting.

"Katie, we have everything prepared and ready for you,

and the pilot said to let him know when you are ready," one of the staff put in. He took her bag and accompanied her aboard.

Katie walked up into the plane and smiled at the donuts waiting for her. "I'm ready to go whenever he is. Thank you."

———

Juntto walked down the street with his hands in his pockets, his face hidden under his ball cap. He had remembered what Katie had said about changing his clothes before he went out, but he refused to change his appearance. He liked Morpheus and felt comfortable in that form. Besides, he was not the type of being to fold under pressure—even if that pressure was coming from Pandora. As far as he was concerned, she could suck it.

The thought made him chuckle as he looked down at the GPS on his phone. Angie had taught him how to use the machine to guide him around the city so he wouldn't get lost. Luckily, there was a GameStop on East Eighty-sixth Street, just a straight shot of eight or nine blocks from the condo.

As he approached the building, he pulled out his wallet and looked at the plastic card inside. Angie had taught him how to use it. "Put card in machine, punch in code 1313," he mumbled.

He grabbed the door handle and went inside, keeping his head down as he entered. He walked to the wall with the green Xbox sign over it and started to look through the games. There were many to choose from, and lots that looked absolutely badass. There were guns and big soldiers on almost every single one.

"Welcome to GameStop. Can I help you find something today?" The sales associate beamed as he approached Juntto, then gasped. The kid almost vibrated with excitement.

Juntto looked up, ready for anything.

The kid looked around nervously, then whispered, "Are you…"

Juntto let out a breath. Right. He was wearing a famous face. He shook his head. "He's my cousin."

The kid nodded and gave Juntto a big cheesy wink, not really believing him. "Okay, gotcha. What can I do for you today?"

Juntto picked up the Halo Master Chief compilation case and looked at it. "I am here to get the new Xbox, and *Halo*. But I think you will show me some more games like that."

"I can do that." The guy nodded. "First-person shooter games. Nice. Well, there is *Destiny*, which is actually created by Bungie. They were the original producers of *Halo* before they sold it to 343 Industries. It's similar, but definitely not the same. If you like *Halo*, most likely you'll like *Destiny*. Personally, I'm a *Halo* guy, but I like the story-line better than *Destiny*."

Juntto nodded. "Okay, I take. What else?"

The associate pulled the *Far Cry Four* box off the shelf. "This is a good one, too. Different from *Halo*, but still a killer game. This is probably one of the most popular games right now."

Juntto was amused by the guy on the cover. "I'll take this too. I like that guy's style."

The associate laughed. "Pagan Min is his name. He is a ruler in the game, but he got there by slaughtering the heir to the throne. He is very flamboyant and out-there, for sure."

Juntto hefted the armful of games. "I was told I cannot take these by force. I will pay."

"Uh. Great. I can ring you up over here."

Juntto followed the kid up to the counter. "How much do I owe?"

The associate started ringing everything up. "Are you a GameStop rewards member? You get rewards, extended returns, party invites for new releases, and a copy of the monthly magazine. I just need your address."

"Not right now. I wait on that." Juntto wasn't sure what his address was but didn't want to tell the kid that.

The associate typed on the computer. "And did you want to buy the warranties?"

Juntto thought about it for a second, remembering that Angie had told him to get them. "Yes, all the warranties."

"Good choice, man. Did you want a pair of Turtle Beach so you can really hear the sounds on the game and talk to other players?"

"Turtle Beach?" Juntto didn't know if he was being made the object of fun. He knew what turtles were, and didn't think they belonged in this store.

The associate pulled a box with headphones in it off the wall. "Yeah, awesome headphones. The best, in my personal opinion."

Juntto nodded. "I'll take them. I can trash-talk those

little assholes on the game better. I was playing computer-style on my Alienware, but now I try the Xbox."

The guy nodded. "I love computer games. Taking it old school. Of course, nothing seems old-school on an Alienware. I personally have a desktop. An Acer for gaming."

Juntto had no idea what the guy was talking about, so he just nodded and swiped his card. He typed in his PIN, then stuck his wallet back in his pocket. The guy put everything in two bags and handed them over. "Enjoy, man, and stop by next Saturday. We're having a gaming tournament."

"Thank you, I will do that." He smiled.

Juntto left the store, overjoyed by his purchases. He pulled out his phone and turned the GPS on. He saw there was a side street ahead that would cut some time off his walk. He was stoked to get back and hook up his Xbox. He wasn't even sure how to play the thing, but he figured Angie would help him like she did with the computer.

As he passed a hot dog stand, he stopped and reached in his other pocket, pulling out a twenty. The guy gave him a hot dog with everything, and Juntto waved. "Keep change."

He took a huge bite of his dog, juggling his bags as he turned down the side street. "Mmm, Angie not kidding. Dogs are delicious."

As he walked down the empty street, he could sense someone behind him. At first, he didn't look. New York was filled with people. There were more beings in this one place than he had ever seen on his planet. He could sense all of their emotions and intentions roiling throughout the city, and tried to block them out most of the time. He finished his hot dog and tossed the trash to the side of the street as he walked.

"You should put that shit in a trash can," one of the guys behind him yelled.

Juntto slowed down. He could hear them continuing forward, and he counted their footsteps quickly. He slowly turned around and wiped his face on his shoulder. There were three men in thick boots. All were smaller in size, and one was carrying a gun. Juntto realized he was being robbed.

"Oh man, you are older than I thought." one of the guys laughed as they stopped a few feet away from him. He wore aviator glasses and was grinning maniacally.

"Yeah, you heading back to the Matrix or something, bro?" another asked. He had a head full of dreadlocks, which Juntto quite liked.

Juntto just tilted his head to the side, a smirk on his lips. He was waiting for the third guy, the one with the gun, to make his move. The third guy licked his lips and ran his eyes over the bags. "Looks like Pops just bought the new system and some games. You rolling in the dough, buddy? I mean, you *did* make all those movies."

Juntto shook his head. "Trust me, just walk away."

The three guys burst into laughter, then fell silent. The guy with the gun held his piece out. His other hand was holding his baggy pants up. "Why don't you just hand over that loot and we might let you walk out of here alive?"

Juntto laughed. "You want this stuff?"

"Yeah," the guy replied, grinning.

Juntto's face got serious, and he set the bags on the ground in front of him. "Come take it, newbies."

14

"Ow, man, let me go," the guy with the cool dreads yelled.

Juntto did not. Instead, he twisted the would-be thief into a headlock and asked, "Do you rob people often?"

The guy grimaced. "Just trying to make a living here, man. What the fuck?"

Juntto narrowed his eyes and punched the guy hard in the stomach, and Dreadlocks wheezed. Juntto tossed him into the wall. He landed with a thwack and slid down into a pile of garbage, grunting and holding his stomach.

Juntto walked toward the guy with the gun, the leader, and smacked it out of the guy's hand. The leader yelped but stepped back into something like a fighting stance, his fists up in front of him. "Stay back, dude. I know jujitsu. I'm serious."

Juntto put his hand to his chin. "Is that karate? I've always wanted to learn."

The leader grabbed his pants so they wouldn't fall,

spun, and kicked Juntto in the side, grimacing as his foot slammed into what felt like a brick wall. Juntto moved like a snake. He grabbed the leader's ankle and twisted hard, spinning him sideways in a circle and releasing. The guy slammed his head into the ground and groaned, trying hard to pick himself back up.

The third guy ran for Juntto, jumped onto his back, and began pounding his fists against the Leviathan's shoulders. Juntto turned in a circle, trying to see the guy. Finally, he roared and reached back with both hands. He grabbed the guy and threw him off. The guy hit the ground hard, skidding through a puddle. His aviator shades were cracked, but he was still wearing them.

The leader was digging through trash, looking for his gun when Juntto stepped over him. He leaped back to his feet and came at Juntto. "Eat my jujitsu, bitch!" He punched him in the stomach and then slammed a left across his jaw. When the leader's fist connected with Juntto's face, something cracked. It wasn't Juntto's jaw. The thief grabbed his hand and yelled in pain.

Juntto grabbed the guy by the wrist, yanking him forward. He punched him twice in the gut—carefully so as not to break him—and pushed him to his knees. "You like the view down there, scumbag?"

Fear floated across the guy's face. Juntto pushed him over and kicked him in the stomach. "That is not how I play this game, fucker. Stay down, or I will put you down." Juntto rubbed his chin thoughtfully. "I am not supposed to kill unless it is absolutely necessary." He brightened. "But I am free to cripple you."

Dreadlocks climbed to his feet. He stumbled for a moment, then pulled a silver rod from his pocket. The rod was little more than a handle. He flicked his wrist and a two-foot length of steel extended outward. He held it like a baseball bat and slammed it across Juntto's back. Juntto grunted and fell to one knee, then lowered his head. Dreadlocks chuckled and raised the rod high over his head, ready to strike Juntto again. As the metal bar fell, Juntto reached up and caught it without looking. He slowly stood and ripped the rod from Dreadlocks' hand, then easily bent the bar in half. The guy stumbled, pressing his back against the wall.

Juntto looked at the metal bar, anger building in his chest. Normally all three of them would be dead by that point, but he had to follow the rules Katie had laid out for him. He threw the bar to the ground and stomped forward, then gripped Dreadlocks' shirt with both hands and lifted him off the ground, growling. The kid's eyes opened wide as Juntto blinked rapidly, his eyes changing from one color to another.

Dreadlocks let out a high-pitched scream and wiggled his legs. Pee soaked the front of his jeans. "How the fuck are you... *What* the fuck are you?"

Juntto gave him a nefarious smile. "Your worst nightmare, bitch."

He dropped the guy to the ground and pinned him to the wall, his forearm shoved under Dreadlocks' chin. "I'm going to let you go, although normally I would pull your fucking spleen out through your neck. You will never hurt anyone ever again. I might not understand how to use the

Xbox controller, but I know how to inflict maximum pain when it is deserved. Do you understand?"

Three shots rang out in the alleyway and Juntto grunted. He let go of the guy, and when he reached around to touch his shoulder blade, his hand came away bloody. He puzzled over the blood dripping off his fingers, then he saw the leader grinning like a jackal behind his gun. The thief had shot him three times in the back, but the bullets were just a pinprick to Juntto. A pinprick that made him want to rip the leader's head off his shoulders.

Juntto walked steadily forward and the leader fired again wildly, missing Juntto entirely. The frost giant grabbed the gun and twisted it from the guy's hand. He looked at it for a moment and then at the leader, who was staring at him with wide eyes. Juntto stood up straight and rolled his shoulders, twisting his back. Three bullets popped from the wounds in his back and clinked to the ground. They rolled along the alley, coming to a stop at the leader's feet.

"Shit."

Juntto gritted his teeth and grabbed the leader's hand. Instead of ripping the guy's arm off, he shoved the gun back into his hand. The guy was baffled.

"My master said I shouldn't kill unless I'm being harmed. You shooting me gives me permission."

The guy's hand was shaking as Juntto held the gun there.

Juntto narrowed his eyes and stepped back, leaving the gun in the leader's hand. "But I hate the idea of paperwork."

He stared at the guy for several moments, and Juntto's

eyes became a hazy gray. The guy looked confused, unsure what to do. Suddenly his eyes hazed over as well, and he stood up. His eyes were half-closed as if he were asleep. Slowly his hand began to curve up, and he pressed the barrel of the gun to his own temple.

The guy with the aviators pulled them off and stood. "What are you doing, man? Stop!"

Juntto's lip curled up. "No."

The leader stared at Juntto for a moment with his hazy eyes and pulled the trigger, blowing his brains all over the alley wall.

Juntto's eyes returned to brown, and he took a deep breath. "Now it is suicide, and I have no paperwork."

He turned around to deal with the other two, but they had taken off running in the other direction. He smiled, knowing he didn't need to chase them. They wouldn't be doing anything stupid for a long time. He kicked the leader's leg with the toe of his boot. Yes, the guy was dead. He walked over and picked up his bags. He pulled out his phone, turned the GPS back on, and started walking down the alley, whistling to himself as he went.

Not a soul had seen the event that he knew of, and Juntto was happy to have followed the rules. He would be glad once he was home playing his new games. The thugs had taken enough of his time. He had aliens to kill and controllers to learn how to use.

Angie climbed out of the taxi with her arms loaded with bags. She had gotten a few things for the pair of condos.

She had neglected many things while trying to take care of Juntto, so she figured it was time to take care of old business. She pulled out her wallet, tipped the taxi driver, and turned to walk in the building. She paused slightly as she walked, seeing the cop car pulled up to the curb in front.

As she approached, she could see the cops talking to the concierge in the entry. The doorman hurried over and opened the door for her, smiling.

"Thank you." Angie sighed. "Should I assume they're here for us?"

The doorman nodded and walked her to the two cops. They both took off their hats and shook Angie's free hand. "Sorry to bother you. We were wondering if Katie was in town. We wanted to talk to her about something that happened earlier today."

Angie shook her head. "No, I'm sorry, she left on business. We aren't sure when she will be back. Is there something I can help you with?"

The cops looked at each other and one pulled out a piece of paper. "There was a shooting earlier today on a side street not far from here. Actually, one of the guys involved in an attempted robbery came and turned himself in. He was incredibly shaken up. His story was all over the place. First, he said a guy shot his friend, then he said the guy forced his friend to shoot himself. It's all kind of muddled right now. Anyway, this is a sketch of the guy they said did it. We want to talk to him and find out what happened. Have you seen this guy around?"

Angie looked down at the sketch. It was an exact replica of Morpheus in a baseball cap. "Is this serious?"

The cop chuckled. "Yeah, he kind of looks like

Morpheus from *The Matrix*, we know. We're assuming the guys were a bit confused. The one that came in was pretty roughed up. Apparently, this guy beat them up pretty bad when they tried to steal his stuff."

"So it was self-defense?" Angie asked.

The cop tilted his head back and forth. "We aren't sure about anything right now. A few guys tried to jack a fourth guy, they got beat up, then a gun was discharged a bunch of times. Three at the victim—and he's the victim, even if he did beat his assailants to hell—then the gun was discharged once more into the robber's head, plus some that went wild. We want to make sure that we don't have a killer on our hands here. Reports of someone looking like this hanging around have come in within the last few days. We figured Katie might know something about it. The concierge said you guys bought the condo across the hall from you and have a guest staying there. Is that right?"

Angie nodded. "That's true, we did, and we do. Why don't you come on upstairs with me? I'll introduce you to him. He's a bit shy and slightly occupied with video games, but he is always willing to help."

They nodded and followed her into the elevator. The ride up was almost exhausting for Angie. She hoped that the man in the picture wasn't Juntto, but she knew better than to hope for that. She really hoped he'd had the good sense to change from Morpheus into someone else. It was going to be hard to get him out of it if he still looked like the sketch, let alone if he did in fact kill the guy. Katie wasn't there to work her magic with the department, and Angie didn't think she had the same clout. Putting Juntto in jail wouldn't be the best thing for anyone. She couldn't control him there.

They exited the elevator, and she led them to Juntto's door. She set the bags down in front of her condo before crossing the hall. She was glad he wasn't screaming obscenities at that point. She knocked on the door but got no response. She smiled at the cops and really banged her fist. Finally, she heard steps approaching the door.

Juntto opened it and leaned on the doorframe. Angie's mouth fell open, but she quickly closed it. He looked like the guy from the cover of Far Cry Four. His skin was pale white, and he had white hair, which hid the ever-present silver streak. He was wearing a pair of purple pants and a white shirt. Angie looked behind him and saw a matching sports coat folded on the countertop. "Can I help you?"

The cops looked at each other and then at Juntto. "Uh, hi. We were wondering if you've seen this guy in the vicinity anytime recently?"

Juntto leaned over and looked at the picture. "Yeah, when I watched *The Matrix* the other day."

All four of them laughed nervously. One of the cops looked at the other and shrugged. "Obviously this isn't our guy."

The other cop nodded. "Yep."

They looked at Angie and Juntto and put on their hats. "Thanks for the cooperation. We didn't mean to take up your time. Let us know if you see this guy. He could be dangerous."

Angie stepped in front of Juntto before he could say anything. "We will, of course. Do you need me to walk you back out?"

The cops were already halfway down the hall. "We got it, ma'am. Thanks. Have a good day."

They stood there smiling until the doors to the elevator closed. As soon as the cops were out of sight, the smile left Angie's face. She huffed and pushed Juntto into the room, shutting the door behind her. Juntto peered around her. "No groceries this time? I'm really starving. You know, that broccoli cheese soup you brought home the other day was delicious. And oh man, the chips! I ate them in like five minutes. Seriously, I am starving."

Angie growled. "Fill your own damn refrigerator, I'm not your maid. I just put food in there this morning. Pandora was right about your food consumption. You need to pace yourself and start buying food with *your* money. And what the hell are the cops here for? I thought I told you to be inconspicuous and not get yourself into any trouble. You were gone for an hour."

Juntto put his hands up. "It really wasn't my fault. I swear I followed all of the rules."

"So the actual Morpheus beat up three people?"

"You look really stressed. Maybe you should sit down for a minute and take a deep breath."

She grumbled as she walked to the table and picked up his shirt and pants. She ran her hands over the blood-splattered holes in the back of the shirt, then touched the blood on his pants. Her head snapped toward Juntto. "Who the fuck shot you?"

Juntto chuckled. "It's a funny story, really. You are going to be like, Juntto, that's hilarious!"

Angie stood there tapping her foot against the floor, holding up the shirt with her fingers through the holes.

There was dried blood all over it. Juntto took a deep breath. He walked to his rolling chair and plopped down in it, feeling like a punished puppy. He wasn't used to answering to anyone, much less a woman. He was a free-roaming Leviathan, or at least he used to be.

"All right, calm down. I'll tell you the story. I went to GameStop and got a bunch of stuff. I decided to take a side street home to get here quicker. I read the map on my GPS, and it was a no-brainer. Anyway, I was walking along minding my own business when three guys came up behind me. They wanted to rob me, and well, I couldn't let that go unpunished."

Angie pursed her lips. "Of course not, but punishment should fit the crime, Juntto. Death and robbery do not balance."

Juntto shook his head. "I know, but just listen. They started to fight me, and I held back all my strength and just kind of beat them up a little bit. If they had stopped, I would have let them run off. In fact, I *did* let two of them run off in the end."

"I know. That's who went to the police."

Juntto scrunched his brow. "They got away, so they went to the police to turn themselves in?"

Angie waved her hands in the air frantically. "One of them did, but that's not the point. How did the third guy end up dead and you wind up with three bullet holes in your shirt?"

"Well, that's the interesting part. I was holding a guy against the wall, telling him he would never rob anyone again or I would find him. That was when his friend shot me three times in the back. I turned around and took the gun from him, then gave it back because I remembered the rule. Then he shot himself," Juntto finished and looked at her with wide eyes.

She blinked several times. "So, you're telling me this robber was so overcome with remorse that he decided to end it all right there in the alley? I don't believe that for a second. You've got ten seconds to tell me the truth, or I'm bypassing Katie and calling Pandora."

Juntto sighed loudly and threw back his head. "*Fine.* I could have killed him right there, no question. But then I thought about paperwork, and I really didn't want to have to do that. Not when I am supposed to be playing Xbox."

"And protecting the city?" Angie asked.

Juntto nodded. "Yeah, yeah, that too. Instead, I simply used my powers of suggestion, and the thief put the gun to his head and pulled the trigger."

Angie's mouth dropped open, and she stared at him. "I actually believe you."

Juntto rolled his eyes. "Because it's the truth."

Angie shook her head, still stunned. "So, you are telling me that you can use the power of suggestion to make people do things you want? I really don't like that."

Juntto shrugged and sat down on the couch with his bags. "It doesn't work in all situations, but since he was already scared of me, suicide became a better choice in his mind. Trust me, it doesn't work on the strong of heart and mind, like you or Katie or Lilith. You three would push it back without even realizing what I was doing."

Angie lowered her shoulders. "Still, don't go doing that. I get it, I do. But, seriously not cool."

She looked down at the shirt and pants and balled them

up, taking them over and dropping them in the trash. "Well, these clothes are a bust. And that was a really awesome shirt and pair of pants, too. I am going to consider buying you cheaper clothes. Maybe not Walmart-cheaper, but definitely cheaper than those were. I can't even try to fix that."

Angie walked to the couch and plopped down next to him. He was busily installing the cords on the Xbox. "Did you get an extra controller?"

Juntto pulled out the extra and tossed it to her. "Duh. I didn't want to walk all the way back when you got mad."

Angie shook her finger at him and smiled. "That was good thinking, my friend. I would have made you do it, too."

She brought the bag into her lap and started pulling out the games. "*Destiny*. Decent game, although not as amazing as they said it was going to be. *Far Cry Four*, of course. I see where you got your outfit. Meh, the game's good but not really my thing. Ahh, that's what I'm talking about, baby. *Halo*, the Master Chief Collection. Nice."

"You play all of these?"

Angie tried to ignore his tone of disbelief. "Sure do. I started when I was with my ex. He played, and when he was out drinking and ramping up to give me a good beating, I would play Halo. I pretended every alien I shot was him. I got pretty damn good at it, and the online play made me feel not so alone. I had a little family. Recently, I just haven't had the time. Been building the dream with Katie. If I had a gaming system, I would be stuck to it constantly."

Juntto laughed. "If anything happens to me, it's yours."

Angie smiled. "Aw, Juntto, that's almost sweet. Now, let's get rolling. Let the little woman clean your clock."

Juntto snapped his head toward Angie. "Is that foreplay?" He grabbed the other controller and opened the bag of chips he'd put next to him on the couch. "If it's foreplay, I mean, I can figure it out."

Angie grabbed a chip. "Don't talk with food in your mouth. What are you, some kind of heathen Leviathan?"

Juntto grinned. "Sorry. When did you become the annoying wife or uptight girlfriend?"

Angie laughed loudly. "First, don't ever refer to me as either of those ever again. I might take offense and use my powers of persuasion."

Juntto looked at her with narrowed eyes, trying to figure out if she was kidding.

She smiled and took another chip. "You can't decide if I'm joking. I'm going to let you simmer on that one for a bit. Now, number two. Let me just tell you that you haven't seen uptight yet, alien-lord256."

Juntto nodded, looking at the screen as the game came on. "I like that name."

Angie chuckled. "Yeah, I saw your gamertag. You are like, so obvious that people would never suspect you. You are that guy people just assume has some weird obsession and lives in his mom's basement eating cheese puffs. Somebody who owns three iguanas but has never had a girlfriend."

Juntto paused. "I *haven't* ever had a girlfriend."

Angie slowly looked at him. "Never?"

"Why tie myself down?" He shrugged. "I like to keep my options *way* open."

179

Angie wrinkled her nose and scooted a bit farther from him. "You are a man whore. An alien man whore. That should have been your gamertag. Do aliens contract STDs?"

"What's an STD?"

Angie chuckled, seeing an opportunity to scare the hell out of him again. "Oh, this is going to be fun."

15

"So, these are the sleeping quarters. As you can see, Stephanie and Timothy put some work in here to make themselves comfortable. Pretty stylish, and nice to sleep in. We appreciate the new beds, by the way. Those old ones were hell on our backs," Korbin explained as he opened the door to Katie's room.

Katie walked inside and looked around the room. It was painted a deep shade of purple, the bed had a black bedspread, and there was lacy Victorian-style décor all over. It had a walk-in closet and a bathroom attached. "Wow, this is pretty amazing."

Korbin chuckled. "Yeah, they really put time in on yours. Stephanie insisted on the color scheme, and Timothy went nuts on the décor. They even built that closet special for you, although I don't really understand all the hooks and hangers."

Katie ran her hands over the special area for her bras and smiled. "They seem to know me well."

Korbin clapped his hands. "I know you just got here,

but let's check out the rest, and then we can talk if you want to."

Katie tossed her bag on the bed. "Let's do it."

He walked her down the hall to the common area. There was a huge flat screen tv and comfortable couches and chairs all over the place. Katie leaned against the wall and smiled. "This reminds me of the first base we were at. Very family-friendly."

"I remembered it and I wanted that same feel, even if the merc team isn't the same as before. We still need a place to gather as a family whenever we can. And we have to be comfortable while we catch up on the soaps."

Katie put her hand on Korbin's shoulder and squeezed. "You did good. It's definitely a comfortable place."

Korbin took a deep breath and led her through the rest of the building, showing her the offices, the different IT spaces, and the training area stacked with workout equipment and a sparring area. Katie wondered if Korbin still had them doing all the workouts she remembered.

Pandora scoffed. *I would hope so. It would do you some good to get in on the action, too. You need to tighten up those moves. And that ass.*

Katie laughed to herself. *My ass is your job, but you're right. Hopefully, while I'm here, I can get in a workout.*

Yeah, right. Most of the time we don't even get a good night's sleep without getting a call. I doubt you'll find time to do a workout, although if Korbin is still a hard-ass, he will make time for it.

"I liked the build of the last base, everything being underground, but this is just as good. We developed some serious defenses, so being here won't be any less safe." Korbin showed her down the hall and back outside.

Katie squinted as she looked across the grounds. There were a couple of diggers still doing minor work. "Korbin, this is great. You really know how to turn nothing into something. I know you probably long for your garden, but I'm glad you're back."

Korbin put up his finger and led her around the corner of the barracks. He put his arms out, presenting a small garden with flowering plants along the edges. "Stephanie and I built it to make it feel more like home. When the spring comes again, we're going to plant veggies in there so we can cook with them."

Katie smiled widely. "That's awesome. I'm really glad you guys are making this place your own. You're a vital part of the team, and I want you to feel that you're at home here."

Korbin looked around the area. "At first it was a big change. I just kept thinking about our little farmhouse and garden. Now, though, after getting those memories back and really working hard on this place, I feel like it's definitely home."

Katie walked up next to him and looked at the armory building. "Good. I'm glad, because it *is* your home. At least one of them."

Korbin motioned toward the armory. "Come on, I'm sure Joshua would love to show you around the place."

Katie grabbed Korbin's arm. "Before we do that, I need to ask you a question. I hate to rush into it, but it's why I came here in the first place."

Korbin squared his shoulders and faced her. "Sure. Hit me with it."

Katie thought about it for a second. "If you were going to do a big hit-and-run on hell, where you needed video, what would you do?"

Korbin rubbed his jaw and looked down at the ground. "I guess that really depends. I don't know anything about hell. What is the climate like? What is the terrain like? Is there a connection strong enough to transmit from that realm to this one, even if a portal closes? Is there a difference in how ordnance works?"

Katie pursed her lips. "That's complicated."

Korbin chuckled. "So is a hit-and-run on hell. I need to know what hell is like before I could really be of any help in that scenario."

Katie put her finger up and pulled out her cell. She dialed her airport contact and put the phone to her ear. "Hey, yeah. It's Katie. I was wondering if my plane is still in the hangar? It is? Great. I'm going to be dropping by for a minute. Yeah. I'm flying in with my wings. Thanks."

Katie stuck the phone in her pocket and looked at Korbin, sizing him up. *You gonna help me keep him up in the air?*

Hell, yeah. I'm always up for a little flight over the desert.

Korbin hasn't seen us in full angel mode. It might freak him out a little.

Nah, he'll be fine. Just make sure he doesn't squirm. I don't want to face Stephanie if we drop him. Bitch be crazy. She'd slit our throats.

Katie stepped back and let her wings unfold behind her, and Korbin's eyes grew wide. "That is very impressive.

They look exactly the way I always imagined they would. I have to say, you make a stunning angel."

Katie smiled. "Thank you, but don't say that too loud. Pandora might drop you."

He tilted his head to the side. "Drop me?"

Katie laughed and flapped her wings, scooping Korbin into her arms. He gripped her tightly as she took off across the base. She tipped her head at the guards as they passed them. Her wings beat furiously behind her as they propelled her into the sky. She could tell Korbin was nervous by the way he was white-knuckling her shoulder, but he slowly began to unwind.

He took in the desert stretching out as far as the eye could see. "Wow, this is the view you get whenever you fly?"

"Usually. Sometimes it's buildings, but either way, it's pretty cool."

Korbin guffawed. "You're telling me. I don't know why you don't fly all the time."

Katie wondered the same internally. "It takes a lot of energy for me to fly, so I use it sparingly."

They flew fast and straight until they were high enough to avoid getting attention from anyone below but low enough to stay clear of any planes flying by, then she zigzagged through the air, making her way to the airport. She was showing off a little bit, but Korbin was grinning.

When they reached the airport, she slowly flapped her wings, lowering them to the ground. She set Korbin down and stepped back, and her wings folded behind her and disappeared. Korbin just stared at her in wonder. "I have to admit, that was not something I ever imagined seeing from you. I am definitely not disappointed, though."

Katie put her arm around his shoulder and walked him toward the plane. "They are pretty awesome. And trust me, when you first brought me back to the base, I didn't think I would last a day, much less be part angel *and* lead a team. A lot of the way I handle things is because of you and the team. The ones still here and the ones gone."

"I feel the same way about all of you."

Katie walked up to the stairs of the plane, leaving Korbin on the ground. She ran inside and grabbed a package neatly wrapped in plain brown paper and tied with a piece of string off one of the seats. She came back outside and handed it to Korbin. "Here, put that on."

Korbin opened the package to find a protective suit inside. He looked at it.

"Trust me."

Korbin put the suit on over his clothes. Katie fixed the headpiece snugly and snapped the oxygen on to make things easier for him. "You ready?"

He gave her a thumbs-up, and she relaxed. Pandora took over, giving Katie dark, jagged claws. She used the claws to tear open a portal the size of a door. She took Korbin's hand in hers and pulled him through to the other side. The hot air hit them both hard and they stood there for a second, letting their vision clear. Korbin slowly walked to the edge of a cliff, looking around at the terrible landscape.

"This is hell?"

"Yes."

"This is where they come from?"

"Yes."

"I can see why they want to leave."

In the distance, he could see several volcanoes, ash blowing from the tops and lava flowing down over the sides. Below were rivers of lava laid neatly within the black stone and lava rock. There were no demons. Katie made sure to bring him far enough out. He leaned down and picked up a rock, rolling it in his fingers.

Katie coughed a bit. She had gotten used to the scenery and was no longer stunned by it. "We can't stay long; we don't have much support. But it's something I can't really explain. It's a sight you really have to see for yourself. This is the outer ring of hell. There's not much action here, and everything is pretty stable. As you get closer to the inner ring, the air gets hotter and denser. It's full of nitrogen-based acids and ammonia. Pandora allows me to travel without a suit, but I should wear one if I want to stay longer. For you and the others, not to mention those that aren't damned, we have developed these suits. We have been fixing them to make them more maneuverable and easier to fight in, but we're still working on them. They were impossible before."

"I can imagine. So, you've been here before?" Korbin asked, still holding the rock.

"Yeah, we came here once to scope out the place and get readings, and then a second time to send out our drones. They are in hell somewhere, flying around sending information back to a lab."

Korbin couldn't believe it. "That's crazy. So, the signal can get through the space between worlds?"

Katie wasn't sure how it all worked; she just knew that

it did. "Apparently. It's been working so far. We have a serious research and development team working around the clock studying hell. They have been vital to the cause, and we're hoping to be able to use the information they have to bring the fight here."

"So that's why you're asking."

"Kind of. This isn't going to be the final battle. We have to show them, though, that they can't fuck with us. They can't attack us and get away with it. We want the people to know that we aren't sitting back and letting it happen."

Korbin bent slightly and started to cough.

That's our cue, baby girl.

Okay, Pandora. Take us home.

Katie waved her hand, and Pandora's clawed hand created a portal straight back to the base. She took Korbin under the arm and led him through. The portal shrank and snapped shut behind them.

Korbin collapsed to the ground, took off the helmet, and took a deep breath in of the cool desert air.

"Sorry, I forget how hard it is on the others. That suit wasn't prepared for a full walk-in."

"I feel like I've been to hell and back." Korbin grinned up at her.

Katie was about to respond when her phone rang.

She pulled it out and saw the general was calling. She grimaced. "Shit. The general."

Korbin laughed. "Uh-oh."

Katie turned on the phone. "Hey, General."

"Katie, we detected two small portals, one at the airport and then one at the base location. What's going on?" the general asked, worried.

Katie wrinkled her nose. "That was me. I'm sorry, I should have told you ahead of time. I wanted to show Korbin hell so that he could help us with a strategy for the mission we've been discussing."

The general let out a deep breath. "Katie, I appreciate that you needed to give him intel, but you could have given the location of the base away. A demon could have followed you back, or someone could have seen you. You have to be more careful."

Katie slapped her forehead. "I'm such a dumbass. I didn't even think about that. I did make sure that no one saw or followed us, though. I'm sorry I didn't think about a risk to the new location. I just jumped without thought."

Pandora snickered. *There you go, jumping without thinking again. I wish you would do that when it came to men. All the pleasure you could be acquiring could cancel out the reprimands you get from Papa Brushwood.*

Katie didn't need Pandora's smart remarks. *No, he's right. I could have compromised the whole thing.*

Pandora sighed. *You humans worry too much. Did he forget that I was there? I would have sensed a demon coming three miles away. He and you need to calm your tits.*

I really don't want to think about the general's tits.

Pandora giggled. *I bet he thinks about yours.*

Ew. Dude, stop.

The general cleared his throat. "All right, I'll let you go. Just try to be more careful."

Katie saluted the air. "Yep. On it, General."

Korbin handed Katie the suit and showed her the rock in his hand. "Let's get inside so I can do some testing on this rock."

Katie walked next to him as they headed toward the main building. "Awesome. I didn't know you had the science gene."

Korbin laughed. "I'm the jack-of-all-trades now. So, you want something dramatic without risking our people, right?"

"Yep, that's exactly right."

Korbin opened the door to the barracks and held it for her. "Okay, I'll have something for you in a day or two."

Angie hummed as she turned a burner to high. She poured oil into a cast-iron pan and scraped the garlic into the oil. Juntto was happily playing his games and she had done everything on her list for the day, so she decided to turn on some classical piano, crack open some wine, and prepare herself a delicious meal. She rarely cooked for herself anymore. She was always taking care of everyone else.

The garlic sizzled in the pan as she chopped up the better part of an onion. She walked back over and dropped it in the pan and moved the pan around, shaking it back and forth and flipping the garlic and onion slightly in the air. She sprinkled in some salt and pepper and turned the heat down.

Angie picked up her glass of wine and took a sip, and as she tried to remember if she needed rosemary for this dish her phone began to buzz. She tried to ignore it but saw Timothy's name.

She wrinkled her nose, hoping for the best, and answered. "Hey, darling. What's up?"

"What's that sizzling sound?"

Angie looked at the pan and took it off the burner. "Was about to fix dinner. What's up?"

Timothy sighed. "Sorry to ruin that, but we've got a portal opening right there in New York."

Angie grabbed a towel, wiped her hands and turned off the burner with a heavy heart. "Okay, send me the location. I'll raise the wolf, and we'll head out."

Timothy paused. "I'm not really sure what the hell that's supposed to mean, but I am on it, girl."

Angie hung up the phone and took her apron off, then burst into Juntto's room. "Hey, time to put down the controller. We have work to do."

Juntto pressed the button again, killing another alien. "Come bursting in here like that and I could be naked or something. Then you would get all huffy, asking me why I'm naked in my own damn apartment. Can't win with you women."

Angie put her hands on her hips and stood in front of the television. "Like you would care if I walked in on you naked. In fact, you've done that to me before. Doesn't matter, we got a hit. Get ready to fight."

Juntto put the microphone to his lips. "Alien Lord has to go save New York. Have a good night and suck my meat, punks."

"Juntto, they're children."

"I said 'good night.'"

He dropped his controller and began to gear up. He wore his purple suit, including the jacket. He pulled out his pistols and holstered them. He stared at two daggers made of special metal, unsure where to put them. Finally, he grew a sheath on either hip and stuck the daggers in.

Angie just shook her head, wishing things were that easy for her when she got dressed every day.

"We need to look into getting me a spear." Juntto looked her up and down. "You got a weapon?"

Angie patted her hips, where she wore two guns like an old-fashioned gunfighter. "Locked and loaded."

They ran to the elevator side by side. The doorman was already on the floor, and he rushed to hold the door for them. Angie smiled at him as they raced out and stopped on the corner. Juntto took two steps back as a cop car came screeching around the corner, its siren on and its lights flashing brightly. The car stopped right in front of them.

Juntto looked at it suspiciously.

Angie flung open the back door. "It's our version of a cab. Get in."

"Ooh, girl, I am so excited about this." Timothy walked into the family room wearing a set of pajamas with pink bunnies and clouds all over them.

Stephanie plopped down on the couch with a bowl of popcorn. She was wearing matching pjs. "Me too. Oh, my God. You know trying to get Korbin to watch chick flicks is like pulling teeth."

Timothy rolled his eyes. "Fine with me. More girl time."

Stephanie laughed. "Okay, what are we watching first?"

Timothy pulled the DVD case out from behind his back. "*P.S. I Love You*, followed by *The Holiday*."

Stephanie squealed. "Oh, those are two of my very favorites. Come on, come sit down."

Timothy giggled and ran to sit next to her. They both put their feet on the ottoman, moving their pink bunny slippers back and forth as the movie began.

By the time it ended, the popcorn was gone and they were both sniffling back tears, wrapped in each other's arms.

Timothy grabbed a tissue and blotted his eyes. "Girl, that would be me. I would have his ashes, singing show tunes alone in my damn apartment. Stepping on pizza, too. That bitch is right on cue."

Stephanie nodded. "That would be my nosy-ass family too. They would let themselves right in. My sister would have been giving me a standing ovation. I can't even. This would be my life if anything happened."

Stephanie's face went dark.

Timothy shook his head and started fanning her. "Hmm, no. Nuh-uh. Don't even let those little thoughts come into that beautiful brain of yours. Korbin and you are life, sister. You will not be taking yourself into any deep depression. Besides, that's rocky-road territory, and I got mint chocolate chunk."

Stephanie laughed. "Mint? Okay, you're right. No bad thoughts."

"Besides, in the end, she gets that hunky new Irish guy who pretty much looks like his friend. Personally, I think it's kind of creepy, but what the hell what do I know? I just want a man with an accent like that."

"That does make the stomach dance," Stephanie pointed out.

Timothy gave her a dainty high five. "Yasss, girl. Yasss."

They finished the movie and took a break to get some snacks. Timothy looked like his mind was off somewhere else. Stephanie stopped and narrowed her eyes at him. "What are you thinking about?"

Timothy groaned. "My job. Sent Angie to an opening portal this evening, and I guess I was worried."

"You've got coverage and she has that Leviathan, so I think it's all good. We have *The Holiday* to watch." Stephanie handed him a bowl of mint chocolate chip ice cream, and they went back to the living room.

They sat down and started the movie. "Girl, I don't mean to bust your happily-ever-after bubble, but I have to be honest. I am *so* glad Katie and Calvin woke you and Korbin the fuck up. I have missed you like hell, and this whole base-jumping thing has been...ugh, so sad without you. I felt lost in my own world, and no one wanted to come and play."

Stephanie leaned over and kissed him on the cheek. "Well, I'm here now, and I ain't going nowhere."

16

S creams and snarls mixed together and echoed through the narrow alleyways and streets of New York City. A portal had opened at the corner of New York Avenue and Kingston in Brooklyn. The portal had blown a hole in the side of an apartment building, and people were scattered everywhere. Demons were pouring out, the fiends grabbing and tearing at anything they could get their claws on. A group of people had started a small resistance, but others panicked and ran for it. Most of them didn't make it.

The cops had been the first on the scene, cordoning off an area. Unfortunately, like so many of the hit-and-runs, the portal hadn't been discovered in time. It was only seconds after the cops arrived that the thing blew open, sending blasts of heat down the streets. The police put their cars on every corner, but the demons didn't abide by Earthly laws. They just plowed into the cars, jumping on top of them and ripping the lights off. Among the demons pouring out of the portal were infected men and women who had heard the call. They had come to help their demon counterparts.

There were red eyes everywhere.

Among the rubble and overturned cars, groups of people huddled together. It was like a merry-go-round of people with guns or sharp objects fending off the demons, only to be swallowed by them. The next man or woman would stand, grabbing anything they could get their hands on. On one corner a man snatched a freshly severed arm, unable to pry the gun out of the hand. He grimaced as he wrapped his live finger around the cold dead one and began pulling the trigger. He managed to strike two of the demons in the head before a snarling beast tore open his stomach with a long sharp claw.

Travers pulled up with Angie and Juntto in the back seat. All three of them jumped out of the car, pulling their guns and running for the fight in the center of the street.

Angie immediately started blasting away, firing on either side of her, striking one demon and missing another. Adrenaline was flowing through her. It took her a moment to realize where she was. In the middle of an incursion, surrounded by demons.

Without warning, fear filled her belly. "Oh, fuck. What the fuck am I doing?"

Juntto ran up beside her. "Don't think, just shoot. Pretend you have my strength and Katie's balls. You will be unstoppable."

Angie nodded and Juntto took off across the pavement, heading for a group of demons gathering in the corner. He fired his weapons until the bullets were gone, then he pulled his daggers. Demons rushed at the newcomer, but he was ready. He slashed through necks and cut off heads so fast that everyone stopped and watched him. Angie continued choosing her shots and firing. She had already seen the show.

Behind them, Travers and Schultz looked at each other in amazement. "Holy shit, that dude is amazing. That's Katie's new sidekick?"

Schultz shrugged. "I'm assuming so."

A huge demon crashed into Juntto, knocking the blades from his hands. Juntto didn't have time to waste. He held up his fists, and they began to grow larger. They looked like huge mallets coming out of his purple coat. He swung them from side to side, knocking the heads off three different demons.

A large demon crawled out of the portal and immediately turned away from Juntto. He had easier prey, a group cowering in the half-demolished corner of the building. When the beast tilted his head back and roared, windows burst and glass showered the frightened humans.

Juntto looked at him and shook his head. "All in good time, big guy. I'll be with you in just a few."

He kicked a demon hard in the chest, sending it flying back until it impaled itself on a broken street sign. The beast scrambled to get off but just sank backward until it finally burst into ash.

Screaming children and the light, muffled music of an ice cream truck grabbed Juntto's attention. He squinted at an overturned truck on one of the side streets. A tall, thin man was walking toward a group of kids.

Something about the man wasn't right.

The guy stopped in front of the truck and hunched

over. His eyes flashed red and his arms began to grow longer, tearing his human skin and revealing the scaly black demon skin underneath. His chin dropped six inches lower than any human's should, and a loud wail burst forth. His long arms reached toward the kids as his legs morphed and twisted, bending backward at the knee.

Juntto's eyes grew wide. "The freakiest shit happens to me. Seriously. They don't have this shit on my planet."

He took off toward the ice cream man. The beast turned around, eyes bright red and teeth sharpened to points. Juntto's fist came down hard on the demon's face and knocked him backward. He scrambled onto all fours and scurried up, clawing his way up the side of the apartment building like some huge, horrific bug.

Juntto waved his arms at the kids. "Run. Go. Get the fuck out of here."

The kids took off toward the cops and were ushered as far from the fight as they could get them. Juntto cracked his neck and brought his hands back to normal size, then looked down and saw his two errant daggers. He grabbed them and motioned for the demon to come fight, and its huge mouth curled into a grin.

The beast leaped straight toward Juntto and tackled him to the ground. The demon latched all four limbs around Juntto and opened his mouth.

"What the fuck?"

The demon began to slash at him with a tongue covered in spikes. He pierced Juntto's cheeks, and Juntto growled deeply. With all his strength, the Leviathan pulled his arm away and jammed one blade into the demon's stomach and the other into its neck. He pushed up to his feet, using the blades to hold the demon in the air.

"You are not an ice cream man," Juntto yelled as he ran straight for the crumbling apartment building.

He slammed the demon into the brick and jammed the knives even farther into him. The demon struggled and moaned, trying to get free. Its red eyes flickered, and a human moan came from his throat before he burst into ash.

Juntto let out a deep breath, and his shoulders slumped. He muttered to himself as he wiped the blades on his pants.

He caught Angie's eye. She was standing there, shocked. Juntto cupped his hands and yelled over the crowd. "They should put that in the game. That shit was wild!"

Angie rolled her eyes and pointed to his left. Juntto looked up just as a demon jumped at him. He stepped to the side and grabbed the demon by the throat, wrestling him into submission. He grunted and twisted the spitting beast's neck, yanking its head off its shoulders. Gooey black blood squirted over his suit, but he didn't care. He could always create a new outfit.

Angie turned to find three demons surrounding a little old lady. The woman kept her head low, waving her walker at them and whimpering. Angie ran at them, shooting each one, careful not to hit the old woman. One by one, the demons collapsed into a pile of ash at the old woman's feet. Angie dropped the magazines from her guns and reloaded before walking to the woman.

She had her head down, and her shoulders shook with fear. Angie reached out and touched her shoulder. "Ma'am, you're all right now. Let me get you out of harm's way."

Suddenly the old woman looked up, her eyes burning red. When she smiled her demonic teeth showed, jagged and yellow. She opened her mouth to talk, and a deep, raspy voice emerged. "Stupid little girl. You are all going to die. All of you."

Angie pulled her hand back from the demon's shoulder and jumped off the curb. She pulled her gun up, but the demon was gone, replaced by a helpless old woman.

"Please help me. Don't kill me."

Without warning, her face hardened and became haggard and demon-like. "You bitch, I'll bite your throat out."

Back and forth the woman changed, her body shaking and twisting as it went.

"Please."

"Die!"

Angie watched in horror for several moments, finally screaming, "*Enough!*"

The old woman slowly lifted her head, and the demon had taken over. Its eyes glistened, and its sharp smile was something nightmares were made of. Angie shook her head in disgust, finally pulling the trigger and striking the woman right between the eyes. Her body fell to the ground, convulsing until the demon evaporated, leaving only the woman's frail and tiny corpse on the ground.

Angie put her hand over her mouth and cried out, closing her eyes as tears began to form. She took a deep breath in through her nose and shook it off, whispering to herself, "Strength of Juntto, balls of Katie. Strength. Balls."

She turned as a smaller demon scurried across the asphalt toward her, his claws at the ready. She pointed her gun at him and pulled the trigger, letting the bullet blow half his head off. He wobbled back and forth like a chicken without a head until she reared back and punted the beast through the air. He slammed into the side of the apartment building and burst to ash.

Juntto had been watching from across the street and gave her the thumbs-up. She smiled unconvincingly and made the gesture back, turning in a daze. She had never been through something like this before. She had only imagined it when Katie had talked about it at the house. Actually being in the situation was totally different. She had to get her wits about her, she knew that, but how?

Just then a loud cackle pierced the air, and the sound of a crying baby filled Angie's ears. She turned toward the sound to find a woman on the ground, her neck torn open. Her dead eyes stared at Angie, a tear still rolling down her cheek.

A demon stood above the woman, lifting a small baby from a stroller. Angie gritted her teeth and narrowed her eyes, shoving her guns into her holsters. As she marched toward the demon, she reached down and grabbed a sharp, jagged piece of metal off the ground. A freckle-faced cop saw what she was doing and moved into position to cover her.

Angie reached the demon and tapped it on the shoulder. The demon spun around with the baby in its arms. Angie quickly jammed the metal into its stomach and hissed, "That baby doesn't belong to you."

The freckled cop shouted, "Now."

Angie yanked the baby from the squealing demon's arms, then rushed away and dropped to the ground, covering the child with her body. Shots rang out as the cop fired at the demon again and again. By the time Angie looked up, there was nothing left of the fiend but a cloud of dust. She turned to the cop and handed her the baby. "Thank you."

Juntto cleared out several large groups of smaller demons and stopped to catch his breath. A large demon was climbing the side of the building, reaching in and yanking people out of their homes. Juntto walked to Travers and Schultz and stood with them as they stared up at the fiend.

Travers held his gun loosely. "We can't fire. There are too many civilians."

"I'll take care of him," Juntto snarled.

The two detectives slowly turned their heads toward Juntto.

Juntto put out his hand. "You mind if I borrow your weapon? It's got the special bullets, right?"

Travers nodded without saying anything, eyeing Juntto's purple suit. The guy was weird, but Katie and Pandora were a little strange too. He handed over his gun, and the two watched as Juntto sprinted across the pavement, leaped onto the hood of a police cruiser, bounced off it and scrabbled for purchase on the adjacent building.

Juntto gulped in air, then leaped to the apartment building. He hit, then clung tightly to the brick next to the snarling demon. Juntto snarled right back. "I'll give you one chance to give up and go back through your portal before I kill you."

The demon let loose a wild roar, and Juntto squinted as spit flew all over him. He wiped the spittle from his face.

Almost as an afterthought, he pulled Travers' gun and shot the demon's knees out from under him. The demon screamed as huge chunks of flesh and bone split from his body and fell to the ground below. The demon still held on, even with his legs dangling uselessly.

Juntto aimed the gun at the demon's arm. "Stupid."

The demon slashed a large catlike claw at Juntto, forcing him back a bit. Juntto hung onto the building, but the demon scrambled up, dragging his lame legs behind him.

Juntto fired at him twice, but the thing was swinging around wildly. He called, "Where you going? We were just getting to know each other."

Juntto sighed and tucked the gun in the back of his pants. With a thought, he morphed his feet into wicked claws and easily sprinted up the building behind the demon. When they reached the top ledge, Juntto leaped over the demon and landed on the roof, changing his feet back to his shiny leather shoes. He dusted his hands off and waited for the beast to poke his head over the edge of the roof.

When the fiend peeked over the edge, Juntto strutted forward and pressed the gun against his head. "Do me a favor. When you get back to hell, tell Moloch I'm coming for him."

Juntto pulled the trigger, putting a hole in the demon's head. The demon held on, dazed from the bullet in his skull but not quite dead. Juntto frowned down at the creature. Setting the gun aside, he grabbed the demon's head with his great hands, placed a leg on the demon's shoulder, and smiled darkly.

With a grunt, Juntto pushed the demon's body away with his foot and pulled the thing's head from its shoulders. The demon did fall, then, tumbling over and bursting into dust halfway down, showering the people below. He looked at the head, not yet ash, and tossed it over his shoulder. He leaped off the building and landed below, running into the group of smaller demons.

Angie was impressed with Juntto's skill; so impressed, in fact, that she didn't see the demon coming up behind her. Suddenly, she felt a burning pain across her back. She winced and arched forward, stumbling over some stones and falling. She turned over and saw the demon coming for her.

"God... Fuck... Shit. Where are my guns?" She looked all around but couldn't find them. They were both gone.

The demon cackled loudly and held up the guns in its long fingers. Angie's eyes grew wide as it dropped one to the ground and turned the other toward her. Carefully, the thing poked its talons over the trigger. She straightened her shoulders, feeling the burn across her back and the weakness in her legs. The warm blood from her wound soaked the stone beneath her, but she didn't care.

As the demon situated the gun, she closed her eyes, waiting for the end. There was a loud boom, and she cringed, waiting for the pain. After a moment, though, she didn't feel anything, and she opened one eye slightly. Standing in front of her was Juntto, holding the demon in one massive hand. There was a bullet hole straight through its brain. The demon turned to dust, and Juntto pulled Angie carefully from the ashes.

"Sorry I didn't get over here sooner. I had to get a busload of elderly idiots out of the way."

Angie looked at the bus carefully parked on the other side of the cop cars. "How did you move it? You don't know how to drive."

Juntto flexed and kissed one of his biceps. "These guns are getting their own show."

Angie blinked at him. "Oh, you mean you have tickets to the gun show. Okay, I get it."

Juntto scratched his head. "What gun show? Should we take Katie with us?"

"Never mind, Juntto. I'll explain it later."

They turned to watch the last of the demons scramble back into the portal. A line of police officers had formed around the portal, making sure none escaped. Juntto grunted. "*Now* they get their shit together."

"You did a kick-ass job here."

Juntto motioned to an ambulance. "You're hurt. Go get cleaned up. I'll help out here."

Angie hobbled to the ambulance, and they started taking care of her immediately. One of the medics told her it was just a flesh wound and she would be fine. She sat on the curb as they cleaned her wound, watching the dust from the falling buildings beginning to clear.

Travers and Schultz walked up to her and Travers winced. "Ouch."

Angie smiled. "Yeah, kind of. I think I numbed it myself when fear took over."

Schultz watched Juntto from afar. "Yeah, I saw him help you. Good to see a bad guy can do good things. I do have to say, he might want to choose a more subtle look, or it's going to be obvious who he is."

Angie laughed. "I'll tell him again, but that's kind of his thing. And as far as being a bad guy, just remember that on his planet that's survival. They don't have the numbers we do, so they don't have the option of debating and examining problems. They just kill. The rest of it? Yeah, he's a douchebag and has no idea how to treat women. He's making up for it, though, one life at a time."

Travers leaned in. "By the way, we saw that freaky-ass old lady. Don't feel bad about that. That shit was straight out of my nightmares."

Angie scoffed. "You're telling me."

Travers whispered, "She looked just like my Nana."

"Really?"

"Yeah. Big yellow teeth and everything."

Schultz and Angie chuckled.

Travers grinned. "I'm not kidding. She was a mean old broad."

17

Katie rolled over in her new bed at the base and smiled. She was in heaven. Stephanie and Timothy had gotten her the good sheets, and they felt like satin on her skin. Even Pandora was knocked out, and Katie could almost swear she'd heard her snoring at some point during the night. Talk about annoying. She couldn't get away from that shit.

Katie pulled the covers over her body, snuggling back in. The vibration of her phone began to echo through the room, and Katie moaned. She rolled over and slapped it as if it were her alarm.

Pandora snorted. *Huh? What? Fuck, you idiot, it's your phone. Stop slapping it!*

Katie sat straight up in the bed and plucked the phone off the nightstand. "Oh shit, it's Angie. She knows the rules about time. Hello? Are you alive? What's going on?"

Angie chuckled. "If I were calling you and I was dead, you'd have other things to worry about. Zombies and demons—what a mix."

Katie groaned. "Don't give them any ideas. Please, Lord. I don't do zombies. That's a new rule of mine. No zombies. We get zombies, I'm going to retire to a bunker somewhere and live out my days in peace."

Angie let out a long deep breath. "So…"

Katie situated herself. "Uh-oh. What's going on over there? I hope it's not Juntto."

Angie cleared her throat. "No, not really. He was actually pretty good. There was an incursion. I, Juntto, and the cops were able to repel it, but it was pretty big. Started in Brooklyn. There were a ton of small demons and one huge one. Then there was the ice cream man and the old lady."

Katie furrowed her brow. "The what and the who?"

"Think of the most terrifying thing you can imagine, and then put a granny's face on it. Or an ice cream man's face. Both were pretty horrific. Dude stretched his jaw down farther than Pandora when faced with her favorite thing in the world."

Pandora laughed loudly. *Bitch over there talking about some dick! And believe me, I can unhinge that shit.*

Katie held back a laugh. "Uh, when did *my* nightmares start popping out of the portals? And the old lady?"

Angie shook her head with a shiver. "She was being attacked by demons, so I helped her, and then she turned into this creepy red-eyed freak and tried to stab me. I put a bullet in her, but I can't stop thinking about that poor little granny, whoever she was. Damn demons are ruthless. When the children of the corn start coming out, I'm handing in my notice. I just want you to know that. It's not just because I don't think I can kill a kid, but creepy kids will fuck you up for life."

She is telling the truth. Have you ever heard the Lizzy Borden song sung by a bunch of kids? Holy shit, that freaks me out and I'm a fucking demon. We get kids in hell sometimes. We just lock those evil little bastards away in the deepest, darkest pits. Nope. Nope. No way.

Katie was perplexed. "I can't believe they attacked New York. I wonder if it was because I took Korbin into hell earlier. Maybe they noticed and implemented a hit on New York in retaliation."

"I don't know, but it was crazy. We're home now, though, and the cops are cleaning up. I'm gonna get some rest, and we can talk later."

Katie nodded. "Yeah, for sure. Get some rest. I'll call you later today."

She hung up the phone and shook her head. Pandora groaned. *I just realized that I'm starving and there is no fucking food here.*

I'm sure the mess hall has something.

There are no donuts, no bacon, nothing. What kind of shitty establishment did you bring me to? All the while Angie's over there killing grannies and eating good food.

Katie looked around her room. *You might be right. This is awesome, but we can't be here for good. I'm going to need to figure out how to get the team on some sort of rotation. That way a few of them can be in the city, too. Otherwise, we'll always be stuck here at the base.*

Pandora scoffed. *Over my dead body. And that was not an offer to kill me. I have been given the taste of luxury and food. I will not go back to bunker living, especially now that we're even farther away from the city. This is why the folks at Area 51 have, like, five-star chefs down there. They would go crazy otherwise.*

Katie looked down at her phone as it rang again. "General Brushwood."

"I didn't wake you? That shocks me."

Katie pushed the covers off and sat on the edge of the bed. "Yeah, Angie woke me. We just got off the phone."

The general was glad to not be the one to give her the news. "Okay, so you know about New York?"

Katie stood up and walked to her mirror. "Yep. Grannies, ice cream guys, and all."

The general was confused. "Are we talking about the same thing here? The incursion in Brooklyn?"

Katie chuckled. "Yeah, sorry. There were some weird details about the attack. Some kind of demon we haven't seen before. Not powerful, just strange."

"I see. Well, if it helps, I agree that so far Juntto seems to be working out. I've heard tales of him saving a bus full of elderly people, killing a giant demon, and rescuing about a dozen kids. I think that was the ice cream man situation. I heard something about that, and the song was playing in the background when I was getting the scoop." He paused a moment, "No pun intended."

Katie shivered as she chuckled. "That's creepy. As far as Juntto is concerned, I figured he would be okay, but be careful with that trust. Everything is fine until he goes apeshit and kills everyone in a bar. Let's not forget that."

"Moooom! I'm *hungry*," Juntto whined.

Angie winced as she looked at the whining Leviathan. Every movement hurt. Even breathing seemed to make her back throb. "I am kind of in pain right now. I am *not* an alien, nor do I have a demon inside me sending super-healing vibes my way."

Juntto sat up on the couch. "Oh yeah, I forgot you aren't Damned. Did you tell Katie about getting beat up?"

Angie grimaced. "Hell, no. She would have lost her mind and gone jumping into hell to kick someone's ass. She'll find out when she gets back. Right now, though, I need you to get your shit together. Here is your mission: choose a restaurant for us. I'm *not* cooking."

Twenty minutes later Juntto met Angie in the hallway. She looked at him grumpily. She was dressed but stiff, and unable to really move her head. "Did you pick a place?"

Juntto smiled. "I want to go to the Infirmary NYC on Second Street. I already pulled it up on the GPS."

"Do you like spicy food?"

He shrugged as they climbed into the elevator. "We'll see. There's a first time for everything. Humans season things strangely. Of course, the food is completely different as well."

They walked into the lobby and out to the curb, where Angie flagged down a cab. Juntto looked down the street. "You don't want to walk?"

Angie chuckled as she carefully got into the car. "I don't even want to move right now, much less walk all the way there."

Juntto got in and gave the cabbie directions the whole ride there. When they arrived, Juntto looked around in amazement at the wooden tables, Louisiana news clippings on the wall, and the general ambiance. He loved it, right down to the jazz playing on the speakers over their heads.

Angie looked at the menu. "Bill's on you, so eat however much you want."

It was all new food to Juntto, so he ordered half the menu. He started with the baked macaroni and cheese and an order of buffalo-style oysters and followed it with a New Orleans sampler that included jambalaya, gumbo, and red beans and rice. He finished up with a catfish po'boy.

Angie shook her head. She could smell the heat of the spices from across the table. She stuck with a watermelon salad and a side of fries, knowing what spicy food would do to her stomach. She pointed her fork at him. "You are a brave man for eating all of that. My father is a spicy food junkie, but he knows when to say when."

Juntto looked at her, slightly confused. "It was delicious." He waved his hands at the remains of what had once been food. "I have confirmed that I love spicy food."

Angie just chuckled, knowing he had no idea what was coming. When they were done, Juntto paid the bill. This necessitated a long explanation of why he needed to tip the waitress at least fifteen percent. "I must leave more money? This is the price of the food, correct? Then why must I pay the slaves? The restaurant owner should pay his own slaves."

She wanted to slap him to make a point. "Juntto, they are *workers*. Workers who prepare your food and bring it to you. They aren't slaves."

"You keep saying they aren't slaves, but they act like slaves."

"This is like any other job, only they work off of tips," Angie explained.

He looked down and blinked at the receipt. Finally,

Angie reached over and filled in the amounts for him. "There. All done. Let's go."

Juntto walked warily out of the restaurant, still not getting it but not wanting to sit through another explanation.

It felt like a tiny amount of paperwork.

They rode back through the city in a cab, staring out the windows at the passing buildings and fall decorations being put up. Juntto didn't say much, and Angie couldn't help but wonder if the food was finally hitting his stomach.

Back at the condo, Angie got out her keys. "You gonna play Halo?"

"In a little bit. I'll let you know."

He shut the door, and Angie giggled, slipping inside her condo. She put her things down and checked the mail stacked on the side table. She threw away the junk mail and grabbed a glass of wine, heading to the living room to get her dose of daily news. It was kind of her routine, although it usually happened earlier. Taking care of Juntto was absorbing more of her time than she would have liked. She was okay with that, though. Katie was counting on her to get it done.

About five minutes later, the front door creaked open. Angie saw Juntto walk in with sweat on his forehead, holding his stomach. She clicked the mute button on the television as he entered. "You okay?"

Juntto shook his head. His face was pale. "There are literal flames coming out of my ass." He grimaced. "Who knew that spices could cause that?"

Angie laughed. "I doubt you mean literally, but it definitely can feel that way. Didn't I warn you? But no, you were dead-set on showing me your Viking stomach."

Juntto waved his hand in the air. "No, literally. Flames. Fire. There is a dragon in my stomach."

Angie sat back giggling as she watched him struggle. Suddenly there was a loud rumbling noise, and his ass practically exploded right in front of her. A flame shot out, burning a hole right through his pants. A puff of grey and black smoke rose to the ceiling.

Her face went straight, and she sat up, eyes wide. "Did your...did your *ass* just explode?"

Juntto's face scrunched in pain as he nodded, standing very still. "I told you." His voice was hoarse and weak. "There is a dragon or something inside me."

Angie slowly got up and walked around him at a distance, going into the hall closet. She pulled out a container of Tums and tossed it to him. "Take like three or four an hour until you feel better. They taste like minty chalk, but it's better than having a flamethrower shoved up your ass and the trigger being pulled if you hiccup. I want to laugh and say it would be an awesome weapon, but... *DAMN!*" She shook her head. "That's too horrific, even for demons." She waved at the front door. "Go explode in your own condo, I don't want you to trip the fire alarm and set the sprinklers off."

His look was so forlorn it was hard not to take pity on him as he shuffled back out her front door.

Korbin walked to the board in the conference room and pointed at a list of weapons. "So, we want to make a big boom, kill their creatures, injure them, and make as big of a point as we possibly can without losing our men."

Katie, watching from the table, put the pen to her lips. "Right. Send a message."

"Good, so we need to be able to drop a quick-build set of defensive gear through a portal as fast as possible. We fill it with missiles, guns, grenades—you name it. This is going to grab their attention and piss them the fuck off."

Katie tilted her head. "Ok, but what is that really going to do besides handing over our weapons?"

"None of the demons will be left to take our gear. The first part of the drop, the big deal, is going to be a large bomb with as much special metal packed in it as we can manage. When it goes off, the ball bearings will rip through all of the demons nearby, killing them instantly. It's like a really big fucking grenade with a kick."

"No one will be able to be there when that happens."

Korbin pointed at her. "Exactly, but that's the whole point. We don't want the teams in there at all if we can help it. And we will make sure that the bomb is detonated remotely, so we can be positive that everyone is out before that happens. Hopefully, we catch Moloch standing next to the bomb. You said there are drones in there, right?"

Katie nodded. "Yeah, a bunch of them."

"See if we can use one for this mission. We will be able to see who is around the bomb when we blow it. That way, we have the ability to be choosy when we press the button. We can have maximum effect with minimal hazard to the rest of the team."

Katie liked the idea, but she knew when it came to hell things didn't always go as planned. Having that kind of firepower in a place where they were going to be was a really risky operation. One wrong move and all of them could be dead in a heartbeat.

Pandora sniffed. *Personally, I think it's a badass idea. I know there are a lot of what-ifs, but we've been playing it safe down there, and it hasn't gotten us anywhere. We need something that is all-out, balls-to-the-wall, flip-you-over-and-fuck-you-some-more crazy.*

She was right, but the dangerous nature of the job worried Katie. *If we all die, that's it. The world will be taken over by demons.*

Not if when we die, we take Moloch and his idiot bestie down with us. Just make sure if we go, we go all the way.

Katie looked at Korbin. "How do we keep everyone safe on Earth while we lure these demons to the trap?"

Korbin pointed to a picture he had drawn on the wall. Katie looked at it sideways, but it was hard to make out. He chuckled. "I'm not really an artist. I covered that too. We spread out a whole bunch of claymores below whatever portal we have. That will take care of the demons that escape. As far as luring, I thought maybe we could play a tape of Pandora egging on the demons like she is in hell."

Pandora asked for permission to talk, and Katie gave it. "Korbin, it's Pandora here. I'd like to personally say welcome back. Now that that's over, I want to be clear about one thing. You are nice and all, but I really only care that your wife is back. She is the fucking shit. Now, as far as a tape? That shit won't work. Remember, we are what you humans call "magical beings." We can sense one another. The demons will know it's a tape without moving from their seats. I have to be there and let them feel my power, so they know it's real."

Korbin rubbed his chin. "How about a small portal? They will be able to sense you and the portal, and when they are getting close, you drop back through. The detonation of the claymores can be your cue. You drop out and close the portal, they are sealed inside, and you are safe."

Pandora looked at his plans. "That might work, actually. I will want to keep in contact with the detonator. Demons could drop before they sense me so it might take me a bit longer. I really don't want to face Moloch in hell, if I don't have to. He's a whiny-ass bitch, but strong as fuck."

"We will make sure the timing is right. You just need to make sure you're out of there when it blows. Otherwise, you'll be a goner."

Pandora grimaced. "Well, I might not die. I'm a pretty tough bitch in hell. If I get caught in the blast and end up with shrapnel in my perfect fucking tits, I will be coming back, and coming for you. You don't want to see me mad with two sagging melons sinking toward my kneecaps."

Korbin choked nervously. "Right, probably not."

Pandora nodded astutely and let Katie take over. "I want you to understand it is vital to this war that we keep Pandora in one piece. She will come back inside of me when it's over."

You care about me, you really do. And you made that whole thing sound so dirty. I like it.

Katie covered the smile on her lips. *You are too much sometimes. If you do this, you better make sure your ass gets out in one piece.*

18

K atie and Pandora took the jet to Los Angeles. Not only did they need to pick up Calvin, but they had the opportunity to satisfy Pandora's craving for some good food. When they landed, there was a car waiting, this time a convertible so they could have a little fun. Pandora loved it, and Katie was just happy she wasn't bitching about it.

They started out by having light snacks at Gjusta restaurant and bakery. Pandora oohed and ahhed over the pastry menu. *Let's do a baklava croissant, a fig and almond tart, two brownies, and the chocolate avocado mousse.*

Katie sighed. *Remember that I'm going to have to drive us around until we make it back to the plane.*

Pandora scoffed. *Please, bitch, I got this. You think I can't handle some pastries? We can take them to the park. I want to concentrate.*

Katie laughed and ordered their sweets. The woman boxed them up and gave her a knowing look. It was hard for Katie to go anywhere without people recognizing her. She was just glad the woman didn't let on too much. She wanted a quiet afternoon in California before starting her trek to hell.

They made their way to the park and sat down at one of the tables. Katie worked through the food, absolutely in heaven. Pandora was so impressed she barely said a word. Katie knew that was a good thing. When they were done, Katie sat back and rubbed her stomach. *I don't know about going to another place.*

Pandora tsked. *Oh, come on. Let me just take care of that really fast. There you go.*

Katie instantly felt better, and her stomach flattened back out. She laughed and gathered the trash, constantly impressed that Pandora was able to do that. *Now where?*

Scratch Bar and Kitchen. We are going to have a six-course dinner, my friend.

Katie's eyes went wide, but she shrugged and made her way to the car. Inside Scratch, they were seated at a table by the window and presented with the special menu of the day. Course one was a Peruvian scallop crudo with lime, grapefruit, cilantro, and fried oysters. They paired it with a glass of brut champagne. Course two was live Maine lobster, pommes puree, caviar, and a delicious and surprisingly sweet Grand Cru Chablis. By that point Katie was just going with the flow, enjoying the lack of donuts on the menu.

Pandora moaned as Katie bit into the lobster. *Why do we not travel to Maine? We need to go there.*

I'll put that on the list.

When the third course of duck breast, confit duck leg, carrot, black truffle, foie gras, and lavender came out with a stout glass of cabernet, Calvin walked in the front doors. Katie waved him over, and he took a seat at the table.

Calvin looked at the empty plate and at Katie. "Let me guess, not the first place you've gone today."

Katie shook her head. "Pandora had her way with pastries before this. She says hey."

Calvin smiled. "Hey there, Pandora. Full yet?"

Pandora laughed. *I've got room for my favorite black Superman.*

Katie looked at Calvin and shook her head. "Not repeating that."

"You ready for this next assignment?"

Katie put down her fork and shrugged. "I don't know. I mean, yes, I'm ready, but it makes me nervous. It has to be done, though. And it will make one hell of a statement."

Calvin and Katie sat there shooting the shit as she finished the last three courses of her meal. When they were done, Katie paid for dinner, and they headed outside. "I have a rental parked just up the street." Katie pulled the keys from her purse.

"Where are we going first?"

"New York. I have to pick up my sidekick."

Calvin rolled his eyes. "Yes, Juntto. Forgot about him."

Katie shrugged. "Don't be too hard on him. He's been really good. For him. Strange, but good."

Katie and Calvin walked up beside a group of guys talking smack to each other. As Katie passed she lowered her sunglasses, flashing her red eyes at them. "Trouble, gentlemen?"

One of the guys gave her a nasty look and reached down to grab his crotch. The guy next to him slapped his hand, hissing, "You *idiot.*" He turned to Katie nervously. "Sorry, ma'am."

Katie winked and continued walking. The crotch-grabber turned to the others. "Yo, what the fuck? You bow down to some chick on the street? Seriously? Bitch ain't shit."

All of the guys went quiet, and one nervously stroked his goatee. "Dude, that's Katie from Katie's Killers. That's the bitch taking out all the fucking demons. She happens to be part angel, too."

All the guys made the sign of the cross on their chests.

Another guy shook his head. "You buck to her, and she would have taken your scrawny ass out. She don't play around. She's got a fucking She-Ra angel-beast sword that falls from the fucking sky. Know when to shut your mouth, dude."

The crotch-grabber watched Katie and Calvin walk away. "She don't look like she all that."

The guy with the goatee shook his head sadly. "Seriously, bro, I've got a date later. I don't need to be pulling my foot out of my own ass because you dissed her. We need to have a talk about your mouth."

The plane touched down in New York, and Katie let out a deep breath. "Damn, it's good to be back home. It's funny how hard a time I had adjusting to the base."

Calvin grabbed his bag. "Nah, you get used to a place. I'm used to my girl's house now. It feels like home there. It feels weird leaving."

Katie smiled at the love in his eyes and followed him off the plane. There were two SUVs waiting for them. "I got you your own ride. Pandora and I are going to hit up our local Krispy Kreme before we go back."

Calvin chuckled. "You are some serious fucking eaters. Okay, I'm along for the ride. Besides, I could use some cream-filled donuts right now. Let's do this."

They piled into one SUV, and the driver drove them to Madison Square Garden. As they went, Calvin looked out at fall coming to New York. "It's crazy. Out in California, it's constantly spring or summer. You don't even think about the changing of the leaves. It's like I flew into the future, coming out here. I have to admit, though, I do miss this time of year. It's the best feeling. Warm, inviting, and everyone is a little nicer to each other."

Pandora laughed. *Has he ever been to New York? I am pretty sure there are more homicides out here during the holidays than any other time.*

Katie shushed her. *Don't ruin the feeling for him. Just go with it.*

Hey, we are going Krispy Kreme. I will shut my mouth.

They walked into the shop and greeted the employees behind the counter. Katie got a dozen donuts and a milk and took her haul to the pizza shop, waving at the guys in the kitchen. Calvin laughed every time she greeted someone. As they sat down, Katie reached in, grabbed a chocolate-covered cream-filled donut, and took a bite.

"We knew we would find you here," a familiar voice broke in.

Calvin and Katie both looked up as Travers and Schultz walked into the place. Katie wondered if they ever thought about the "cop in a donut shop" stereotype. Probably not, because this was a pizza shop, but she always had donuts.

Calvin stood up and shook both their hands. "How are you guys?"

Travers nodded. "Not too bad. Glad to see you back in the city."

They all sat down at the table and chuckled at Katie finishing her donut. She wiped her mouth and looked at the two of them. "What's wrong now? I know you boys don't usually come here."

Schultz laughed, taking a donut. "No, but we heard you were back in town, so we figured we would try to catch up with you."

Katie shook her head. "Damn, news travels fast. I literally just landed and headed over here to get donuts. You must know someone at the airport."

Travers sat up straight and dignified. "We have our contacts, that's for sure."

They all chuckled. Katie picked up another donut and took a drink of her milk. "So, how is my *partner* doing? I heard he was part of the incursion in Brooklyn."

Schultz looked impressed. "He was definitely a huge help. He killed a big fucker, although he did cause quite a bit of damage. Then again, he is your protégé, so that does not surprise us at all. You aren't really the merc who rolls in trying to protect private property."

Katie giggled. "No, I protect the people. You guys can rebuild the buildings. What about his off-time? Did he behave himself?"

Travers nodded. "There weren't any killings that could be attached to him while you were gone. There is one stranger we've been trying to track down, but he just kind of disappeared into the wind."

Katie just stared at them, blinking. "What does he look like?"

Schultz put in, "He looks like Morpheus from *The Matrix*."

Katie cleared her throat and glanced between the two cops. "And what is he wanted for?"

Schultz shook his head. "Not really wanted. He could have some information for us. He wasn't the one who actually killed the victim. It looks one hundred percent like suicide, and that's based on an eyewitness statement. Thing is, the witness also said that this Morpheus character used, and I quote, "Jedi mind tricks" to make this guy kill himself."

Katie almost spat out her milk. She coughed and wiped her chin with a napkin, then dabbed up a bit of milk from the table in front of her. "Wow, how much crack did this guy smoke before turning himself in?"

Schultz laughed, handing her another napkin. "Right? Anyway, we aren't looking too hard for him, anyway. He is probably out of the state by now. There was no trace. That was how we first met Juntto. We got word that the Morpheus guy disappeared into your condo, and Angie took us up to meet him. He looks like the guy from *Far Cry*. He should consider doing cosplay in one of those competitions. He would win some money."

Katie wiped her lips. "I'll make sure I tell him, although I don't think I want to send him to a convention like that. He might get confused and start a battle with a ten-year-old dressed up as the Joker or something. He hasn't really gotten the whole make-believe versus real thing down quite yet."

Travers chuckled. "Most of those people haven't either. But hey, I'm not one to judge."

Schultz glared. "Oh yeah, we can smell the bullshit from that one, you judgmental prick."

They all laughed and changed the subject to Calvin, talking about California and how they had always wanted to go out there. Katie was glad to get them talking about anything but Juntto. She made a mental note to ask him about the suicide in the alley. She wasn't above threatening him with paperwork for the rest of his damn Leviathan life.

Moloch and Baal stood over the table with the large map on it. They hovered over the United States, looking at all the different places they hadn't touched yet. Baal moved back away from the table, looking at the world as a whole. "So, what's the plan this time? Are we going all-out?"

Moloch put a pin down on the edge of the map. "We are going to have a major incursion, yes. But I think we are going to do something a little more tactful. We'll focus on the USA this time, no other countries. And instead of one large gate, what do you think about lots of small ones?"

Baal smiled. "I love that idea. You can see if that cuts down on the response time of the humans."

Moloch nodded. "Exactly. On top of that, we can see how hard it hits the home team. They won't be able to respond to every single attack. It will make them scatter, which will make them less useful. Or, better yet, they could all respond to one attack, making it easier to kill them, and easier for us to cause some serious destruction in other parts of the country. There has been no response to any of our incursions. That must make the humans doubt the mercs' ability to protect them.

Baal laughed evilly. "And when they lose faith, they will turn to whatever or whoever offers them a chance of survival."

Moloch clapped his hands together. "Precisely. So, I am thinking small gates. We will use heavy manpower all along the West Coast. Then, at the same time, we drop several hordes right into the middle of the Midwest. Burn the cornfields, burn the farms, burn the factories. While those are simmering, we launch a wide-scale attack on all of the major East Coast cities. New York, Washington, Philadelphia, and Boston."

Baal perked up. "While in Boston, I request a pie."

Moloch chuckled. "Absolutely. In the end, you will be able to have all the pies you want. Shit, look up the best piemaker on Earth, and we will make them your slave. The world will literally be ours to do what we want with. The US not only holds our major hitters, but it is also an Earthly superpower. If it falls, it's only a matter of time until the rest of the world does too."

Baal was getting really hyped up. "How will the attacks go?"

Moloch ran his finger across the board. "I want a mad-dash scenario. A shock-and-awe and all-you-can-eat effort.

Baal nodded. "Fresh food gets the boys riled up every time. Will we drop them all at once?"

Moloch pressed his finger against the board. "We will start with Massachusetts, then let everything else loose like falling dominos. I will command from Massachusetts. If all goes well, I will tip the scale with the other attacks."

"Why start there?"

Moloch sighed. "Fewest guns per capita."

Baal scrunched his face.

Moloch rolled his eyes. "It's *math*. I know that probably blows your mind, but try to stay with me."

Baal huffed. "I know what math is, thank you very much. I also know what per capita means. If you haven't forgotten, I did statistics for Lucifer for two years."

"Okay, smart guy. If the population of the United States is 320 million people and the GDP—gross national product, by the way—is \$16.7 trillion, how do you find out the per capita income?"

Baal blinked at him and licked his lips, putting his finger in the air and waving it around on an invisible chalkboard. "You would divide 16.7 trillion by 320 million. Carry the zero, move the decimal point." Moloch yawned, looking at his fingernails. Baal gave him a nasty look. "\$52,194 per family. Of course, that is an average and will fluctuate between areas, poverty levels, and those who hold the primary amount of American wealth."

Moloch nodded his head, impressed. "What is the difference between per capita and median income?"

Baal cleared his throat. "Median income is the number right in the middle of the list of incomes. Therefore, it is a more accurate picture of what is going on in the country."

Moloch sighed. "I suppose you *do* know what you are talking about."

Baal smiled and crossed his arms over his chest. "To be honest, I was just impressed that you took the time to research the gun statistic. You are usually so gung-ho, you forget those things."

Moloch rubbed his claws together. "Yes, well, we have more to lose this time around. I've done even better than research guns. I've researched the town in that movie, *Witches of Eastwick*."

Baal retorted. "What, Eastwick?"

Moloch's face fell. "No, Cohasset, you Neanderthal."

Baal made a face mocking him like a child. "Wow, four syllables this time!"

Moloch put up his fist. "What is wrong with you today? You are extra spicy. Did you not get your warm cup of kitten blood last night?"

Baal's face dropped, and he kicked at the floor. "Maybe. I had terrible nightmares about humans running through a field hand-in-hand. The sun was shining brightly, flowers were blooming. There was laughing and singing." His voice quivered. "And even *dancing*."

Moloch shook his head. "Dear Lucifer, stop. That sounds absolutely horrible. I am going to have nightmares for weeks now. Try eating a gerbil full of Ambien next time."

"That shit makes me sleepwalk. I wake up eating from the pit of souls and don't even know how I got there. Dreadful."

Moloch put his arm around Baal. "Come on, I can lift your spirits. Let's go open some small gates and get this party started, shall we? We want to be prepared."

Baal instantly perked up.

19

It was fall in Cohasset, Massachusetts, the most exciting time of the year for the small-town residents.

They held fall festivals almost every weekend, welcoming the tourists and getting the town ready for the leaf season. The leaves had already begun changing, and the weather was a cool and crisp sixty-five degrees. The breeze off the water kept everyone in windbreakers as they rushed around the town setting up the different stations for the first fall festival of the season.

All the residents from the town came out to help, bringing decorations, booths, and food to the event. The children ran around in the main square, jumping over each other and rolling through the grass. Laughter echoed throughout the entire town, and the warm scents of spiced apples, ciders, and baked treats fluttered through the air. The entire town smelled delicious to both humans *and* demons.

Across the field, the men of the town worked building the firepit they would light at the end of the day. The kids would roast marshmallows and tell historical ghost stories. Amongst the hugs and the exchanges of kind words, they didn't even see the attack coming.

The sound of small portals tearing open in the distance didn't register to anyone. A small girl chased her ball toward the South Hill Art Center, and it bounced up in front of her and disappeared into a portal in the grass. She tilted her head to the side and stepped closer as a wave of hot air hit her hard in the face.

A swarm of demons leaped from the portal and rushed around her, barely noticing the small girl. She screamed at the top of her lungs and clamped her eyes shut, frozen in the burning grass, unable to move. The demons disappeared into the distance.

The girl let herself breathe again.

When she opened her eyes, there was a grinning demon right in her face. "Boo!"

The little girl disappeared into its arms.

The demons crept slowly to the edge of a hill that gave them a perfect view of the town. None of the humans knew what was happening. A woman walked up the hill, enjoying the fall breeze. She was calling her little girl's name. As she reached the crest of the hill, she let out a loud shriek.

In the town below, men and women paused at the piercing wail.

The woman choked on her words for several moments. She had seen her daughter's pink lace dress torn to ribbons on the ground, covered in blood. "*Demons!*"

Timothy typed on his computer frantically, then ran his finger across the screen. He jumped up and took off down the hall, grabbing his cell phone and dialing Katie. He didn't give her a chance to say a word, just blurted it out as soon as she picked up. "Incursion, several portals in Cohasset, MA. Because of how small they are the estimate is six minutes, and there are at least five portals."

"Shit," Katie yelled, taking off out of her room.

The whole world began to stand still as the word was spread across the wire. The small town had absolutely no warning. By the time the phone rang at the local police station, the place was empty. Patrols were already out to investigate the reports of portals popping up all over the place.

In her apartment, Katie slammed into the side wall with a groan and turned into the kitchen.

Angie looked up with a spatula in her hands. "What's going on?"

Katie caught her breath. "Incursion, a ton of small portals opening in Cohasset. We need the plane fueled and ready to go."

Angie dropped the spatula and tossed the hot pan in the sink.

Katie ran across the hall and burst in on Juntto, who was playing video games. "Suit up. We have a big one."

She grabbed her phone and dialed Korbin. "Hey, get with Timothy and get Brock's team on a plane over there now. I need them in Cohasset. You, Stephanie, Timothy, and Joshua, stay there and protect the base. We don't want to get ambushed."

Korbin understood. "Got it. Be careful out there."

Katie ran back to her condo and called Timothy as she geared up. "What are we talking here?"

Timothy pulled up satellite images. "There is some sort of festival going on. Uh, people everywhere. There are five portals right now, smaller demons pouring into the town. We are looking at incursions at the Cohasset Central Cemetery, the South Shore Art Center, the yacht club, the historical society, and a small portal right in the center of town on North Main Street."

Pandora was pissed. *Those sons of bitches are using buffet-style tactics.*

Katie curled her nose. *What?*

It's used all the time. Starve the small demons, then set them loose on a fucking buffet of humans. With all those humans out for a festival, it's a smorgasbord for them. The festival is huge in that town; I was there when they filmed Witches of Eastwick. *There are pets, children, old people, and everything else you could think of.*

Katie shoved her two large pistols in their holsters. *This is madness. Just absolute fucking madness. Okay. Let's get there as fast as we can, and we can talk tactics on the way.*

Pandora scoffed. *We can try. The best tactic is to drop and start killing. These fuckers are going to be ravaging that festival, and I promise you apple pie is not on their menu.*

Katie stopped for a moment and rubbed her hands over her face to compose herself. She had to remember this was no different than any other incursion. She would go in, save who she could, and inflict serious damage to the demons. She prepared herself for the carnage, knowing that by the time they got there things would be dire.

The television flashed to a special report. The newscaster looked slightly disheveled. She tapped her papers on the desk before staring directly into the camera. "We are sorry to interrupt your regularly scheduled programming, but we are coming to you with breaking news. A large incursion has broken out in the small port city of Cohasset, Massachusetts. Five small portals have opened. Anyone from that area would know that today is their first fall festival of the season, which makes the town an especially prime target. For a view of the events unraveling right now, we will take you to Skycam 8, traveling over Cohasset."

The screen changed to shaky footage taken from inside the helicopter. The camera focused in and out on the five different portals surrounding the town. Demons were pouring out of the portals, looking even more savage than they normally did. Every time they pounced on someone, the camera would jerk away.

The screen flipped back to the inside of the newsroom. "Information is coming in now that there were a massive number of people already there for the festivities. The five portal locations are the following: Cohasset Central Cemetery, South Shore Art Center, the yacht club, the historical society, and one right in the center of town on Main Street. If you are in Cohasset and you are watching this, please get to a safe location—a shelter or basement—as quickly as you possibly can."

The reporter held her earpiece with one finger and nodded, then spoke to the camera. "We just received cell phone footage from the area. It was uploaded to us, but we have not been able to get hold of the sender. These images are extremely graphic and are not appropriate for minors. Viewer discretion is advised."

The screen showed video footage of someone running across a well-manicured lawn. They panned their camera to the right, capturing images of three demons leaping on the town priest. The woman taking the footage screamed and turned into a grocery store. She hurried through the aisles, stopping and shakily filming another attack right in the center of the store. Slowly she walked into a dark room and turned the camera on herself. "Help us, we are under attack."

Her head shot up, and her eyes grew wide right before the camera cut out. The screen shifted back to the reporter, who was struggling to swallow a drink of water. "Again, that was footage from Cohasset, Massachusetts. We have word that the mercenaries have been dispatched, but the warning on these attacks was minimal. We hope that...hold on, something is happening down below."

The small portals shimmered and stretched as more small demons poured out onto the grass. As soon as their feet hit the ground, they began sniffing out their first meal of the day. They rummaged tables, destroyed buildings, and pulled citizens screaming and kicking from their homes.

As the smaller ones feasted, townspeople armed themselves and fought back. They managed to take down a few of the beasts but barely made a dent in their numbers. Bodies lay all across the grass, chunks of their flesh missing. It was a feast for kings, and the smaller demons weren't the only ones that were going to have the opportunity to eat.

A loud rumble shook the ground beneath the demons' feet. They paused in their meals and looked at their respective portals. While small demons continued jumping out, a larger portal began to tear open over the town. Heat billowed out of the portal, scorching the grasses and crisping the flesh of those dead or dying on the ground. Slowly, large demons began to grip the edges of the portal and pull themselves through into the cool air of Earth. Steam spiraled off their scaled black skin, and their mouths were stretched into terrible jagged smiles.

One by one the giants leaped forward, running through the casualties. They swung their great arms from side to side, smashing into buildings small and large. When they found a human to devour, they would eat them, but in the meantime, destruction was the name of the game. They focused on the churches dotted throughout the town, slamming their giant fists into the steeples. Dust flew as the towers began to fall. The bells of the Catholic church were sent rolling loudly across the cement, taking out three people in their way.

A loud explosion from a shotgun folded a smaller demon in half, and a middle-aged man in a plaid shirt reloaded his weapon. There was blood on his face as he ran through the streets, firing and reloading. He pointed his gun at every demon he passed, blasting some of the smaller ones' heads off their shoulders. He slowed as he approached a large beast that was gnawing on a woman's thigh. The man with the shotgun swallowed hard and racked a round. The demon saw him and growled.

The man let fly, shooting the demon once in the side of the chest and once in the head. His bullets weren't special metal, so the giant demon just swatted at the pain. He threw the woman's leg to the ground and set his sights on the man in plaid. The man fumbled for more shotgun shells but he dropped them, and then it was too late. The demon lifted him and threw the man as hard as he could. The guy soared through the air, crashing into the side of a bank, then falling to the ground. He left a smear like a huge bug on the building.

The whole town was in chaos, large demons smashing and small demons feasting. There would be no festival that day, or any day for a very long time if Moloch had his way.

"This is Mariah Donaldson, interrupting your regularly scheduled program with continuing coverage of what is now being called the Cohasset Massacre. We'll take you back to Skycam 8 for aerial coverage of the event. Viewer discretion is advised."

The screen switched to the footage with a reporter speaking over the images of the town. "This is Donald Hyatt on Skycam 8 flying over Cohasset, Massachusetts. There are large portals over the town now. We have reports of several huge demons destroying everything in their paths. The smaller demons are continuing to pull people from their homes as we watch. It's a... What was that?"

The image of the town shimmied side to side. The

reporter could be heard mumbling in the background. "Oh shit. He's throwing those boulders at us. Go up. Go—"

The feed skipped and became fuzzy, but the cameraman kept filming. Below, three large demons were lobbing stones at the chopper. The helo swayed, successfully dodging them. Another boulder flew directly at the camera and the sound of the pilot and reporter screaming filled the helicopter.

The feed froze on the face of a large demon with red eyes staring directly up at the chopper. The newscaster came back on screen, looking pale and worried. "We have lost footage from the Skycam, but we will check in and make sure that everyone is all right in just a moment. To recap the situation at hand: We have a major incursion happening as we speak in Cohasset, Massachusetts. Several portals tore open within minutes, spilling demons into the small town. There was a popular fall festival about to kick off, and we cannot know the true extent of the damage at this moment. Mercenaries are on their way, but these portal openings have taken everyone by surprise."

The newscaster put her finger to her ear and listened to her comm. "We are getting some statistics. The death toll is undetermined at this time, but we do know there are roughly 8,500 residents, not including the thousands who flock to the town during this season. Since the incursion occurred earlier in the day, unlike the normal nighttime attacks, we are hoping a majority of the people have gone to ground. Again, if you are in Cohasset, please take cover in any shelter you can find. Do not go outside."

Angie, Juntto, Calvin, and Katie rushed through the streets in a cop car driven by one of the locals. The car sped through the back gates of the airport and straight up to the hangar where their plane was kept. People were rushing around, loading the last of the ammo and equipment into the plane.

They jumped from the vehicle and sprinted aboard the plane, then sat down in their seats and caught their breath. Even Juntto was breathing heavily, but more from the adrenaline pumping through him than anything else. Katie motioned to the flight attendant. "Please tell the pilot we need to take off as soon as the door is shut. We have no time to lose."

The flight attendant sprinted to the front and entered the pilot's cabin, closing the door behind her. Cohasset, Massachusetts, was approximately two hundred and thirty-six miles away, and the plane had to get there as quickly as it could. They would need to land, then take a military chopper to the town. They would be cutting it close, but that was the best that they could do.

"Rock and roll," Juntto yelled, still dressed like Far Cry with his purple suit and white hair.

Pandora sniffed as the plane took off. *This is going to be a big one. Prepare yourself. Think Incursion Day.*

Katie shook her head. *Every day is Incursion Day now.*

No one spoke during the entire ride. They were too focused on what they were going to have to do. When they arrived at the local Cohasset airport, Brock and his team were already there. They were checking their gear near one of the choppers, and Katie waved to them as they boarded. They knew what was ahead of them. She put on her headphones and waited for the chopper door to be shut before giving the pilot a thumbs-up.

"Just to tell you, I've made a trip over there already. I'm going to drop you on the outskirts of town. Some of the larger demons took out a news chopper earlier. They have their eyes out for helos in the area," the pilot warned.

Katie understood. "That's fine. I want to get a good idea of what I'm walking into before I do it anyway."

Pandora snorted. *No crazy jumps from the chopper this time?*

I have a team to think about now. I gotta make sure they all get to the zone safely.

Pandora sighed. *We need to get them wings.*

As the chopper flew over the small town and circled around to land, Katie could see the massive amount of warfare going on in the area. The cops and local reserve units were on the scene blasting everything they could, but there were so many demons.

The teams jumped out of the helo and ran toward the line of vehicles waiting to hustle them into town. Katie hugged Angie around the shoulders. "Keep safe. You got this."

She took off ahead of the vehicles, spreading her wings and flying into the carnage.

20

When they reached the town, the team jumped from their vehicles and raced into the fight. They loosed their weapons and began to blast any demon they saw. Brock and his team went to the right toward the cemetery, hoping to slaughter the demons as they flooded out of that portal. Angie and Juntto took Main Street. Calvin moved toward the art building, pulling his large swords from his back and slicing heads off as he ran.

Above them, Katie circled to the hardest-hit area and landed. She pulled out Tom and Harry and fired, taking chunks out of the skulls of several large demons congregated there. More demons rushed into the hospital and were met by screams of panic. The demons were slowly picking away at the patients as they went through the floors. Katie's heart fell when she heard the frightened shrieks coming from the place.

Pandora was confused. *Why are you struggling with this? What's wrong with you?*

Katie breathed heavily as she jumped onto one of the

demons' backs, pulling its head to one side and jamming Tom in the thing's skull. The fiend's head exploded. *Nothing. Nothing is wrong. I'm just a bit more sensitive to the carnage today, I suppose. I'm getting tired of this bullshit. These demons think they can just kill our people. Eventually, this has to stop.*

Pandora quieted down. She knew Katie wasn't talking about her, but she figured her attention was better spent amping Katie up as much as she could.

The teams battled through the incursion, trying to take down the maximum number of demons in their initial sweeps. There were so many they could barely see down the streets, much less figure out who was where and who needed help. A serious extermination of demons was needed, but the portals were still open. More beasts took the place of those the mercs slaughtered.

Brock walked along the street blasting his gun. He carefully stepped over the mangled bodies and random parts strewn everywhere. He stopped halfway down the street leading from the cemetery and stared at a kid's lemonade stand that had been knocked over in the rush. Lemonade dripped to the ground, mixing with a splash of bright red blood and pooling in the grass. There were no bodies to be seen, but something terrible had happened there.

Calvin ran through the tall grass behind the art center, slicing through the smaller demons chowing down their afternoon snacks. He stopped abruptly, staring at the tangle of pink lace and blood. He swallowed hard and gritted his teeth, slicing as hard as he could into a demon chewing on a small leg.

Across town, Katie crept through the streets. This side of town had already been hit hard. She could feel every muscle in her body tingling as she waded through the carnage. She was too late to stop it. She had prepared herself for Incursion Day, but what she was finding was ten times worse. There were bodies everywhere, some frozen in fear, others shielding the children still lying in their arms. Her heart thumped so loudly that even Pandora could hear it, and the angel in her was begging to come out.

There was too much destruction for the angel to be silent.

She stopped as she turned the corner into a residential street. A group of small demons was huddled ahead of her, snarling and snapping at each other. She moved quietly, trying to see what they were surrounding. She stepped off the curb and caught sight of what used to be a body. The demons were fighting over it like crazed hyenas, ripping the flesh from the bones and attacking each other for every last morsel.

"Like there isn't enough to go around, you fuckers," she grumbled to herself as she approached.

She lifted her guns up and began to shoot, making sure to aim for their heads. The six demons tried to flee, but she took them down where they stood. In a moment there was only ash. She looked away from the mutilated body on the ground.

Pandora's voice was soft in her ear. *Wait.*

I've seen enough.

No. Listen.

From her right, Katie could hear whimpering. Human whimpering. She tracked the sound through the yard to a small shed. Carefully, she reached for the door and opened it. Inside, a mother was huddled with her two young boys. The woman cowered in fear until recognition fell over her. "Help us."

Katie nodded and bent down. "You get on my back. Boys, climb into my arms."

Katie spread her wings outside the small shack, a beacon of hope in the carnage. She took the children in her arms, and their mother climbed between her wings.

Katie's wings lifted them over the town. She held the kids to her so they wouldn't see the devastation below and flew to the hill where they had set up emergency services. She landed, and the mother embraced her children.

Katie left them to fly back to the scene.

She landed in the front yard of that house and took a step toward the sidewalk. Loud barking and wailing echoed from the back of the house. She burst through the gate and found that a hulking demon had cornered a Lab. Instantly her eyes flared. Maybe it was the children, maybe it was the blood all around her, or maybe it was the whining of the terrified dog, but Katie was furious. She flew through the air at full speed and slammed her fist into the demon's head. She pulled out her short sword and grabbed the demon by the top of the head.

Katie gritted her teeth and looked it in the eye. "Don't fuck with the dogs."

She sliced the demon's throat, and it turned to ash. When she opened her arms, the dog rushed to her. She flew to the top of the hill where emergency services were gathered. One of the boys she had just saved was still standing there looking down at the city. Katie landed in front of him, and he yelled with joy. "Benji. Thank you!"

The dog whimpered and licked the boy's face. Katie sighed and took off again, ready to find as many survivors as she could.

Juntto laughed as he pulled a demon's skull in half, the brains and blood oozing down in globs to his feet. "That's what you fuckers get for playing against me on Halo. Calling *me* fucking names? Who's a fucked-up noob now?"

Juntto knew the demons weren't actually the ones playing him, but he could use that as an excuse to get all his anger out. He faced another demon with a huge overbite. "You, *demon*! I shall name you LIckmyBalllzzz and imagine you are the pain in the ass who mocked me during my second time playing Destiny!"

He cracked the demon over his knee and ripped him apart at the waist, throwing the pieces to the ground. He shifted right, plowing through a group of the fiends, swinging his huge hands. Demon parts splattered against houses and into yards. Juntto's ragged laughter could be heard for blocks. He didn't even need any weapons; he had his hands to break the necks of every beast he came across.

As he wiped the black goop from his cheek, he spotted a demon trying to make a break for it. "Oh, fuck no, little shit-goblin. You're mine."

He ran full speed, soaring over a privacy fence and landing right on top of the demon. The two of them tumbled wildly across the ground and came to a skidding halt in someone's backyard. He reared his fists back and began to beat the demon senseless. He knew it wasn't going to kill him, but he wanted to inflict a little pain first.

When the demon had all he could take, Juntto pulled a knife from his belt and stuck it into the demon's chest, zigzagging down its sternum until its intestines flopped to the ground. The demon squealed and burst to ash, leaving Juntto laughing, covered in blood and dust. He went to step forward and stopped.

In the center of the backyard was a swimming pool, but instead of beach chairs, float toys, and blue water, it was a charnel pit. The water was red with blood, and the pool was stuffed with human bodies and pieces of bodies. On top was a young kid with long blond hair. He was stout but muscled—like a Viking.

Something inside Juntto snapped. He gripped his fists tight and raised them in the air, screaming wordlessly at the top of his lungs. Lightning shot across the sky above him.

He lowered his arms, breathing heavily.

The frost giant kicked the fence down and left the backyard to find his prey. "Every last one of you will meet Juntto's wrath."

Calvin kicked the door to the art center open and lifted his gun, looking right, left, and overhead. He had killed about fifteen demons outside, but there had to be more fiends lurking in the shadows inside the building. The art center was relatively unscathed compared to the human blood splattered across the artifacts. Small scratches could be seen on the floor, left there by demons' claws, but everything else was as it had been just moments before the incursion. In fact, it was so still in there it was almost creepy. It sent chills up Calvin's spine.

He carefully opened the door to one of the back hallways and began to search. He looked into each room, making sure there were no demons hiding there. Every room was clear. Finally, Calvin stood staring at the last door at the end of the hallway. He crept closer, paused, and pressed his ear to the door. He could hear slight movement and quiet whispering. That was when Calvin realized he had found survivors.

"Open the door. My name is Calvin. I'm a mercenary," he shouted.

The door slowly opened, and Calvin let out a breath. There were at least twenty kids and a dozen or so adults hiding in the dark room. Calvin put his hands up and calmed them down. "I want you all to stay in here. I'm going to close these doors and then barricade you in. When the demons are gone I will come back for you, okay?"

They all nodded and an older gentleman reached up to take Calvin's hand. "Thank you, young man. We are in your debt."

Calvin closed the door behind him and pushed desks, cabinets, and anything else he could find down the hall, stacking them all tightly against the door.

The sounds of scratching behind him gave him pause and he spun, his guns out. Six demons stood in front of him, now snarling and screeching. One stepped forward and Calvin pulled the trigger, blasting half its head off. "Back up, motherfucker."

The other demons lunged, attacking Calvin ferociously. He kicked a demon in the chest and then shot it between the eyes. He emptied his magazine, taking down three more. They dropped hard and turned to ash, clearing Calvin's way to the last one. The beast turned to run, but Calvin shook his head.

"Where do you think you're going, little fucker?"

Calvin jumped forward and grabbed its ankles, slamming it to the ground. He climbed up and straddled the demon, then looked into its beady red eyes. The demon bucked, swinging its arm and slicing Calvin across the cheek.

Calvin put his hand to the wound, his eyes flashing red. "Oh, hell no. That is my motherfucking moneymaker."

He grabbed a dagger from his belt and kept stabbing the demon in the throat until the thing's head was almost completely severed from its body. He spat into the demon's ashes and sheathed his dagger. "Fuck with a man's face, and that's what you fucking get."

Juntto ran from the backyard of the house, his hands huge and formed into rough, thick spears. His jaw was clenched, and his eyes changed colors rapidly. He rushed past Angie, who was reloading. She had heard the reverberating sound of his bellow, and could now see the anger flowing through him. She wasn't sure what had happened in that backyard, but he was apparently on a mission to take down every-thing in his path.

Juntto growled and slammed his shoulder straight into an approaching demon she hadn't seen. The demon flew back thirty feet and Juntto followed it. He stabbed the beast with both of his spear hands, then ripped it apart. Angie looked away as the blood spattered and checked her gun. She was good.

She pushed down the fear that was radiating through her. It wasn't as bad as it had been at the subway, but it was still almost paralyzing. To the left, a demon burst out of a house and into the yard, carrying a half-eaten cat. She raised her gun and pulled the trigger three times, striking the demon dead. To the right was another demon who saw the falling corpse of the cat and dove for it.

Angie stepped onto the curb and put one bullet right between the beast's eyes. "Poor kitty. Nothing is safe here."

She continued down the street and around the corner. The immediate area was mostly clear, but at the end of the block a church was burning brightly. The front of the building was all but gone, so she could see all the way to the pulpit. A demon had a priest by the neck and was slashing at him. Angie took off running, pulling up her gun and aiming carefully. She leaped through the broken debris of the church and jumped on top of a pile of shattered pews.

The demon turned just enough for her to get a shot off. The bullet flew through the air, going through the demon's brain, out the other side, and into the wooden cross behind him. He dropped the priest and burst into dust. Angie ran up and went to her knees, cradling the priest's head in her arms.

He looked at her and reached his hand to her forehead, making the symbol of a cross in his blood. "God will protect you. You are his warrior."

With that, the priest quietly left the world. Angie sat there in the rubble and flames, holding the priest and looking at the crucifix above her.

She slowly stood up and wiped the blood across the front of her shirt. "It seems that God has abandoned us."

"Go left, Turner. Take the other two with you. I'll go right, and we'll meet on the other side of the building," Brock yelled as they walked toward the historic building.

The heat from the portal radiated, sending waves across the street like it was high summer. Turner and the others moved low to the ground, their guns ready. They knew there was a group of demons on the other side, and they were about to ambush them. As Brock glanced into the open door of the historical building, he spotted an older woman curled up under a table. He put his finger to his lips

He stepped to the edge of the door and took a deep breath. Turner, Eddie, and Sean fanned out, ready to demolish the bastards. Before Brock could give the signal, Juntto dropped from the roof of the building right on top of the beasts and began tearing them apart. Brock could see that he was almost rabid. His eyes were glazed and spittle flew from his mouth. His clothing, his face, and even his hair were stained with black blood.

When the last of the demons was gone, Brock took a step forward and reached for Juntto's shoulder. Juntto spun around, grabbing his arm and slamming him to the ground. Brock's gun flew up and Juntto's spear-shaped arm angled toward the soldier's eye. "Juntto, wait. It's me. It's Brock. I'm on your team."

Juntto shook his head and recognition came over his face. Slowly he lowered his arm, still pinning Brock to the ground. "It's okay, buddy. There is a lot of death here. I know what it's like to lose control. You can't hurt your own people, though."

"Juntto!" Katie yelled as she landed next to them. Her wings folded back.

Juntto swung his head around to Katie and backed off Brock. Katie held Tom and Harry loosely, ready to take on the Leviathan if she had to.

Juntto wiped blood from his face. "Same team. I got it. Just had a moment."

Katie looked the soldier over. "You okay?"

Brock nodded. "Fine. I'm fine."

Turner gave Brock a hand up. "Wow, so you almost get killed by demons and a Leviathan at the same time. Do you ever do anything low-key?"

Brock laughed and slapped Turner on the back. "It's okay, buddy. I promise you will have your day."

Calvin turned the corner with Angie in tow. Katie looked at all of them. "One last push. You guys finish up the demons out here, and I'm going to close the portals. You ready?"

They were more than ready.

21

K atie stood on top of the main courthouse building, looking out over the town. Her wings were spread wide, and her angel armor sparkled in the sunlight. The gold threads of her sash gleamed with their holy nature. The gauntlets on her wrists glittered, sending flickers of light on the dome below her. She could feel the energy pulsing around her and see all her friends fighting the last of the demons below. The wind whipped wildly through her hair as she scanned the town, spotting all the portals.

Pandora broke the silence. *Hold up. Aren't you being just a tad dramatic here? I mean, seriously. You are acting like a damn diva. Just close the fucking portals.*

Katie stood boldly with both hands on the hilt of her sword. *Can I not have one shining moment on this pillar of justice?*

No. Close the damn portals.

Katie rolled her eyes. *Fine, whatever.*

Katie sheathed her sword and closed her eyes, pulling energy from all around her. It pulsed down her arms and pooled in her palms, ready to explode. She pulled her arms way back and then flung them forward, slapping her hands together. An enormous surge of energy blasted outward, and when it slammed into the portals they wavered, shimmered, and dissolved.

Katie opened one eye and looked around. *Did it work?*

Pandora scoffed. *Are you telling me you just did all that bullshit and you didn't even know if it would work? In the amount of time you did that, you could have leisurely walked around and had me shut the damn things. I seriously think you have issues.*

I don't know, it was in my gut. I figured since that worked before I got my armor, it would work again. Hey, look, the portals are shut!

Pandora let out an exhausted sigh. *Yes, dear. The portals are shut, and the last of the demons are being slain as we speak. This incursion is clear, although the damage isn't something they will be able to clean up anytime soon. It looks like a bomb went off in this town.*

It kind of did.

Katie took a seat on the roof, watching the energy waves ripple outward, then calm. The sounds of battle stopped, and there was no more screaming. The seagulls returned to the ocean's shores, and for a moment, if you closed your eyes, you wouldn't know anything had happened there. However, the destruction was deep, deeper than any town had seen before. Katie took off and set herself down on the ground next to the rest of her team.

Calvin chuckled. "That was pretty sweet, closing those portals like that."

Katie looked around, stunned by the violence that surrounded her. "Are the demons taken care of?"

Calvin put his hand on her shoulder comfortingly. "They are. We can help look for survivors if you want. I know this is one of those battles that is not easily walked away from. I could barely look down when I was fighting earlier. I think every one of us felt that anger at some point."

Katie nodded absentmindedly, not really hearing anything he said. She stood at the end of the street, with fires burning and bodies stretched all the way to the ocean.

Families began to slowly emerge from their homes, turning their children's eyes away from the carnage. They may have ended the battle, but they hadn't won it; that was for damn sure. The demons would regroup. As far as the people lying dead in the streets went, the demons had won. Their souls had already departed.

Katie scanned the yards, hearing a quiet, muffled sound. A small child's cry. A tiny four-year-old girl wandered into the bloody street, still wearing a nightgown stained with syrup from that morning's pancakes. Her feet were bare but red with whatever blood she had trekked through. She looked lost and scared, and there wasn't a sound coming from inside her house.

The girl's tight blonde curls floated around her as she looked back and forth. "Momma? Daddy?"

Tears began to stream down Katie's face and she grabbed her chest, feeling unbearable heartbreak. She opened her mouth and cried out, the sound echoing like a voice from the heavens. Everyone stopped and watched the angel run through the bodies toward the little girl.

She didn't even stop, just scooped the small child into her arms and lifted her high into the sky, covering her eyes from the carnage. Katie's glistening tears flowed over her cheeks and down onto the girl, creating a spark of light.

As she flew toward the medical area, the little girl looked up in wonder and curiosity at Katie. She wasn't like everyone else; she had never seen Katie on television. She accepted Katie for who she was immediately. The girl touched Katie's cheek. "Are you an angel?"

Katie smiled, the tears still coming. "Partly."

The girl tilted her head. "Why do you cry? Mommy says angels are our guardians. Are you taking me to heaven to see Jesus?"

A lump built in Katie's throat, but she held it back. Even Pandora could be heard in the background sniffling and trying to keep herself together. Katie gently floated to the ground and looked into the girl's eyes. "Not today. You have a long time left here on Earth. I cry for those whose time is done."

The girl kissed Katie's cheek and whispered in her ear, "Don't cry for them. They are in the great kingdom."

Katie pulled back and looked into the little girl's eyes. A woman from the rescue team came over and put out her arms for the girl, but Katie stared into her bright blue eyes until she disappeared into the tent. She let out a deep breath and felt her knees buckle beneath her. Two strong hands grabbed her elbows and slowly guided her to the ground. Her wings collapsed behind her, but they did not disappear.

Calvin pulled her to him and hugged her tightly. Katie

was wracked by sobs as she let out all the anguish and terror of that day.

As Katie wept, the angel in her was free to mourn. Her great angel wings wrapped around her and Calvin as the reality of it all beat into her heart. A crack in the clouds sent a ray of light cascading over them, and for just a moment every foot and every voice froze in remembrance.

Everyone went to work helping to clean up the small town.

They searched for buried bodies in the fallen buildings, swept sidewalks after the bodies were removed, and counseled families with the support teams that had arrived. None of them—not Juntto, not Angie, Brock, Calvin or the rest of the team—were comfortable leaving the town to be cleaned up by anyone else.

They felt responsible.

Katie soared through the town doing an aerial survey, trying to find any signs of life from above. She felt better after letting go, but she was slightly embarrassed. *I'm sorry for losing it, Pandora. I don't know what happened. I have never felt sadness that great before. I felt like I was breaking.*

Pandora spoke gently. *It was the angel in you. Angels break when they watch the suffering of humans. They are God's angels because they loved humans as much as God did. You have part of that in you, and let me tell you, it is strong.*

Katie narrowed her eyes. *So that was why you were upset?*

Pandora cleared her throat. *I wasn't upset. I was having an allergic reaction.*

To what?

Shellfish.

Katie chuckled. *Oh, okay. Gotcha. Sorry, didn't mean to confuse you with someone who cared.*

Pandora yawned. *It's all right. It happens from time to time. I'm a demon, though. Evil, horny—the whole bit.*

I'll remember next time.

People forget, and all of a sudden they're projecting onto me.

Katie's phone began to vibrate in her pocket, so she landed on a rooftop and answered it.

"Katie, are you all right? I saw footage of you on the hill." The general's voice was concerned and sincere.

Katie took in a deep breath. "I'm okay now. It's an angel thing, I'm told."

General Brushwood's voice was as tired as she had ever heard it. "No, Katie. It's a heart thing. We all cried. The whole country gave a collective sob watching the footage of this battle. I'm sorry you had to see all of it, walk through it, and clean up after it."

Katie looked at the sun setting over the water. "It's my job."

The general cleared his throat. "That's right. And it's my job to push you, as much as I might not want to. Moloch and his crew have devastated our country. They have taken the lives of thousands today, and countless others in the past. We can no longer sit by in good conscience and allow it to continue without rallying our troops and striking back at them. These demons need to know they will not break us with one blow, or two, or even a hundred. The American spirit is stronger than it has been in decades. We face our enemies, and we don't allow ourselves to be bullied into submission. I know you just got done with this, but we need to move quickly into retaliation mode."

Katie stood up and gathered herself. "General, I couldn't agree with you more. I not only want this world to be safe from demons, but I want revenge for every ounce of blood spilled, for every life taken, and for every animal sacrificed. I want Moloch to know we will not back down from his advances. We will not cower under his tyranny. No one has ever been more ready and willing to take this fight to that bastard."

The general slapped his hands together. "There you are. Damn right, Katie. I couldn't have said it better myself. Now, tell me what you need."

Katie thought about it for a minute. "Give me twenty troops to start with, then I need a shipment of RPG-7s with PG-7VL ammunition, and an RPG-18, although I know it's hard to find. I will also need a shit-ton of frag grenades, obviously using our metal if we have them. Also stick grenades, and whatever we have left of the special metal smoke grenades. Make sure we get our usual barrage of automatic rifles, shotguns, and submachine guns. Those will be put to use by the troops I am taking with me."

The general stopped writing. "I thought we were teaching them a lesson, not invading the place."

Katie grimaced. "If I have learned anything over the past few years, it's that plans only go so far. When the fighting starts, things change quickly. I don't want to be caught with my pants down this time. I want everyone to be able to defend themselves, no matter what. We have lost enough good people over the years. If we do this, we're going to do it right. If that means being overly-fucking-prepared, so be it."

The general wrote down the rest of the list. "Good thinking. Now, what about the major explosive?"

"Get with Joshua; he has already started on that. It's going to look like a hodgepodge mess when you see it, but trust me, it's built to do the job. My main concern is detonating that thing after we get our infected troops out. I don't want to come back to you with an order for coffins, General."

"And I don't want you to."

Katie clapped her hands. "Oh, and I want drones that can shoot video and send it across a portal. I'll teach these motherfucking demons they can't play with Earth. Doctor Thorough and Alice should be able to help with that, since we already have similar drones in hell. He may even be able to reroute some of the ones he has, which would make it a lot easier."

Pandora laughed. *The fire has been lit under your ass. I like it.*

Just wait for the explosion. It's going to be a showstopper.

Katie dropped a large piece of broken lumber into a pile of rubble and rolled her neck from side to side. It was late, and they had been helping clean up for hours. All of the rubble had been gone through, and the bodies they found had been taken away for identification. Katie had checked on the little girl, but her parents still hadn't been found.

She walked over and grabbed Juntto by the arm. "Can I talk to you?"

Juntto smiled and tossed a large stone onto the pile. "That was some damn good demon-killing today. I think I took out over a few hundred of those little bastards. I just kept picturing them like my games and went to town."

Katie nodded. "Listen, you went a little wild out there. Angie said she can pinpoint the moment you lost it. Now I don't know what happened to set you off, but you got Hulk tunnel-vision hardcore. You went absolutely berserk. You turned on one of my friends."

Juntto held up both hands in protest. "But I didn't. I heard his voice, saw his face, and stopped myself. That has never happened to me, or probably any of my kind, before. There is a difference between making a mistake and *almost* making a mistake."

Katie let out a deep breath. "I know. Trust me, I've been there. I've been so blinded by the hate flowing through my veins that it wouldn't have mattered who I killed as long as everyone was dead. Of course, I felt differently when I came out of it, but those moments are incredibly dangerous. We have to worry about what demons are going to attack us, and how many of them there will be. We have to worry about whether we are strong enough to face them. In the midst of that, we have to worry about getting innocent people to safety. We can't be worried that one of our own is going to trample us in a blind rage."

Juntto shook his head angrily. "It wasn't a blind rage. Besides, I'm *not* one of you. I'm a ward. I was brought here to kill, and that is it. You give me nice clothes and housing, but I know better than that. I am not one of you. I see it in everyone's eyes."

Katie spoke fiercely. "Listen to me. If we fight beside you, celebrate with you, and cry next to you, then you are *one of us.* We don't discriminate, and we have all gone out of our way to leave your past in the past. We have all stepped up and started looking at you for what you do *now*, not what you did *yesterday*. That is how our team works. We all have secrets or pasts, but none of that matters here."

Juntto nodded. "Thank you."

Katie waited for a moment before she spoke again. "However, we are about to go to hell again to pay them back for all of this." Juntto perked up, but Katie put her hand up. "I'm not sure you should come."

Juntto was taken aback. "What? Not come? That is why I was brought here. I am just as good a fighter as anyone else, and I can withstand hell better than even you. I am perfect to go in there. I can put myself in the most dangerous situations and spare your human and infected lives. I don't understand."

Katie shook her head. "It's not because you can't fight or that you aren't an asset. It will hurt me not to take you in. I'm just not sure you will break off when I tell you to. I need to bring everyone back, and that includes you. We don't leave our men behind, but at the same time, if you take matters into your own hands and run off chasing demons, I can't afford to sacrifice others' lives to find you."

Juntto ran his hand through his white hair, stunned. "I don't even know what to say, Katie. I have done nothing but what I've been told from the beginning. You think death scares me? You think that standing in that field, I chose to join you because I didn't want to die? Death is the next great adventure. Today, standing in that backyard, I looked at a pool full of dead bodies. On top was a young man who reminded me very much of me, except he was dead and no longer able to be a Viking hero. *That* was why I lost it."

Katie went to say something, but Juntto shut her down.

"I joke, and I have fun killing demons because it feels good to show them pain. But more than that, in every dead body on this street, I see my team's faces. I am the only one here who is, well, like me. Except for Pandora, but she is a demon. I believe in what we are doing, and if I can have one more swing at those bastards for what they did to this town, I want it. I want to stick it to them where they stuck it to me. Where they stuck it to all of these people. I want to stand with the humans as a willing ally. I was not tricked into this. My honor should not be questioned."

Katie looked him in the eye and could see that he meant everything he was saying. Finally, she nodded. "Okay. You can go. Not because I'm telling you to, but because you want to."

Juntto smiled and pulled Katie into an awkward hug. "You won't regret it. I'm going to fuck them up like a twelve-year-old playing Fortnite."

22

A few hours later they were on their flight to the base in Colorado, where they would be opening the portal. Katie talked to Angie on the phone. "I know you wanted to fight more, but you have done your duty. Besides, you have one of those frail little human bodies, and it needs rest."

They both laughed, and Angie conceded. "Okay, I'll hold down the fort back here. Tell everyone good luck, and tell Juntto I'll get his Halo rank up."

Katie smiled. "I'll tell him. Watch for our videos, and I'll see you in a couple of days."

The flight was strangely quiet. Everyone was silent, absolutely exhausted from the fight and the cleanup. Katie was not sure if she had dozed when the plane touched down. The lights on the side of the runway flickered as they sped by and the plane slowed and curled around, coming to a stop.

They unloaded their gear and headed to the hangar.

Katie called to them as they walked away, "Get a good night's sleep. You're going to need it."

Pandora cleared her throat for attention. *I know you got all this shit coming in on planes, but you need to get your rest too. Going down to hell is hard on both of us, so I need you at one hundred percent. The people here will take care of the loadouts.*

Katie didn't want to leave. She needed to supervise the men loading and unloading the shipments. She yawned, feeling Pandora reducing her energy levels.

I'm serious. Get your fine ass to bed.

Tricky bitch.

Night-night, girl.

She made her way to her room and plopped down on the springy mattress, but instead of complaining, she curled into a ball and fell asleep.

The moonlight shone through her window as Katie drifted through a dream world. She dreamed about her past, long before she was Damned.

She dreamed about the fight, and about the future where humans were free from demonization.

Her next dream took her off-guard. She found herself standing in a dark room, but she couldn't see the walls or floor. Standing in front of her was the little girl with the bright blue eyes.

Katie leaned down and stuck out her hand. "Come on. I can get you somewhere safe."

The little girl just stood there staring at her. Katie slowly stood back up and wrapped her hands around her shoulders as an icy chill went through the room. She looked at the little girl and jumped. Blood was running down her neck, and the girl's eyes had turned black. The little girl put her hand out. "You can't help me. You are Damned, and you will damn everyone you care about."

The girl flew back into the dark and Katie screamed, running after her. She slammed into the wall and stumbled back, shaking her head. All around her a white mist floated. She held up her hands and found them dripping with blood. She screamed, but no one could hear her.

Katie sat up in the bed breathing heavily. Someone was pounding on her door. She threw her covers off and opened the door. Calvin and Brock stood there with their guns out. They rushed into the room, ready for anything, but they found nothing. Calvin lowered his weapon. "We heard screaming. What is going on?"

Katie looked down at her hands. They were perfectly clean. There was no trace of the blood from her dream. "I had a dream. A really bad one, I guess. I'm sorry, I didn't mean to freak you out."

Juntto was standing behind them chewing on a tooth-pick, unworried. "I told them you were fine. Pandora kicks nuts all day long. But no, they had to be your rescuers."

Calvin scoffed. "You ran faster than the rest of us."

Juntto waved his hands and headed for the hangar. "Come on, there are donuts."

Pandora perked up. *Fuck, yes. Exactly what I need to get that demon child out of my mind. Seriously, your brain is freaky sometimes.*

Katie locked eyes with Brock and shook her head. He nodded. She waved to Calvin. "I'll be out in a second."

Katie geared up and headed out to the hangar, where she grabbed a couple of donuts to shut Pandora up. Lined up behind the donuts was a shitload of ammunition for the big day. Everyone stood around the donuts talking, eating, and drinking coffee. When everyone was done, Katie jumped up on one of the large pallets of ammo and put her hands up to get everyone's attention.

Calvin and the others, including the twenty troops and the people who worked at the base, gathered around. Katie chuckled and looked at the crowd. "I've always hated making speeches, but I figured this one was important. Yesterday we walked through the final resting place of two thousand, three hundred and eleven souls. We battled their attackers, but we were too late for them. Today we are going to hell itself and we're going to give those mother-fuckers the payback they deserve."

She reached into the top part of her shirt and pulled out a very old, wrinkled piece of paper. Calvin recognized it immediately. Katie unfolded it and looked at her team. "After every great battle, I used to read this. In honor of those who lost their lives yesterday, and in honor of our friends and family before Incursion day, I'd like to read it again."

She cleared her throat.

"We are the ones who did not make it home.

We are the chosen.

The infected,

battling our demons night and day.

Protecting the uninformed from reality.

We fight where the stupid meet the clueless to perform the asinine for our teammates every day.

We are cops, military, special forces, and SWAT,

medical techs, priests, and clergy.

We are the dimensional derelicts,

the legion, the host, the forgotten.

The *feared*.

The sheep can sleep at night because we don't.

We fight for humanity—yours—and for our own.

We are the Damned, and death is our enemy,

our escape,

and our *tribute*."

Everyone stood perfectly still, tears in their eyes as Katie folded the paper back up and put it into her shirt. "Usually, we would mourn our friends or our loved ones who had passed. Now, though, we are going to go to hell and *deliver our reply*."

Everyone was pumped up as they prepared for the fight. The room was no longer sullen and thoughtful. An air of determination flooded each and every one of them, including Katie. She marched through the halls of the barracks and out into the hangar, greeting every soldier she passed. She walked to the map Dr. Thorough had created from the data they had gotten so far.

Katie scanned the rocks and volcanos. *Okay, Pandora, you're up. Where are we going? Let me get their attention, then take over.*

Katie waved the captain, Calvin, Brock, and Juntto to the table. "Pandora is going to take over for a minute or two and put in her two cents."

She closed her eyes and let Pandora slip forward. It was becoming easier for the two of them to work together. Pandora stood up tall and shivered, then took a deep breath, still holding Katie's form. "All right, gentlemen. I have a new place for us to land." She slammed her finger down in the area of the map that was relatively blank.

The captain peered at the spot. "But what is there?"

Pandora smiled. "There is a drone on its way there now. I gave the directions to Dr. Thorough. This is closer to the inner ring than we've ever been before, but it is very defensible. A demon by the name of Rector owned this castle two hundred years ago, but he was thrown into the abyss by Lucifer. It was an ugly scene. Rector disagreed with Lucifer about something, words were said, and *poof*—he was gone. Anyway, he is still climbing out of the pits to this day, but his castle still stands there. It is a ruin, Lucifer's minions saw to that, but it stands. It will be the perfect place for us to start our incursion."

The captain rubbed his chin; he wasn't sure. Alice came over, pushing a monitor on wheels. "I've got it up."

They all looked at the screen as it displayed the live footage from a drone.

The captain nodded in understanding. "I see what you are saying now. That is very nice. They can set up weapons all along this outer wall, and they'll have good visibility. Very nice. Uh, thank you, Pandora."

Pandora gave him a mock salute. "Thanks. On top of that, Moloch won't be able to turn his head after we've invaded his territory. I know him too well. He'll have to don his ridiculous armor and come out to fight. It is exactly what we need."

Pandora dropped back, letting Katie take over. Her eyes flashed to blue and then brown again, telling the group

Katie was back. "Does anyone have any questions? The new suits should protect you while we are down there."

The captain saw no one had any questions and asked, "All right, Katie, why don't you give us the rundown."

Katie nodded. "Okay, so getting there is relatively routine for most of us. With Pandora's help, I will open a portal that will lead right into the castle. Our force will don their suits and simply step through. We'll have teams pushing carts of our equipment while others will be carrying armor and weapons. Once in, we need to clear any and all demons from the area. We can expect to walk in and make immediate contact. They won't know we are coming, but our entry point is so close to the inner ring that we won't be able to avoid them. They will come from all directions. The last few times we went, we had some advanced warning, but that's an advantage we won't have this time. We basically won't see them coming."

Pandora chimed in over Katie. "They will be of all shapes and sizes, too. It's possible a few might slip through, so you have to be prepared. It's going to get hot in this tin can."

Katie cleared her throat. "Exactly. Now, once the demons are cleared from the castle, we will immediately move to set up the defenses and traps. We want to keep the demons as far away from the castle as we can. We don't want them to see what we are doing. We don't want them accidentally setting off any of these traps while any of us are still in there. You would be sitting ducks."

Calvin made a check mark in the air. "Careful with the explosives, check."

"We will be under extreme pressure. There will be no

perfect time to evacuate. We will be under heavy attack. You can expect wounded, and possibly casualties. We will have to work under those circumstances to get everyone out. We are the A team, people. We are responsible for getting every last human and Leviathan life out of there. We leave no man behind."

Everyone nodded, but Juntto put up his hand. "What if that is impossible?"

Katie looked at him for a moment, not having thought about it. "We go in with a full team, and we come out with a full team. Dead or alive, nobody is left behind. This will be hard on a lot of the men, but this is our chance. We go in today, and we let those demons know exactly where we stand. Failure is not an option. Our world depends on it."

The troops lined up in ranks across the hangar bay. They were outfitted in their new atmospheric suits and bore custom rifles made to withstand the heat of hell. The equipment teams had their carts of supplies and explosives. In front of the ranks stood Calvin, Juntto, Brock, Turner, Eddie, and Sean. They had their helmets in their hands, ready to begin the mission. The hangar was as quiet as a mouse, and Katie knew they needed something special to knock the nerves out of them.

She came to the front of the crowd. *Pandora, I need you to take this one. Give them a speech that will send them running into hell. These boys need to be powered and amped.*

Pandora smacked her lips. *Oh yeah, I got this one.*

Pandora took front and center and put her arms high in

the air. "Today, we march. This reminds me of a speech given by Hannibal when he addressed his soldiers after crossing the Alps in 218 BCE. '*On the right and left two seas enclose you, without your possessing even a single ship for escape. The river Po around you, the Alps behind, hem you in. Here, soldiers, where you have first met the enemy, you must conquer or die; and the same fortune which has imposed the necessity of fighting holds out to you, if victorious, rewards than which men are not wont to desire greater, even from the immortal gods.*' That is some serious shit."

Pandora put Katie's hands together and paced back and forth. "You will not find riches like gold and gems, but you will find something even greater. Today, we send a message to these disastrous pricks that we won't stand by and let them wage war on our soil. We won't bury our children and stand back in fear. We won't be bullied by a half-cocked imbecile from hell. We will bring demise and destruction to their door and see what they make of it."

Everyone cheered and Pandora nodded Katie's head, still pacing. When they had quieted, she continued, "Hell needs to be taught a lesson. What better soldiers to teach him than those created by the hand of God himself, led by an angel, backed up by the Damned. Together, we're going to take that red-hot poker Lucifer holds between his claws and ram it right up their asses! Dispel your fear, boys; you won't need it in here. It's hot and it's sweaty, but when those demons fall, they fall to the pits of hell. When Moloch falls, he will fall right into the hands of Lucifer. I can tell you now, that is not a comfortable place to be. Put one boot forward and take it home for all humanity!"

The whole place went up in cheers.

Pandora put her back to the crowd and held up her hands. "Are we ready?"

"*Hell*, yeah!" everyone yelled.

Pandora closed her eyes, and her hands morphed into demonic claws. She slashed the air, creating a large portal in the middle of the floor. The guys held onto each other as a strong, hot wind blew through the hangar. They all had their suits on, but they could see the metal around them shimmering as the room heated excessively.

Every single one of the guys knew that it hadn't been Katie talking then. They knew it was Pandora, but they all loved it. She had become a leader amongst the men.

She was a demon turned, a lost soul on the right side for the first time in history.

She was the dark to Katie's light, like a perfect yin and yang.

Pandora stood at parade rest as the soldiers walked into the portal to hell. First Calvin, Juntto and Brock's team, then the brave volunteers. The last soldier ventured a glance at Pandora and winked at her before hopping in. Pandora giggled, but Katie took back over. *Sorry, lover girl. We got business to take care of.*

Almost immediately, shots began to ring out. The battle had started as soon as the first soldier stepped through the portal. The demons scattered, not expecting the intrusion. Some fought back while others ran for cover, dodging the special metal bullets they had come to fear. Katie directed the equipment teams as the weapons and ammunition were carried across the castle floor and mounted on the walls.

She took a deep breath and turned toward the view.

Hundreds upon thousands of demons milled about the inner circle below. Lava boiled through molten rivers. Thunderous explosions from the volcanos shook the rocks beneath their feet. They were deeper in hell than they had ever been, and they had a job to do.

Calvin began pulling out the drones and switching them on. He set them free one at a time until they had enough out flying to capture a full view of the battle. Katie pulled her gun and put out her arm, stopping Calvin as he was about to grab another drone. She pulled the trigger and a bullet whizzed past him, striking a charging demon between the eyes.

Juntto put his hand on Katie's shoulder. "We fight until they no longer stand, but we retreat when we hear your call."

"Protect everyone, Juntto. You are the powerhouse here. Together we can do this; make them pay for the pool full of bodies you stumbled upon. No one fucks with us."

Juntto slammed his fists on his chest and roared, "No one fucks with us! No one fucks with the humans or Juntto!"

He grabbed a demon and ripped it in half, slamming it to the ground.

Katie raised her guns and began firing. There was no denying it.

The fight had begun.

23

"Fuck you, scum," Brock shouted as he slashed his long sword, cutting off three demon heads at once.

Turner flipped his daggers over and flung them at two demons climbing the castle wall. They stuck in the demons' skulls, and he yanked them out as the demons dropped. Brock and his team had taken to the ramparts of the castle to try to make sure the entire place was clear. They didn't want to worry about demons coming up behind them when they were in the middle of a fight.

Several of the soldiers had followed them, using their rifles to blast holes in the demons as they went. Brock liked having extra men with them, especially in a situation like this.

A lanky two-headed demon dropped in front of him. Brock bent back as far as he could, barely missing the swipe of a demon's claws. The demon's two heads snarled in unison as it walked like a bird across the castle ramparts, almost like it was protecting its turf.

Turner put his daggers away. "What the fuck is this, a

chicken? My grandma taught me how to kill a chicken. You want to see?"

Brock smirked and nodded. Turner dodged the demon's slashing claws and grabbed one of the beast's long, thin necks. He began swinging the demon around over his head, yelling like a cowboy. The demon's body slammed into the crumbling brick wall, its eyes spinning in its head.

Turner slammed it to the ground and put his boot on its neck, then pulled out his dagger. "Then, if that doesn't do it, you lay him down just like this and *chop*! His head comes right off."

He sliced through the two thin necks and let the body up. The guys laughed and watched it run around while its two heads lay on the ground. Finally, it toppled over, turning to dust.

Juntto had gathered a dozen smaller demons that had been hiding in various corners of the castle. He came out onto the overlook, dragging them behind him. He walked up to a soldier setting up a mounted machine gun. "You want practice shots?"

The guy grinned. Juntto started throwing demons out in front of the gun one at a time, letting the guy blow them to pieces. Chunks of demon flew everywhere, smacking some of the soldiers in the head. When they turned around to see what it was, they couldn't help but laugh at the scene. Juntto threw another demon, but he felt someone tapping him on the shoulder.

Katie cut her eyes at him. "Can we get serious here? There are about a thousand demons heading this way. We need to be secure."

"This is practice. This *is* making us secure." Juntto gave

her a forced smile and tossed the rest out, letting the guys go nuts.

A young soldier fired his rifle until it clicked empty. The demon in front of him had four arms, and it was using all of them to try to disembowel the young man. Calvin yelled and leaped over the soldier, startling them both. He blasted the demon in the back of the head just as it was about to slash the soldier in the stomach. The guy nodded and ran off, grabbing another batch of ammo. The soldier immediately reloaded and began firing, taking out a line of demons with one swipe of his rifle.

Brock and the other guys came running out of the front gate to the castle and stopped in front of Calvin. "The castle is clear. From what we can see, this is the only way in. Unless they slip by us, it is protected."

Calvin slapped him on the shoulder. "Good work. Let's help them get the Gatling guns set up. Those mother-fuckers are heavy."

Brock's team helped set the massive machines up on the edge of a wall. Eddie held one in place while Sean stacked stones and fallen bricks around it.

Sean wiggled the gun. "Secure?"

"As secure as it's going to be." Eddie called the gunner over and they moved on, setting up three more guns the same way. They had four in total, and they were all vital to the battle.

Juntto picked up three missile launchers as two soldiers struggled to lift one. He nodded at them and walked to the front lines. The frost giant propped them on a crumbling wall, then found three guys and showed them the launch-ers. "You launch missiles. Okay?"

The guys looked at each other and then nodded excitedly. Juntto helped each of them steady a missile launcher on his shoulders. Katie tapped three more guys to join them, pointing to the cases of missiles. The soldiers began loading the missiles into the backs of the launchers. They flipped safety switches down and tapped their comrades on the backs, then took cover.

As the guns began to fire into the approaching crowds of demons, the RPGs let loose, launching missiles into the horde. It looked like a scene from a civil war movie, explosions going off all over the fields. Demon bodies flew in pieces in all directions. Ammunition shells clinked against the black stone as the Gatling guns fired hundreds of rounds one after the other.

The drones flew high above them, watching the battle and the soldiers fighting it. In the castle, Katie walked up to an overlook. *There are a lot of fucking demons down here.*

There are a lot of fucked-up humans up here. Kind of equals out. I'm pretty sure there's a demon somewhere in this crew that infected that tyrant Hitler you guys talk about so much. His demon flesh was carved with the swastika as a constant reminder of his failure on Earth.

Katie scoffed. *Failure? He killed hundreds of thousands. Millions.*

Pandora laughed. *Takes a lot more down here to impress his diabolic highness and his slew of whores.*

The bar in Boston was packed to the gills. People were observing a day of mourning for those lost in the attacks on Cohasset. They drank beer and took shots, toasting the victims. They droned on about the demon invaders, and what they would do if they could get their hands on them. Little did Boston know, they had been on Moloch's list. He simply hadn't made it that far.

"Fuckin' demons. Send 'em all back to hell where they belong!" someone yelled, followed by a rousing cheer and the clinking of glasses.

The bartender climbed up on the bar. "Everyone shut up. There's a special report!"

She turned up the television and the whole bar fell silent. The newscaster looked wildly at the camera. "We are getting a special report from the United States government. There has been a retaliatory strike made by the US in conjunction with Katie. It's hard to describe this event, so we will now bring you footage straight from the government, recorded in...hell."

The screen flipped to drone footage of hell. Demons were swarming up the side of a cliff while troops stood on the edge firing guns and missiles down into the crowd of beasts. One drone panned to Katie, who was standing on a crumbling castle wall firing her twin guns into the crowd below. Everyone in the bar cheered as soon as she came on the screen.

The video continued to play as the newscaster talked. "It is being reported that we have, in fact, attacked hell. The strike force includes three mercenaries, four Special Ops Damned, and twenty troops. They went through a portal into hell just moments ago. They are armed with the best equipment the military has available. We have not been told what their mission is, but we *can* confirm that we have attacked hell."

The people in the bar were silent, but then a voice cut through the quiet. "We finally fucking did it. *We attacked hell!*"

Someone raised their glass. "I knew the government wouldn't fail us. They've been researching this shit all along."

The newscaster watched the footage in awe, along with the audience. "Now remember, folks, if you are sensitive, you might want to look away. This footage is being streamed live with no edits."

Everyone in the bar began to cheer on the battle. The camera captured a soldier falling under an onslaught of demons, then being pulled from danger by a group of rifle-carrying soldiers. The wounded man was carried back through the portal behind them. It was a bad scene for sure, but it gave hope to any human who was watching.

One of the older patrons stood up. He was wearing a Vietnam Veteran hat. "God bless our soldiers and their sacrifices."

"Hear, hear," the whole bar yelled.

Moloch was celebrating in his lair with Baal by his side. The two of them were surrounded by goodies from live kittens to deep-fried gerbils. They had dipping sauces for everything, and several empty bottles of wine were lined up on the table. Servants scurried in and out as they collected empty dishes and replaced anything that was running low.

The mood in the lair was jovial, to say the least.

"My compliments to your chef."

Baal waved the compliment away. "He turned out quite nicely, didn't he?"

Moloch swallowed a gerbil, then held up his glass and smiled. "To us. We may not have hit all our targets, but I think over two thousand dead is pretty impressive. The Killers and that bitch Pandora didn't even know what was coming. They showed up when the carnage was almost finished."

Baal laughed loudly and a kitten tried to jump from his mouth. He chomped down on it and swallowed hard, clanking his cup with Moloch's. "The beauty of the looks on their faces—it was priceless. My favorite part was when the demons were first discovered because of that nasty child in her pink dress. The mother looked like she was about to drop dead right there."

Moloch held his belly as he laughed. "Oh, Lucifer, it was magnificent. The demons attacked her like a pack of wild dogs. I loved that. I knew it would be good to keep them caged up and hungry. They were even more feral than when they first became demons. I can remember a time I was that bloodthirsty. I was beautiful."

Baal pointed at the television. "Let's watch some more clips from the news. They can't stop playing them."

Moloch waved one hand to turn on the screen. An old woman was shaking like a leaf. "And then my Harold grabbed his gun, kissed me like we were twenty, and ran out the door. They say he killed two before he was taken down. He is a pure hero to me, just like back in the war."

Moloch made a pouty face. "Oh, poor Harold. I'm pretty sure Harold's body will be recovered in pieces. I saw an old man ripped apart."

The demons burst into laughter.

Baal choked on his gerbil and hit his chest, sending it flying across the room. "Oh, I can't. This is too much. Remind me again why we didn't attack the other places?"

Moloch waved his hands. "That one was more successful than I ever thought possible, and my revenge was satisfied. Not a peep from those assholes since then. They are scared to death."

Just then the screen flipped to the newscaster. "I'm sorry to interrupt this recap, but information is coming in fast. Apparently, there is a video feed being routed to us as we speak directly from the government. Hold one second, the details are streaming to me right now."

The newscaster listened for a moment and then looked at the screen with wide eyes. "Reports from the White House have been verified. The government, in connection with Katie and the Killers, have put together a task force. As you are watching this, an elite strike force is fighting a battle in hell itself."

Moloch spat out his half-chewed bunny and leaned forward. "*What?*"

"We take you now to the live feed."

The screen flipped, and Baal and Moloch both sat there with their mouths open, watching the troops fighting on the terrace of the old castle. They had all kinds of weapons, and were really putting a hurt on the demons racing toward them. Moloch slammed his hands on the chair arms and jumped up, running to the window.

He squinted into the distance as hordes of demons raced from the inner ring, heading in that direction. Moloch's entire body clenched and he marched to the closet, swinging open the door. He pulled his armor out and gripped his great spiked club tightly in one hand.

Baal nervously approached him. "You shouldn't. They are trying to lure you out."

Moloch roared. "Good! I'll stick my foot up that bitch's ass so far I'll be able to open and close her mouth with my big toe!"

Baal knocked a platter of kittens to the floor, and the servants scurried everywhere trying to collect them. Baal pulled the napkin from his neck and stood as tall as he could. "I will come with you, then."

Moloch waved him off. "You are too old for battle, Baal. Sit here and keep an eye on things. If anything happens to me, though, you better come out there and save my ass." Moloch turned to his head servant. "Go sound the alarms. I need all my biggest demons front and center for this. If Pandora and the other humanoids want to bring war to my doorstep, I will meet them with the best I've got. This bitch is going to be buried so far beneath the lava that she will never climb out."

Moloch stomped out of the room, leaving Baal perplexed and nervous. He turned back to the television and slumped down in his chair, then picked up a guinea pig and popped it into his mouth, watching intently as the war waged on the screen in front of him. Demons were being blasted in all directions. Baal had been around long enough to know that even if Moloch survived, he was going to have to answer to Lucifer. There was no way the king would let this intrusion slide.

Katie fired into the demons as she approached a squad of soldiers, waving a dozen men to her. "Men, grab your weapons, but also take bombs for the traps. We are rolling the big guy down there right now, but we need the small ones farther out. They will set off a chain reaction. In order for this to work, you have to fight the demons back as you go. The men up here will cover you to the best of their ability, but keep your eyes open. We don't want to start setting this shit off early."

The men agreed and ran off to gather supplies. Brock came up and looked at Katie. "What can we do?"

Katie pointed at the front line below. "Help them set up, and then get out of there. They could use some cover, too. We're doing the best we can from up here, but there are demons slipping through. I need those men to concentrate. I don't want to blow up today. That isn't on my schedule."

Brock chuckled. "Mine either. We'll go down and hold the line. You want the men back through the portal when they're done?"

"Yeah, we want to have to evacuate as few men as possible when it comes time. Once all the traps are set, we will start relieving the front riflemen and missile launchers."

Brock saluted her. "Yes, ma'am. We've got your back."

Katie grabbed Calvin as he ran past. "I want you to start

evacuating all nonessential personnel through the portal. We are setting up the bombs below. When they are in place, we have to get the hell out of here."

"What about the weapons? We can't leave them here for the demons, can we? I mean, we don't really want that shit falling into their grubby claws."

Katie shook her head. "With the kind of explosive firepower we have, everything will be blown to bits."

Calvin gave her a thumbs-up and ran off. He paused long enough to lift two injured soldiers off the ground and help them through the portal.

Pandora sniffed the air. *Uh-oh, something is stirring. I can smell it. Do you feel that rush of heat?*

Katie closed her eyes and let her senses feel around. *Yeah. It's like a warm breeze on a fucking sizzling hot day. What is that?*

Pandora sighed. *Something or someone is on their way up from the inner ring. I can promise you he will not be traveling alone. We need to get these traps set up* right now.

24

"Move them to the right," Katie yelled as she fired into the crowd of demons.

She jumped off the ledge, landing between two claymores, and glanced at Calvin with wide eyes.

Careful. Don't start the party early.

Nope. No party here.

She leaped again to the front of the demon line and started throwing them out of the way. The ground shook beneath her feet, and almost as one, all the demons stopped and stared into the distance.

Pandora groaned. *This* cannot *be good.*

Katie followed their gazes about half a mile and her breath came short.

Moloch was rushing toward them in spiked iron armor, carrying a huge spiked club in one gnarled hand. Behind him were legions upon legions of large demons, all carrying some sort of crude weapon. Katie took a deep breath, readying her nerves.

Fuck fuck fuck fuck fuck.

No, this is exactly what we wanted.

Katie spun and pointed to the soldiers holding the RPGs. "Blast him with missiles! The big fucker! Get him!"

The line of soldiers took aim and fired, sending missiles in his direction. He batted two away with his great club, but the third got through and exploded against his knees. He tripped and tumbled down the hill. He rolled head over feet, smashing smaller demons and crumbling large chunks of rock. "Fuck, dick, fucking shit!"

He cursed the entire way down the mountain, every human and every demon watching in horror. The demons knew he would be pissed as shit when he finally stopped, but the rest of them found it kind of amusing. Not only that, but the large idiot demons behind him figured that was what they were supposed to do. One by one they stopped on the hill, scratched their heads, and then leaped forward, tumbling down the scorched incline.

Pandora laughed. *Holy hell, that is the funniest fucking thing I've seen in a long time.*

This is amazing. I'm speechless.

Those fucking morons. Oh, and Katie...

Yeah?

You might want to get the fuck out of here.

The ground started to rumble, and a horrible sound filled the air—the shrieking of tens of thousands of demons as they came rolling over the hills from all directions. The sounds of horns blowing could be heard all across hell, and every able demon was answering the call. The army was massive. It was nothing Katie or even Juntto could handle.

Katie ran toward her soldiers. "Retreat! Fucking *run!*"

The soldiers began to jump across the killing field and run for the castle steps. Some yelled as they leaped through the portal. Others looked back, stealing one last glimpse of the army of hell. It was a sight that no human, and precious few angels, had ever seen before. There were thousands of them in all shapes and sizes—a great, writhing, clawing, screeching horde that descended upon the castle.

Calvin was stone-faced, staring at the demons. He was mesmerized by the sight of them. It was like a scene from a movie. They reminded him of giant ferocious ants, but ants that had the ability to rip him to shreds. He shook his head. "I think we pissed off the ants!"

Pandora chuckled. *Yeah, you knocked their queen down a fucking mountain. They know they are going to get it for that one.*

Katie slapped Calvin on the chest. "We gotta get everyone the fuck out of here so we can blow this shit."

Calvin lifted a wounded man in each arm and rushed for the portal.

Katie pulled another soldier to his feet, putting his arm over her shoulder. They limped forward as fast as possible, but the demons were starting to gain on them. Katie took out her gun and fired into the crowd. A few demons dropped, but they kept rushing forward. Katie was slowed by the man she was carrying.

He shook his haggard face. "It's too late."

"Fuck that."

Katie propped the soldier against the wall, then stepped away from him and summoned her angel energies. Pandora ducked down inside of Katie. *Oh hell, Slut Girl is fucking* pissed *now.*

Katie screamed as she pushed the energy from her chest, exploding a ring of pure power outward. It slammed into the first ten rows of demons and sent them flying backward, toppling others like dominos.

"See? No fuckin' problem."

She grabbed the wounded soldier and rushed him toward the stairs. Eddie and Sean were at the portal helping soldiers through, and they took the soldier from Katie. "Should we go?"

Katie dusted off her hands. "I've got some scores to settle." She grabbed a missile launcher from a stack of weapons, then caught the eye of a soldier guarding the ammunition. "Toss me a missile."

He hesitated. "Toss it?"

She waved her hand and nodded. He grabbed one and carefully threw it to her underhand. She loaded the launcher and swung it onto her shoulder, then took aim and pressed the button. The missile flew out of the launcher and slammed into the fifth row of demons, blowing more than a hundred of them to bits.

But still they came.

With a warrior's scream, Juntto leaped from the castle walls. He raised two impossibly large fists high and sent them crashing down into the demons as he landed. He swung his hands like hammers, knocking demons in all directions. He laughed loudly, loving the fight.

Katie shook her head and pulled her short swords as the wave of demons met her.

Juntto fought hard and fast, smashing demons apart as they jumped at him. They stabbed their long talons into his skin, but he kept going, taking the blows in stride and giving them right back.

In the distance, Moloch had gotten to his feet. He had rallied his giant demons and was charging toward them at a damned fast pace—too fast for her liking. His eyes were gleaming red, and he was madder than fuck. He was staring right at Katie. She knew he was coming for her and Pandora. "Come and get it, you big fuck."

Pandora cackled. *Big fucking idiot, small fucking dick. I mean, even for his size, you can barely see it when he runs.*

Katie wrinkled her nose. *There you go again with the giant demon dicks. We talked about this.*

Watch out!

Katie ducked as a demon sliced his claws at her. She stabbed one sword into his belly and then yanked up, cutting him completely in half. The demon screeched and burst into dust, which flowed into the cracks in the rocks at her feet. She swung her short swords right and left, taking several heads off and watching them roll toward the oncoming hordes.

Juntto was making his way back toward the team, falling to one knee as he flung demons off his back. He growled out and slammed his body upward with force, sending beasts flying all over the place. He gritted his teeth as he ran for the castle, blood pouring from a dozen wounds, and streaming from the corner of his mouth. They were all bleeding, all struggling, but Moloch was close. Their objective was almost complete.

In her mind, Katie could see that little girl's blue eyes shining. She just had to push herself harder.

She had to make this work.

The whole world was watching, and she had to send the message that no one was going to mess with her people and get away with it.

Calvin tripped, cursed, and pulled himself to his feet, then turned quickly, shooting a demon in the face. He grabbed one of the last wounded soldiers and ran him to Brock, who took him up the stairs and through the portal. Calvin sighed and wiped the dust from the front of his mask.

He was more than ready to get the fuck out of hell.

He took a step forward and grunted, feeling a clawed hand around his arm. He tried to pull away, but the demon was strong and grabbed his other arm. Across the line Katie saw what was happening and slashed her swords, trying to get to him, but the crowd of demons had grown too thick.

Another demon jumped in front of Calvin and grabbed him around the neck, holding him still. Calvin twisted, staring the demon in the eyes while trying to get free.

Katie slashed her sword through the demons, only getting an inch closer to Calvin each time. He struggled to pull his short sword, but a huge demon wrapped him in a great bear hug, pinning his arms to his sides. Katie sliced wildly, trying to push through the crowd of demons. The fiend in front of Calvin pulled back one large claw, ready to strike him dead where he stood.

Calvin shut his eyes tightly and prayed. Katie screamed.

Juntto came forward, ripping the head off the demon behind Calvin. The demon fell to the ground. Juntto slammed a huge fist into another demon's mouth, breaking his jaw and sending him sprawling. Free to move, Calvin pulled his gun and fired five shots into his attacker's head and neck. Ash billowed around him a moment later.

Juntto put out his fist for a bump and Calvin chuckled, impressed. "Nice. Getting with the times, my man."

"Time to get the fuck out of here," Juntto whispered, grabbing Calvin by the waist and throwing him toward the portal.

"Thaaaanks, asshoollle," Calvin yelled as he soared through the portal and out of sight.

Katie laughed and mouthed, "Thank you" to Juntto as they stood there in the sea of demons. He gave her one of his big smiles, but it only lasted for a second. His body jolted as Moloch reached out and grabbed Juntto by the waist. He lifted the frost giant to his face. "Well, well, you aren't dead after all. And we killed that poor Arnold guy, thinking he was the mystery fellow."

Juntto gritted his teeth. "You killed the Terminator?"

Moloch tilted his large head back and laughed loudly, squeezing Juntto even tighter to keep him from growing.

Katie couldn't just let Juntto die like that. *Pandora, are all the rest out?*

Pandora sniffed. *Sure are. You thinking what I'm thinking?*

Katie chuckled nervously. *I don't know, but it's fucking nuts.*

Good. It's about damn time.

Katie swiped her hand toward the portal, and it slammed shut.

She was alone in hell.

Katie's eyes blazed blue, and she ran to Moloch. She

raised a hand and summoned her angel sword, casting a heavenly light in the dim glare of hell. She lashed out and stabbed Moloch in the leg. He grunted and kicked at her, knocking her to the ground. He threw Juntto down to look at the glowing wound on his ankle. "Fucking angels. How dare you come in here?"

He grabbed Juntto again before the Leviathan could get himself together. Katie stood up and held her sword in front of her, letting her giant wings unfold. The hordes of demons stopped and quickly backed up in fear. "I won't let you hurt any more humans or their allies, you big ugly bastard."

Katie's knees began to buckle as the pressure of hell, and her angel powers wore her down. *Fuck, I don't have enough, Pandora. I just don't.*

Pandora pulled her strength inward. *Don't worry, sweetie. Momma's got this one on lockdown.*

Pandora leaped from Katie's chest, immediately growing as tall as Moloch, who turned toward her in surprise. In her true form, Pandora was beautiful and nightmarish at the same time. She reared back, slapping him hard across the face. "That's for calling me a bitch, you fucking dickwad."

She snatched Juntto from Moloch and set him on the ground next to Katie. "Get her up top. I'll be with you in just a second. I got a dear old friend to get reacquainted with."

Juntto scooped Katie's exhausted body into his arms and ran around the two giant demons, taking the stairs two at a time. He stopped with his back to the wall of the castle and covered Katie's head with his arms to protect her. He had waited a very long time to see what he was about to see, and it wasn't only because Pandora was about to fight butt-ass naked.

Pandora circled Moloch, her eyes narrowed. "How dare you come to my planet, pick on my friends, and think I wouldn't come knocking on your fucking door?"

Moloch swung his club wildly and missed. "Oh, I knew you *would* come knocking. In fact, I was counting on it. I'm sure that your husband would love to take a look at you now. He's got a torture cage all set up for you in his lair. You've been a bad girl, Lilith."

She slapped the club out of his hand and grabbed his shoulders. "One, he's my ex."

She slammed her knee into his groin. "Two, I only like it when a sexy man tells me I've been bad. You just make it *creepy*."

She reared back and slugged him hard across the face, sending him down on one knee. He rubbed his cheek and growled. With great effort, he pushed himself up and back-handed Pandora hard across the face. She stumbled back and shook the shock out of her vision. "Why does it not surprise me that you would hit a woman?"

Moloch laughed. "You're *not* a woman. You are just a common fucking fallen-angel whore. In fact, I heard God actually threw a party with Gideon when you left. He no longer had to deal with a charity case."

Pandora's eyes shone bright red and she charged Moloch, slamming her fists on his shoulders, then kicked him in the stomach over and over until he fell to his knees. She stepped back and backhanded him across one cheek, then the other, then did it again. He looked up at her with black blood coming from his mouth, laughing loudly. "Don't you understand, Lilith? You are no longer the *queen*. We no longer have to fear you. You are nothing but another dirty demon, infecting humans to get your kicks."

Pandora screamed, grabbing a boulder and slamming it over Moloch's head. He rose to his feet, dusting the ashes from his shoulders. Pandora walked up to him and put her finger in his face. "You come to Earth again and I'll come down here and cut the dick off every demon in this place, feed them to you, and then castrate you for the world to see."

She kicked him hard between the legs and took off running, shrinking as she climbed up the stairs. She stopped in front of Juntto and looked down at Katie. "Come on, let's get the fuck out of here. I'm ready to blow this dickhole to shreds. I'm starting to feel that hell might just be a little too goth for me."

She opened a small portal and grabbed Juntto, pulling him and Katie through it and slamming it shut behind them. Juntto held on to Katie as Pandora ran naked across the hangar bay, everyone staring at her wildly.

Calvin gave her a glance and then looked at the monitor. Pandora took a deep breath. "It's time."

Calvin handed her the switch. "Oh, girl, this is your treat. I'm pretty sure you have the longest-running beef with that fool."

Pandora watched the monitor. In hell, Moloch stood up laughing. "What, Lilith, are you weak? That wasn't a portal. I'll show *you* a portal from hell."

Pandora shook her head. "Maybe next time, fuckface."

She pressed the button, and the claymores began exploding all around him. The explosions came closer.

Moloch tried to leap away, but an explosion caught him in mid-air.

The bombs blew like fireworks, shaking and rattling the drones in the sky. The shockwave sent many of them spiraling to the ground. Only one continued operating. There was fire and smoke, then nothing. After a moment, a large chunk of meat came out of the smoke and stopped right in front of the drone.

It was Moloch's giant fucking arm. The thing was surrounded by great heaps of ash and scores of severed limbs. The surviving demons retreated as fast as they could. They didn't know if Moloch was dead, but not a single one of them waited to find out. If he wasn't dead, he was going to take it out on anything he could find.

The whole hangar erupted in cheers and Calvin hugged Pandora tightly, lifting her into the air. Slowly he pulled back and put his hands up, signaling that he hadn't touched anything he shouldn't have. He had forgotten she was completely naked.

Pandora looked at him, surprised. "You weren't exaggerating after all. I knew it all along. Didn't doubt you for a second. Long Dong Silver—that's your new name."

Calvin narrowed his eyes. "Don't you have somewhere to be? You know, keeping someone alive?"

Pandora followed his eyes to Katie. "Oh, shit, yeah. Bitch can't survive without me...what can I say? I guess I can't really survive without her, either, so I think we're square."

She ran across, all the guys watching her body bounce

like a porn version of *Baywatch*. As she dove back into Katie's body, she flashed a smile to the guys and blew them a kiss. Calvin followed her and knelt next to Katie. She was breathing but unconscious. Juntto stood over them looking worried.

Calvin had seen it before. "Pandora has to heal her. Give her a minute. She will come back to us. You okay?"

Juntto shifted slightly, holding his breath. "Yeah, yeah, Juntto's fine."

25

***

The base was absolutely silent. The halls were still. The soldiers, freshly returned from hell, did not joke or brag. The computers sat unused. Brock crossed his arms nervously on his chest and stood over Juntto. Katie's body lay in Juntto's lap, her eyes still closed. Turner and their teammates bunched together, unsure what to do at that point. No one could fathom the idea of Katie not waking up.

The captain held his phone in one hand. He had promised General Brushwood that he would call at the first sign of Katie moving. Those soldiers who were not wounded had finished taking the bodies of the fallen to the medical building and now came back, sitting silently on the floor and waiting. All anyone could do at that moment was wait.

Even Pandora didn't make a sound or try to move. Inside Katie, she used all her powers to bring Katie back to a conscious state.

The clock ticked on the wall, the first time anyone had noticed it. The heat had dissipated from the room. Soldiers had long since hung up their atmospheric suits.

Calvin knelt next to Katie, patting her hand. "Come on, girl. Wake up. We're all here waiting for you."

Her hand twitched in his, and he looked up at Juntto. Juntto adjusted her head, and she let out a small groan. Her eyeballs moved under her eyelids, and they flickered open. She gripped Calvin's hand and let out a deep breath as if she had been holding it all that time. Her eyes opened and she blinked, trying to focus them in the harsh light of the hangar.

"Hey, hey, take it easy. You're right here with us," Calvin whispered.

A small smile moved across her lips. Calvin grinned.

Pandora let out a sigh of relief. *Holy hell, bitch. Seriously, I thought I was going to be stuck inside a damn vegetable for the rest of my life. Why would you freak a bitch out like that? You have got to learn how to be a better friend.*

Did we get him?

Pandora chuckled. *We blew the shit out of that fucker. Didn't see his body. Well, except for his severed arm.*

Nice.

She shifted her gaze to Juntto, who looked like he was in pain. He stared down at her with his eyes shifting colors. They turned a brilliant blue, then shifted to green, then yellow, and back again. His arms trembled beneath her, but he didn't say a word. He forced a smile onto his lips and lifted her to a sitting position. "How are you feeling?"

Katie smiled and gave him a thumbs-up. He leaned in,

whispering to her, "Don't think I don't know you could have left me. And don't think you will be getting rid of me now." He cleared his throat and raised a fist. "Not when I still need to learn how to kick ten-year-old asses on Xbox."

He covered his mouth as he coughed, trying to hide the blood coming from his mouth. "I have been practicing Halo now for about a week, and I think I will be a champion soon. I decided, though, that emperoring isn't really my thing. I just like to fight and kill bad guys. Or, at least kick villain's asses. Or any ass, really, but in my current position, I'll say villainous asses. I can kick anyone's ass on a video game, though."

Katie laughed and put her hand on his chest, straining her voice. "Good. Oh, and I think Angie is starting to miss you being there. She told me that while you were gone, she was going to get your Halo character a higher ranking so you would enjoy the game better when you got back."

The thought nearly brought a tear to his eye. "She was a great choice. You did good with her. She is a badass, but human too. Don't forget she's human."

Katie furrowed her brow. "You can tell her all that when we get back. She would love to hear that, even if she says differently."

He smiled, and there was blood on his teeth. "Deal."

Calvin helped Juntto to his feet. "Why don't we get Katie to medical to get checked out? You should come too. You are pretty beat up, brother."

Juntto shook his head. "I heal fast. I'll be fine. Take care of Katie first. All these people depend on her. They need her to save the humans, right?"

Calvin chuckled. "That's for damn sure."

Calvin nodded at the medical team standing by. They rolled the cart down and helped Juntto and Calvin pick Katie up and carefully lay her on the gurney. She gripped Calvin's hand tightly and smirked. "We stuck a bomb up Moloch's ass."

Calvin laughed. "I know. Motherfucker didn't know what to do with himself. When you get better, you can watch the playback."

Katie pointed at Calvin. "You better get a copy of that shit. We can watch it on family night."

Calvin turned and towered over the medics. "You make her comfortable. No scratchy fucking blankets. Whatever she wants, you get it for her, and that includes donuts. Listen to her when she's telling you something. Her demon is healing her. If you have a television, bring that shit in, too. She likes the soaps."

Katie giggled. "I'm not scary. Just ignore him. The way my demon works, I'll be back in action in two hours. But I *would* get the donuts if I were you. She tends to get grumpy without them. Thanks, Calvin."

The medics wheeled her up the ramp and into the building. Calvin let out a deep breath, putting his hand to his chest. "This job is going to kill me yet."

Just then, Juntto fell to his knees, groaned, and collapsed on the floor. Calvin's eyes went wide, and he dropped down next to him. "Just lie still, buddy. We'll get you some help."

Juntto shook his head, reaching up and taking Calvin's hand. "I'm sure my body will heal. If it doesn't, I have lived a life worth a million stories." He coughed, blood splattering his palm. "Stories they would make songs about where I come from. Have I ever told you about my home, Calvin?"

Calvin sat down next to him, glancing up at Brock. "No, man. Tell me about it."

Juntto smiled. "It's fucking beautiful. Clear purple skies and deep blue oceans surrounded by lush green grassy hills. We have creatures that change colors depending on the temperature, and villages built for families. We were all family, caring for each other despite any blood relation. We had enemies, but that was how I became a warrior."

Juntto's voice faded, his eyes slipping shut. Calvin tightened his grip. "Tell me about your family."

Juntto opened his eyes and smiled. Not a vicious smile, but a soft, wistful one. "They were wonderful. And then there was Lucivia. She was a beautiful girl who lived in the next village over. She had the bluest eyes and the brightest smile. She died when we were young adults, but she was my one love. Ha. Imagine me with a love, right?"

Calvin smiled. "Oh, man, we all gotta love someone."

Juntto coughed again, barely shaking his head. He shut his eyes.

Calvin shook his shoulder lightly to try to wake him. He leaned over and listened to the Leviathan's chest.

Brock stood there concerned. "Did he..."

Calvin shook his head. "No. He just fell into a coma, I think."

Calvin jumped when Juntto's body began to morph. He grew longer, his skin forming cold blue scales. He was reverting to his original twelve-foot form.

Calvin stepped back and watched the change. "He sacrificed himself to save me, then did the same for Katie. I never in a million years thought he would be as loyal as he has become. I guess everyone needs a family to show them the right way."

Brock sighed. "I saw the recognition in his face when he jumped me at the incursion. I could see the pain in his eyes when he thought he hurt me. He cared about all of us. He was wild, and that was hard for us to understand."

Calvin looked up at everyone standing around. "Maybe this is how he heals."

"We don't have a big enough space for him in the barracks, but we can at least try to make him comfortable here." Brock gestured to his team, and Eddie, Sean, and Turner grabbed blankets from a medic's cart.

Brock spread out the first blanket and the others followed suit, layering them over his body. The captain walked down and handed Brock two pillows. Brock and the others knelt next to the sleeping giant and lifted his head, gently laying it back down on the pillows. Calvin stood up and looked around at the soldiers. "I will say this one time, and one time only. This was a brave man. He saved my life tonight. He saved Katie's life tonight. And he damn sure saved yours, even if you don't know it. If I see one video of him making the rounds on the internet, letting the world know he is alive, I will make it my life's work to hunt down whoever took it. Let him rest and try to get through this in peace."

Calvin looked down at the silver streak in the frost giant's hair. "I think we owe him that at least."

Exactly one week had passed since the deadly portals opened in Massachusetts, setting in motion a plan that would change the way the world looked at the war. Things had been crazy since, with media, news, and riots across the country. People tried to make sense of something as insane as invading hell.

On that particular day, though, things were different.

All across New York City, the cars stood still. Tourists didn't crowd the streets. Vendors closed down their carts for the day. In the center of Times Square, the Jumbotron stayed on without advertisements, and people sat quietly in chairs in the middle of the road, watching coverage of the event on screen.

Flags at half-mast waved in the fall breeze. The sound of fabric flapping filled the streets, something that those streets probably had never heard and would never hear again. This day in New York was for the heroes, and no one was going to step out of line for that.

But it wasn't just New York; the heroes were being celebrated all across the country.

Tractors sat still in the late-afternoon light. Toys were idle in yards, and parks were completely deserted. Bars were open, but there was no joyous music or loud conversation, just the television tuned to the memorial service.

From small town to big city, valleys to mountaintops, and coasts to islands, the entire nation stopped to remember what they had lost, and why it was so important. People sat together regardless of creed, nationality, sexual orientation, or any other triviality.

They put aside their differences, put aside their red hats

and blue hats, set down their protest signs and stilled their hateful chants, and just sat side by side, thinking about what was and what would come to be.

There was a stillness in the realization that humanity was all one race, all one species, and all one kind. It had taken an event of massive proportions to bring that realization to the fore, but when it did come, the country saw peace for one shining moment. All around the condo where Katie lived, people sat cross-legged in the streets holding candles in their laps. The doorman had locked the doors to keep people out, but no one tried to enter.

The hall leading to Juntto's and Katie's apartments was absolutely silent. No yelling or cursing, no laughter or tears, and no smell of bacon or donuts wafting out. The remote sat on the coffee table with the television off, and the radio was shut down. The kitchen was empty.

Angie walked quietly through the hall, her black dress perfectly fitted and pressed for the occasion.

She went to the windows and looked out over the park. She wondered if things would have been different if she had been there. She had never lost anyone she cared about, even if she didn't know it at the time.

The sound of footsteps approaching from behind caught her by surprise, and she turned, wiping a tear from her cheek. Calvin walked over with a smile and wrapped his arms around her, kissing her on the top of the head. He rubbed her arms and pulled back, looking into her eyes. "You ready to go? They will be waiting for us."

Angie nodded and let out a deep breath. She followed Calvin, shutting the lights off as she left. They rode a short distance to Madison Square Garden, and the chauffeur helped her from the car. They were ushered through the quiet halls into the grand area at the back. As they stepped down the walkway, the people in the seats turned to them. Angie stared ahead, her heart broken.

In front of her were twelve beautiful caskets draped with American flags. Katie stood at the podium and silently nodded as they entered. Angie nodded back and moved to one side, sitting down next to Calvin. Perched on the top of each of the caskets was a picture of the fallen soldier. Most of the pictures were of them in uniform, but a couple were images from their everyday lives. The casket on the end had a strange picture. It was not a man in uniform, but it wasn't exactly of a man at home and at ease either.

The picture made Angie chuckle through her tears. She held a tissue in front of her mouth.

On top of the last casket was the insert from the *Far Cry Four* video game case. It was Juntto's last disguise.

Angie whispered to the picture, "Goodbye, asshole. I'll be beating your scores on Halo."

Baal sat back in the huge armchair in Moloch's lair, sipping a glass of whiskey and smoking a cigar. He had never been in that chair before, but it felt good. It felt right. He blew smoke rings high over his head before reaching over and popping a toy poodle in his mouth. He chomped away, leaning back and enjoying the sound of jazz playing on the record player in the corner. He couldn't remember the last time he had been that relaxed. It had probably been before the whole taking over Earth nonsense had arisen.

He tapped the cigar in an ashtray and looked over as a servant entered with a tray. Baal took off the lid and inhaled deeply. A whole roasted human head sat on the platter. The top of the head had been sawed off and replaced, making it a sort of lid. Baal lifted it up and inspected the boiled brains inside. They were peppered to perfection, with slices of orange and lemon on top.

He put the lid back on and nodded. "That's perfect. Just set it on the table. Service for one, please."

The servant bowed and scurried off. Baal put his cigar in the ashtray and stood up, stretching his arms over his head. The light from the fire of souls caught his attention, and he bent down, looking at the writhing bodies inside. "Well, hello there. Bet you are just dying for someone to torture you. Sorry I have been preoccupied lately."

He laughed, patting his belly as he made his way to the window and looked out over hell. The chaos from the fight had ended and all the demons were back to their daily grinds, collecting souls and bringing them back to hell. Business had been slow after the deaths of all of those humans, everyone beginning to mind their bibles. Baal knew it wouldn't last forever, though. It never did. Humans were like clocks. They would go through some-thing traumatizing, but a few weeks later they'd forget all about the sins they had promised never to commit again.

The only thing that made Baal nervous was the silence from the top. Lucifer hadn't said a word to anyone, and all meetings had been canceled. He had stayed locked up in his lair deep below, where the fires burned the hottest. Baal couldn't remember that happening since Lilith had run away. Even then, he'd snapped out of it long enough to torture a few humans. He shrugged, figuring that this too would pass and eventually things would get back to normal.

He stood next to the head of the table for a moment, his hand on the massive chair. He was about to sit when a deep bellowing roar stopped him. *"Baal!"*

Baal jumped away from the table, sighed, and lumbered over to a great door. He stopped at the doorway and straightened, then took a deep breath and put on his most pleasant smile.

A small servant demon scrambled across the floor, gathering dirty gauze and sutures. He glanced up at Baal, sweat pouring from his scaled forehead. He yelped and ran from the room.

Baal shook his head and approached the huge bed. "You can't keep scaring away all the servants. You need someone to take care of these wounds. Look, you screwed up the sutures on your arm again."

The creature in the bed growled. Moloch's scales were cracked and bleeding; his whole body had been crisped by the explosion, and his right arm was gone. He groaned in pain. "What does it matter? She took my good arm. You know I am useless with my left hand. And look at this ridiculous gash. The angelic magic is just not allowing it to heal. Not to mention the missile that blew a hole in my damn thigh. I look like parts of a fucking demon."

Baal chuckled as he picked up the gauze and began wrapping Moloch's arm. "I told you that you shouldn't have gone down there. You weren't ready for it."

Moloch huffed. "Do you always have to be so right about everything? You are supposed to tell me I will get better and be eviler than ever."

Baal smiled. "Of course you will. That is just how you are made. I told you there was a good chance your arm might grow back in a few centuries, and until then we can get you a badass metal one. Won't that be nice?"

Moloch pouted. "I don't want to be a fucking robot. I want my limbs. That fucking bitch set me up. Thank God I jumped when I did. I only took half the force of that blast. If I had just stood there like an asshole, the shrapnel would have taken off *all* my limbs. Then where would I be? I'd be a goddamn chicken nugget."

Baal tried to hide his laughter. "No, those are brown and crunchy. You are scaly and black."

Moloch's eyes darted toward Baal. "You are enjoying this, aren't you? You are enjoying running my position right now. I bet you don't want me to get better."

Baal furrowed his brow. "That's not nice, Moloch. I have been a trusted and true friend to you all these centuries. I would never do such a thing. Besides, your job doesn't interest me. I am happy with what I do. I am only holding your place until you return so no one can claim your spot on the board."

Moloch looked remorseful. "I'm sorry, Baal. I'm just so... Ugh. I sit here day after day, trying to heal as best I can. Meanwhile, I'm stuck either watching replays of the battle, including my arm scene, or the funeral that is happening today."

Baal's eyes lit up. "That's something to be happy about, right? We finally killed Juntto. He has been a hard one to nail down all these years. I was afraid that with him joining Lilith, we might never take him down."

Moloch shook his head. "I guess, but I'd rather be watching Lilith's and Katie's damn funeral. Have you heard any word from our master?"

Baal shook his head. "No, but that's a good thing. Give him time to simmer after everything. Something will happen, and he will forget all about you and your... uh...mishap."

Moloch snarled. "It wasn't *my* mishap. It was the fucking *humans'* mishap. They brought that drama here."

Baal clicked his tongue. "You know that someone will have to pay the price for it. At least, that's how it usually works. But fear not—no news is good news, at least down here." Baal finished the wrap and looked at the other wounds, which were already cared for. He washed his claws in a bowl of water on the dresser and dried them off, then sat down next to the bed.

Moloch clenched his remaining fist and growled. "I swear, one day I am going to make that bitch pay. She is going to find herself so deep in hell she will never get out. I would kill her, but nothingness is too good for her. She deserves to suffer for an eternity in the pits. I am so *angry*, Baal. I can't wait to get out of this bed and find that bitch in the street. I will take her down when she is least expecting it."

Baal opened his mouth to talk but stopped when he heard a knock on the door. He sat up straight in his chair. An elaborately dressed demon strolled in, the insignia on his cloak sending a shiver through Baal.

The demon walked over and laid an envelope on Moloch's bed, then cleared his throat. "Lucifer would like to see you...*right away.*"

The messenger bowed his head and backed out of the room, closing the door behind him. Baal watched Moloch closely, wondering if he was going to blow. Moloch's face twitched slightly, and he let out a growl. "Great, I'll just hop my way down to the deepest level of hell so I can be tortured for eternity. I'm going to get that bitch if it's the very last thing that I do. Mark my words. *I will do it.*"

"I don't know," admitted the scientist, looking at the strange-looking alien in the freezer. He turned to the woman next to him. "You've got connections. Why don't you ask someone from up above?" he asked as he pointed a finger toward the ceiling.

The woman nodded, "That asshole Gabriel owes me a few answers for all the shit I've been through. I'll see if he knows anything we can do to save him. It's the *least* I can do."

She walked out, and the scientist sighed. He was itching to dissect the alien, but he knew that if he so much as cut one hair off the great blue body without her permission, he might find his dick cut off and rammed up his ass without lube or pain medication.

And that was just what her demon had threatened to do.

He closed the special vault and checked the settings. The thing would stay frozen. The body would be kept safe.

FINIS

Before I explain what is going on, let me say THANK YOU for not only reading this book, but these author notes, as well!

Today is Wednesday, and I had lunch with a LONG time fan Heath Felps (Go Navy!) and two of his friends (Aaron Colantino and Brendan Gillespie. One has probably read MORE of my stories than Heath (according to Heath), and one is a complete newb. Fortunately, they enjoyed Jessie Rae's and we have successfully impressed Mike (the owner) with the fandom's efforts to come into his shop ;-). As a note, I refuse to out who had not read my books. I'm cool that way (lol).

Mike (of Jessie Rae's) says to tell everyone interested, that they are SO close to having God Sauce available for purchase... they hope.

Below is a duplicate from another author note (TUMB 11) – HOWEVER – it is important for those who enjoy Fan Pricing (it explains the whole story. For those who have read it already, I'd be curious to read (in the reviews you place on Amazon, OR just send to me in the Protected by the Damned Facebook Group (group, not page) what you think should happen in the future with the stories.

Ad Aeternitatem,

Michael

--- FOR THOSE WHO HAVE NOT READ THIS IN BROWNSTONE #11 ---

LMBPN has set this BHAG (big hairy audacious goal) of releasing four hundred titles next year. To make this happen, we had to get cracking and bang a few brain cells together to figure out how to streamline our process.

Which, you know, was probably said last year, but I didn't FEEL like being responsible last year. As the owner of this company, I didn't want to be told when I had to have stories in. The whole concept made the obstinate part of my personality stand up and try to figure out who to flip off. (Editor's note: HAHAHAHAHAHAHA! Serves you right.)

In the end, I had to give myself the finger.

Way to fuck yourself over, Michael.

Why? Because it's one thing to have two or three (at most) books coming out in a week. But, when we started doing full weeks of books (well, five days, not weekends) the challenges exposed themselves.

One of the issues is fan pricing. How do we continue the pricing while reducing the effort? With four hundred books we have a LOT more to do, and emails are a serious time and effort suck. We already send too many.

FAN PRICING ON SATURDAYS

We are moving to releasing our books at $3.99 (a $1.00 less than regular price) during the week, then on Saturdays pricing all new releases (except box sets) at $0.99 for that day only. On Sunday, they go up to regular price.

This way you always know what day to look, and we are able to send two emails during the week focused on book releases. One on Sunday / Monday that announces what books are coming out (and when) for those who (for whatever reason) care, and then again on Saturday with the books and the links to the Amazon website (we don't always have these a week before.)

We are HOPING to put more content on the LMBPN Publishing website about interesting stuff that might apply to you (including games, Anime, backstory on stories and authors, etc.) When we get this working, we will start releasing a special Wednesday email to highlight our blog posts.

[Note from Steve: We're starting to post new content already. If you haven't checked out the site, please do so, www.lmbpn.com]

Soon, I will be reducing my *Author Notes* in the back of collaboration books. There is no freaking way I can put out five-hundred-word (or more) *Author Notes* in the back of four hundred books. So, my plan is to do a Mad-Libs sort of deal where the core is consistent, and I can add in one or two unique items and see how that goes.

Making 2019 happen at four hundred books is a mountain-type goal for me. I suspect in 2020 we will reduce the number of books released as we use what we learned in 2019 to cut the chaff.

However, for those who follow us, we appreciate your shouts of encouragement as we try to accomplish something (to my knowledge) NO Indie Publishing Company is doing.

Bring it on, 2019, bring it on!

Ad Aeternitatem,

Michael Anderle

CONNECT WITH MICHAEL TODD

Want more?

Find us On Facebook

https://www.facebook.com/Protected-by-the-Damned-193345908061855/